ALSO BY KIT FRICK

Before We Were Sorry
All Eyes on Us
I Killed Zoe Spanos
Very Bad People

THE RED

THE REUNION

A NOVEL BY

KIT FRICK

Margaret K. McElderry Books
New York   London   Toronto   Sydney   New Delhi

MARGARET K. McELDERRY BOOKS

An imprint of Simon & Schuster Children's Publishing Division

1230 Avenue of the Americas, New York, New York 10020

Text © 2023 by Kristin S. Frick

Jacket illustration © 2023 by Levente Szabó

Jacket design by Debra Sfetsios-Conover © 2023 by Simon & Schuster, Inc.

MARGARET K. McELDERRY BOOKS is a trademark of Simon & Schuster, Inc.

For information about special discounts for bulk purchases, please contact Simon & Schuster Special Sales at 1-866-506-1949 or business@simonandschuster.com.

The Simon & Schuster Speakers Bureau can bring authors to your live event. For more information or to book an event, contact the Simon & Schuster Speakers Bureau at 1-866-248-3049 or visit our website at www.simonspeakers.com.

Interior design by Irene Metaxatos

The text for this book was set in Adobe Garamond Pro.

Manufactured in the United States of America

First Edition

10 9 8 7 6 5 4 3 2 1

Library of Congress Cataloging-in-Publication Data

Names: Frick, Kit, author.

Title: The reunion / Kit Frick.

Description: First edition. | New York : Margaret K. McElderry Books, 2023. | Audience: Ages 14 up. | Audience: Grades 10–12. | Summary: In Cancún, Mexico, the Mayweather family gathers for a family reunion to bring them all together, but each brings their own agenda, old grudges, and dangerous secrets that ultimately lead to murder.

Identifiers: LCCN 2023005714 (print) | LCCN 2023005715 (ebook) | ISBN 9781665921466 (hardcover) | ISBN 9781665921480 (ebook)

Subjects: CYAC: Family life—Fiction. | Family secrets—Fiction. | Murder—Fiction. | Cancún (Mexico)—Fiction. | Mystery and detective stories. | BISAC: YOUNG ADULT FICTION / Thrillers & Suspense / General | YOUNG ADULT FICTION / Mysteries & Detective Stories | LCGFT: Detective and mystery fiction. | Novels.

Classification: LCC PZ7.1.F75478 Re 2023 (print) | LCC PZ7.1.F75478 (ebook) | DDC [Fic]—dc23

LC record available at https://lccn.loc.gov/2023005714

LC ebook record available at https://lccn.loc.gov/2023005715

This one's for LSWC.
How did you get this access?

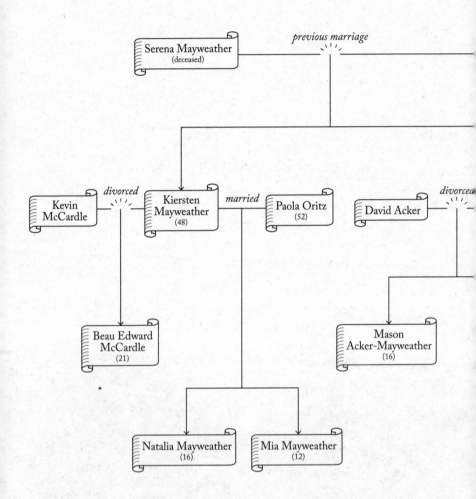

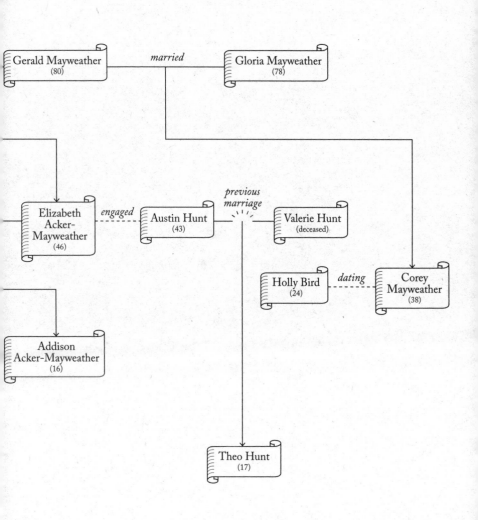

THE MAYWEATHERS

THE REUNION

1

THE RESORT

LA
MARAVILLA
HOTEL RESORT

Tuesday, January 2
From: Resort Management
To: All Guests

With sincere apologies for the disturbance to your stay at La Maravilla Resort Cancún, we are writing this morning to inform you of a search currently underway for a resort guest who went missing last night from a private engagement party on the Vista Hermosa terrace. Rest assured, this is no cause for alarm. We anticipate a prompt and happy conclusion to the search, and we will keep all our valued guests updated.

In the meantime, you may see uniformed members of our police around the resort, conducting this investigation. Please do not be alarmed! Under the orders of the Policía Federal Ministerial, La Maravilla staff have not been authorized to release any further information about the missing guest or the circumstances surrounding the search at this time. However, we do expect their efforts to come to a swift and successful result, and we encourage you to continue enjoying your stay in beautiful Cancún, Mexico!

Attached to this memo, you will find complimentary passes

to La Piscina *Splash!*, our partner water park just ten minutes down the beach. The sun is shining, and today is a perfect day to take the whole family on an aquatic adventure. If you wish to stay close to the comforts of your home away from home, a reminder that all eleven of our acclaimed restaurants and bars remain open, as do our Teen Lounge, Kids Kamp, spa, gym, lap pool, outdoor pool, and our numerous other amenities. We look forward to continuing to make your stay at La Maravilla truly marvelous!

Finally, if you should happen to have any information to share that could assist in the search, please see Ana or Yessica at Guest Services, beneath the palm arch, just off the main lobby. They will be happy to connect you with the appropriate authorities.

With our sincere thanks,

Your friends at La Maravilla

ADDISON

The Acker-Mayweathers are accustomed to breezing through life's annoying little lines—at the farmers' market, the post office, the florist where Mom buys fresh-cut lilies on Sundays "to brighten up the breakfast nook." People know us in Rhyne Ridge. People let us through. But the Cancún International Airport is six hours and one connecting flight away from New York's Hudson Valley, and here, we are three cogs in an epic crush of sweaty, stinking bodies, everyone trying to make their way from the arrival gate to the six men and women in their little plexiglass huts checking passports and releasing exhausted travelers into the bright Caribbean sunshine.

"This blows." My twin brother, Mason Acker-Mayweather. For the third time in the last five minutes, he lets his backpack slump from one shoulder to the floor.

"Mason, don't say 'blows.'" Our mom, Elizabeth Acker-Mayweather. She twists her shiny brown hair behind her, then pats her wrist fruitlessly for a hair tie. The air-conditioning is blasting, but it's no match for the sheer magnitude of body heat in here.

We landed approximately forty-five minutes ago, an arrival time apparently shared by every other international flight touching down in Cancún on the day after Christmas. After half an hour inching along a corridor stretching from our gate to a single escalator, we descended into the massive sea of travelers already jammed into the Passport Control hall, everyone jostling to join the six long lines snaking their way toward the agents at the front. I do a quick head count of the travelers in my general circumference, then multiply by eighteen, the approximate quantity of similarly sized areas in the hall. Roughly, there are nine hundred people inside, all waiting to see six agents.

An airport official glances at our customs slips and ushers us toward the end of line five. Give or take, one hundred and fifty people wait ahead of us. We're going to be here a while.

I click open my red roller case and pull out the novel I need to have finished for Miss Dern's class when I get back to school next week. Then I flip my suitcase on its side and take a seat.

"I don't know how you can read in here," Mason says, squatting down next to me. "It's loud as hell."

"White noise." I shrug. I'm good with words, but lit has never been my favorite. I'm a science and math girl. So the faster I can get through this book, the less of the trip I'll spend with it hanging over me.

But Mason clearly isn't going to let me read in peace. "Have you tried the Wi-Fi? I can't get past terms and conditions."

I shake my head. "Reading."

"Can you try it, though? Or give me your phone."

I dig it out of my pocket and hand it over. There's nothing on my phone my brother and cousins can't see; I made sure of that before this trip. "Help yourself. But there are nearly a thousand people in this room alone trying to log on. The network is overloaded."

The line inches forward, and I scoot my suitcase up a foot, then sit back down. Mason pokes at the screen and scowls, clearly getting nowhere. When we were little, people always wanted to know if we had that "twin thing," which seemed to mean something between a deep empathetic understanding of one another and straight-up telepathy. We didn't, even then, but we were close in the way many little siblings are close. And we looked a lot alike, for fraternal twins. Dusty blond hair, which we got from our dad, small noses and wide-set blue eyes from Mom. And we were both short for our age.

That changed in sixth grade, when Mason shot up and filled out, shoulders and chest broadening faster than most high school boys, and I stayed five feet flat. Soon Mason needed glasses, and I didn't, and by the time we were thirteen, we were barely recognizable as siblings. Thirteen was the year we began to grow apart, too, until our physical differences mirrored even bigger changes on the inside. Sometimes I wish we could go back in time.

I scoot my suitcase again and try to finish my paragraph. James Joyce is so obscure.

"We should have been at the hotel by now," Mason

grumbles. He drops my phone into my lap, letting my book catch it. "I should be on the beach."

Mom glances at her delicate gold watch. "Austin and Ted—*Theo*—were scheduled to land a few minutes after we did. Can you see them anywhere, hon?"

Mom only has an inch or two on me; "hon" is definitely directed at Mason, who towers over both of us.

He gives the crowd a cursory glance, then shakes his head, shaggy hair flipping back and forth before it settles in his eyes. "If there was any service in here, we could text them."

Mom sighs, and the queue inches forward again. It's been ten minutes since we joined line five, and we've almost reached the first curve. Eight belted lanes between us and the gate agent at ten minutes per lane; my guess is we'll be out of here around two thirty. I don't share that with Mason.

"I just wish I knew they got in okay." Mom twists her hair back again, and I climb off my suitcase and unzip it to find her a hair tie.

"I'm sure they're fine," I say, holding out an elastic.

Gratefully, Mom pulls her hair through it. Honestly, I could go a little longer without running into Austin and Theo—known to his father as Teddy, a habit Mom's trying to break after Theo made it clear the nickname's off-limits. Ahead of us stretches an entire week of enforced bonding with the new step-fam. Austin Hunt is Mom's fiancé; they're getting married in Rhyne Ridge this June. Theo Hunt is Austin's seventeen-year-old son, a senior at a high school about forty-five minutes away from the school where Mason's a junior. I'm about an hour and a half south, in my junior year at Tipton Academy, a private school known for, among other things, its cutting-edge science program. Austin and Theo seem fine; I've only met them once, last month, when I came home from school and we all got together for Thanksgiving. I'm not opposed to getting to know them, but a whole week together at an all-inclusive Caribbean resort with the rest of the Mayweathers is going to be *a lot*.

We round the bend to the line's second lane, and Mason bounces up and down on the balls of his feet, then pulls out his phone to check the Wi-Fi once again. My brother never could sit still. I don't know him like I used to, before playing Division 1 hockey became his entire identity and I moved away from home to study biology and attempt to figure out what being a Mayweather means without my twin brother and my cousin Natalia constantly by my side. But some things haven't changed. Mason needs to be in motion always, and he has the attention span of a fly. He's also fiercely protective of Mom, ever since she got out of a bad situation with Dad, and Dad lost custody.

"How well do you really know Austin?" Mason asks her for what is clearly not the first time, judging by the expression on Mom's face.

"Hon, you don't need to worry. Austin's a very different man from your father. I'm so happy we're going to have this time to really get to know one another."

"You've only been dating for a few months, though. How do you know he's the one?"

"Eight months," Mom says. "And still another five until the wedding. And I just know, I suppose. He's attentive and smart and kind, and he's fantastic with Theo. I think you're all really going to hit it off."

I close my book, giving up, and crouch down to unzip my suitcase again. I hope Mom's right, that we're *all really going to hit it off*, although it's Mason and Natalia I most want to spend time with. It's been far too long since my brother, my cousin, and I have truly talked.

I'm tucking my book back into my suitcase and digging around for a snack when my fingertips brush against something that definitely shouldn't be inside. Something I'm sure I packed in a different suitcase—one safely locked in storage back at Tipton.

A golf-ball-sized lump lodges in my throat, and I peel back a layer of neatly folded shirts to be sure. The wooden cigar box is right here, in *this* suitcase, in Cancún, where it definitely should not be. Quickly, I smooth the shirts back in place and re-zip my suitcase, making a point to keep my gaze cast down, away from Mom and Mason.

This is bad. Very, very bad.

How did I let this happen? Everyone in my dorm had to clear out our rooms last week so Anders could be used as housing for the Hudson Valley Student Leadership Conference, which Tipton is hosting over winter break. My bookcase, my mini-fridge, and most of my belongings are in campus storage, which is where I meant to leave the box I usually keep tucked away in my dorm room. But somehow, in the rush to get home for the holidays and probably precisely because I was so nervous about keeping it safely locked up over break, I packed the box into the wrong suitcase. *This* suitcase. The one with my vacation stuff, which is now irrevocably here in Mexico with the exact people who absolutely cannot find out what's inside.

I force a grin up at Mom. "I'm sure we will. Hit it off. Mason and I can't wait to spend time with the Hunts this week."

THEO

Dad's in a hurry the moment we touch down, eager to meet up with Elizabeth and her kids. My soon-to-be family, which is beyond weird to think about. It's been ten years since Mom died, ten years that Dad and I have been a unit of two. What we have works fine, but I'm trying to keep an open mind. Elizabeth makes Dad happy, and she seems cool enough. It's the other Mayweathers—eight on this trip alone—I'm not so sure about.

We trot down a short hallway with the rest of the passengers from JetBlue Flight 1127, then take the stairs one level up to a small arrivals hall. I've never flown internationally before. Jay said to brace myself for a long wait at Passport Control and customs, but it looks like we're in a wing of the airport only serving a couple of airlines. A guy in uniform checks the customs sheets we filled out before landing. He taps Dad's at the bottom and reminds him to sign.

"Ah, silly me." Dad rubs at the brown-and-gray stubble at the back of his neck, and the official points him to a counter with a row of ballpoint pens chained to the top.

"Can't believe I forgot to sign," he mumbles when we've joined the end of the line leading toward passport check. It's moving pretty quickly, the minutes separating me from a plunge into the deep end with the entire stepfamily shrinking fast. Too fast.

Dad's a copyeditor for a business magazine that rates snow

equipment and winter gear, and he's also a registered notary, both of which require a close attention to detail. I can't remember the last time he forgot *anything*. But when Dad's nervous—especially when he feels out of control—he gets irritable. It's been years since his temper really flared up, at least that I've seen, but something tells me I'm not the only one whose nerves have been set on edge by the week ahead.

"Not too late to turn back." I give Dad a weak grin. We're halfway to the front of the line now, and my passport feels slippery in my hand despite the air-conditioning blasting in here.

He nudges my shoulder with his in an attempt to lighten the mood. "It's going to be fine, Teddy. Dare I even say *fun*?"

"Sure, sure. But can we stick with *Theo* on this trip, please?"

"Right." Dad gives a crisp nod, the skin around his dark brown eyes crinkling in concentration. "I really am going to try. Honest."

"Thanks." We take six more steps toward the front. I should have broken Dad of the habit years ago, but the truth is, the nickname reminds us both of Mom. At home, just the two of us, Teddy is fine. But to the rest of the world, it's Theo. It was embarrassing enough when I learned Elizabeth had been calling me Teddy to her kids before I even met them. If she hadn't, maybe I wouldn't have gotten off on the wrong foot with Mason this fall. Then again, the cards were already stacked against me when it came to my new stepsiblings. Mason's a hothead, quick to assume the worst in people and not shy about expressing his views. My stomach clenches at the thought of spending the next seven days as his roommate. The guy clearly hates me, and he's huge.

Addison seems nice enough, if a little stuck-up. I get the impression she's used to being around a certain type of person at boarding school, and I'm not that type.

Dad's right. This week is going to be *so fun*.

"Next." The agent in plexiglass hut number three is beckoning. We step up and hand over our passports and forms. I'm prepared to answer a volley of questions about where we're staying and the purpose of our trip—more advice from Jay—but the agent gives our paperwork a quick review, then slaps her stamp briskly onto our passport pages and hands them back with a curt, "Welcome to Mexico."

Dad grabs his giant suitcase at baggage claim, then we head toward the door marked NOTHING TO DECLARE. No one stops us. Everything I brought fits easily in my duffel; years of camping trips and ski weekends have taught me how to pack light, a skill Dad's never quite mastered. He's all about *gear* and *extra socks*.

Soon we're stepping through wide glass doors and into the bright midday sun. I slip on my shades and run one hand through my short brown hair, glad I remembered to get it cut before this trip. It could be worse—in December, the highs here top out in the mid-eighties—but I'm not built for the heat. My pasty skin burns no matter what SPF I apply, and I'm not the world's strongest swimmer. I'm not afraid of the water; hanging out in the shallow end of a pool is fine, and I can wade out in a lake to fish, but the ocean is not my friend. Even in salt water, somehow I sink.

If I was home, I'd be skiing with Jay right now. Unfortunately, my dream of spending break with my boyfriend of nearly six months evaporated into sunshine and salt air as soon as Dad announced this trip—a reunion for the Mayweather clan, culminating in an engagement party for Dad and Elizabeth on the final night. My attendance was mandatory.

It's only been a few hours, and I'm already homesick. New Courtsburg is a forty-five-minute drive from super-trendy, everything-artisanal-and-handcrafted Rhyne Ridge, where the Acker-Mayweathers live. The place I'm from is bigger, less artsy, more "economically stressed." A postindustrial town with mediocre schools, an A&W drive-in, and mini-golf may not be most people's idea of paradise, but it's home. Jay's there. And we have killer slopes. I'm extremely pro-nature when nature means the woods or mountains of snow.

Sweat beads across my neck and runs down my T-shirt, and I can feel my jeans sticking to the backs of my knees. Hot. I jam my hands into my pockets and help Dad look for Activo, the transport company that's going to be shuttling us to the hotel.

"Can you get on the Wi-Fi?" he asks.

I pull out my phone and search for the airport network. "We're too far from the terminal. The only networks showing up are locked or people's hot spots. But—there's Activo." I nod toward a black-and-white sign to the left of Margaritaville, an open-air bar bumping with American tourists getting loaded on Mexican booze one more time before their departing flights.

Dad frowns. "We're supposed to be sharing a van with Elizabeth and the kids, but I'm not sure how to reach her. I was planning to extend our wireless coverage for the week, but she thought everywhere would have Wi-Fi." He looks stressed. Again.

Before he starts to spiral, I dump my duffel at Dad's feet

and tell him I'll run back into the terminal to see if I can get any service. "Hang on."

It's a failing mission. I find the network, but it's maxed out, and I can't get past terms and conditions. By the time I find Dad again, he's speaking with a young Mexican guy holding a clipboard and wearing a black Activo T-shirt.

"I'm Jorge, your Activo captain," he greets me in perfect English. "First time in Cancún?"

"First time out of the northeast US," I say. Dad and I do fine, but the fun money from my part-time job at Aldi's goes to skiing, and Dad's never had a lot left over for things like vacations. After college, I'm going to travel.

"I understand we're waiting for Ms. Elizabeth, Miss Addison, and Mr. Mason," he says.

"I don't know." I turn to Dad. "I couldn't get on the network inside the airport, either. Were they on JetBlue?"

He shakes his head. "American Airlines."

"Ah," Jorge says. "JetBlue, you're lucky. Different terminal. American Airlines, one o'clock arrival?" He taps at an Apple Watch. "They're gonna be in there a while. Let me take you now; Activo has many vans. We'll bring the rest of your family separately, don't worry. I'll alert my driver." He switches on a walkie-talkie and speaks to someone on the other end in rapid-fire Spanish.

Your family. Jorge's words clang around in my ears, but Dad doesn't flinch. He gives me a wide grin and wraps his arm around my shoulders. My T-shirt clings to my skin.

2

MASON

When we've finally been approved and stamped by the agent at hut number five, it's almost two thirty. I'm starving and my phone battery is nearly drained, not that the Wi-Fi ever worked. Piece-of-crap public network. Mom and I collect our suitcases from a huge pile dumped by the baggage carousel while Addison fiddles with the zipper on her carry-on.

"Anyone need a bathroom?" Mom asks like we're still five.

My sister slings her purse across her shoulder and jerks her roller case toward customs. "All set."

"Yeah, me too."

"I can't believe how long that took," Mom says as we follow after Addison. "Although it is a holiday week, so I suppose I should have expected it. Remember the passport line in Zurich the summer after second grade?"

"First," I correct her.

"I thought you were going to have a legendary meltdown."

I clench my teeth until my jaw ticks. Does Mom need to resurrect this story every time we fly? Sure, I come off smelling like roses, but it's a reminder that I was in better control of my emotions at six than I am at sixteen. Mom wouldn't be singing my praises if she knew the truth about what happened this fall. She'd look at me with that *so disappointed* face and get really quiet and sad.

Which is why she won't find out. She can't.

"But then the toddler in the line next to us *did* have a full-blown tantrum," Addison adds, "and his mom was losing her mind trying to get him to quiet down."

Mom picks it up from there. "Until Mason leaned across the belt and said, all serious, 'Hey kid, you think I like this? We're all miserable, but you don't see the rest of us screaming.'"

Then they both deliver my final line of dialogue in unison: "'Give your mom a break and *chill out.*'"

Mom laughs. "It worked! The toddler stopped crying, and that mother looked so grateful. I could have hugged you for hours." She reaches up to ruffle my hair, and I let her, even though I've been tall enough to dodge her affection for years. Even though I really don't deserve it.

"Please wait."

My head snaps up at the rough voice. We're almost at the door marked NOTHING TO DECLARE, but two uniformed guards with pocket holsters and a big German shepherd on a thin chain leash step into our path. The dog gives Mom's suitcase a cursory sniff, then mine, and one of the guards gestures for me to place my backpack on the ground so he can sniff that, too. But the dog isn't interested; he's already straining toward Addison's roller case. My sister freezes, and all the color drains from her face. She knots her fingers into her long, ash-blond hair as the dog sniffs her suitcase along the zipper line, then down at the wheels.

One guard says something to the other in Spanish, and I can't follow the words, but he's definitely gesturing to Addison's suitcase. If possible, she goes even paler, and I choke down a laugh. Obviously I don't want her getting thrown in jail, but if she has a vape or something stashed in her bag, I will never let her live this down. It would be so out of character, so *shocking*. Or maybe this is who Addison is now. We used to know everything about each other, but the truth is, I hardly know my sister at all anymore.

When we were kids, Addison was such a little rule-follower. I was constantly getting in trouble—fighting, not listening to the teacher, not listening to Mom and Dad. They signed me up for every team sport under the sun, mostly to get me out of their hair, but I have to give them credit, because I found hockey. Hockey saved me from my worst self, or so I thought.

Addison, on the other hand, has always been a classic over-achiever. Reading at three, gifted program at six, off to a fancy boarding school at fourteen to pursue her passion for biology and genetics. Sure, I'm proud of her, but if she's the one who does something to embarrass Mom on this trip—and before we even get to the hotel—I will never stop laughing.

"Ven." The guard holding the leash gives it a tug, and just like that, the dog loses interest in Addison's suitcase and returns to its handler. He nods at the three of us, and we've been released. Guess Addison's off the hook.

She's still pale as we cross out of customs and into the arrivals lounge, then out into the bright afternoon sun. I suck in the warm air—finally.

"What was that all about?" Mom asks, frowning down at Addison's suitcase.

"No idea," she says, voice tight.

"You can tell us," I say, hip-checking her just hard enough to make her skip a step. My sister is tiny; I'm not trying to knock her down. "You packing heat? A kilo of heroin?"

Addison rolls her eyes. "Those dogs are trained to detect all sorts of things. Like fresh fruit, which can carry invasive bugs or crop disease. I have some dried mango in a Ziploc, which is not illegal to bring into Mexico, by the way, but that's probably what he was interested in."

"I'm just glad they didn't make us open up our luggage," Mom says. "We're already so late to meet Austin and Teddy."

"Theo," Addison and I say in unison.

"Right." Mom gives her forehead a dramatic slap with her palm as we pass by some cheesy airport bar called Margaritaville. At Mom's instruction, the three of us are looking for the transport company she hired to shuttle everyone to the hotel. "I one hundred percent respect that he goes by Theo," she says. "It's just Austin was calling him Teddy for months before I met him, and it's hard to get out of my head."

I grimace. Mom has no idea how much stress Teddy slash Theo has already caused me.

"There!" Addison is pointing to a black-and-white sign for

Activo, our transport company. Mom ushers us up to the guy with a clipboard.

It doesn't take long to figure out that Austin and Theo left without us almost two hours ago.

"How'd they get through that line so fast?" I ask.

I don't expect a real answer, but Jorge, our greeter, says something about a separate terminal. "Don't worry, though. Another van is on the way. Ten minutes."

Mom smiles and thanks him, and I follow my sister's lead, turning my suitcase on its side and taking a seat. The sun is hot on my back, through the thin fabric of my Knicks jersey, but at least it finally feels like we're in Mexico. In half an hour I'll be on the beach. When I close my eyes, I can almost feel the hot sand on the soles of my feet.

NATALIA

From the moment we arrive at La Maravilla Resort, it's clear our group is getting the VIP treatment at an already swank place. A middle-aged man with a salt-and-pepper mustache and impressive biceps whisks our bags from the back of the van and onto a luggage cart, while a younger guy gestures for us to follow him out of the foyer, where the regular guests are checking in. We walk down a short hall, and a vast lobby unfolds to our right. People wearing everything from swimsuits and beach covers to casual shorts and tops to pressed linen suits and dresses with plunging necklines lounge on couches and chairs, playing cards, sipping cocktails, and chatting. I touch my phone through the pocket of my cutoffs, itching to log onto the resort's guest network. I haven't gone this long without chatting with Seth since we first started talking, over a month ago.

We round a bend, crossing beneath an arch of palm fronds, and arrive at a light-filled room with GUEST SERVICES etched in English on the glass doors.

"Yessica will get you settled in," our escort tells us, opening the door and nodding to a young woman with medium brown skin and light blond hair seated at one of three reception desks. Mom hands him a folded bill. The air in here is perfumed, papaya and salt water. I think it smells like paradise, but Seth would hate it; he thinks papaya smells like baby vomit, a fun fact I learned when we were video-chatting at lunch last week. I make a mental note to tell him about the air freshener as soon as I get the Wi-Fi password.

Beside me, my little sister Mia bounces excitedly from foot to foot, while Mom and Mami walk up to the desk. My twelve-year-old sister is probably more excited about this vacation than anyone else, except maybe Uncle Corey, who's apparently bringing a hot date. Yessica gestures for us to take a seat in the open chairs before her and accepts Mami's driver's license with a smile.

"Welcome, Ms. Ortiz." She types, flexing her fingers so her long peach nails don't touch the keys, then looks up from the screen. "I have your party down for seven nights, checking out on Tuesday, January second. Two adults—Ms. Paola Ortiz and Ms. Kiersten Mayweather—and two minors—Natalia Mayweather and Mia Mayweather. We have you in rooms 506 and 507, both booked with Maravilla Resort Group points, from the account of Gerald and Gloria Mayweather. Is that all correct?"

"Sí, es correcto," Mami confirms. "¿Necesitas la identificación de mi esposa también?"

"Sí, por favor." Yessica smiles up at Mom, who digs into her purse for her ID.

Mami launches into a series of questions about the lap pool hours, and where we can eat on the beach, and soon I'm lost. I turn to Mia, and she shrugs, bony shoulders tapping her long silver earrings. How long will we be here before someone assumes I'm fluent and I have to awkwardly correct them? Mia and I are half white (Mom's side) and half Puerto Rican (Mami's side, via a sperm donor). I've taken Spanish in school for years, but growing up in Rhyne Ridge, there wasn't really anyone to practice with aside from Mami, and I've never gotten any good.

But Mia and I are both clearly Latina—light brown skin, dark brown hair, brown eyes—so strangers assume. Since we moved to Portland, Oregon, three years ago, I've had a few awkward exchanges on the bus, but here, in Mexico? I listen to Yessica and Mami go back and forth and realize it's going to be A Thing on this trip.

"Girls?" My head snaps toward Mom. She's holding out two key cards, which Mia plucks from her hand. "You're in 507 with Addison, but Yessica says the Acker-Mayweathers haven't checked in yet. Leave her some room in the closet, okay?"

"Can we go up?" Mia asks.

Mom nods, and her brown hair swishes against her chin. The new bob makes her look like a suburban soccer mom, but I'd never say that to her face. She's made her opinions about my short, wavy cut perfectly clear, and I'm not about to start that conversation again.

Mia is already on her feet, our key cards clutched in her fist. She tugs at my wrist with her free hand.

"Is there a network password?" I ask Yessica, who nods and jots it down on a key card envelope for me.

"Don't forget dinner," Mami says as Mia tugs me toward the door.

"What time?" I ask, allowing myself to be pulled. Before we left, Aunt Elizabeth, Mom's little sister, sent an all-Mayweather email setting up a group dinner for the first night at El Mar, one of the resort's several restaurants.

"A las sies," Mami replies. Between my practice schedule for flute and Mia's constant rotation of activities, six o'clock is at least two hours earlier than we usually eat at home, but the hummus and pita chips I grabbed at the airport weren't much of a meal, so I'll probably be hungry.

"Come to our room at a few minutes of," Mom instructs. "Room 506, right next door. We'll go down together."

Mia pushes on the door, and I give Mom and Mami a wave.

"'Kay," I agree. "Hasta después."

As soon as we're out in the lobby again, I pull my phone from my pocket and log onto La Maravilla Guest, exhaling in relief as the full set of bars appears at the top of my screen.

"Remember when we went to visit Gigi and Pop-Pop in Florida a few years ago and we met those girls from Nebraska at the pool?" Mia asks. "I wish you were doing Kids Kamp with me; we're the best at making vacation friends."

"I'm too old for Kids Kamp," I remind her, eyes glued to my screen. I have three new messages from Seth. "But you're going to love it. Like you said, you always make friends."

"You can still come hang out with us, though, right? The resort isn't that big; come find me tomorrow, okay?"

Landed in paradise! I start to type, then erase it. I should wait until I've changed out of my gross airplane clothes and send Seth a poolside selfie instead.

"Natalia?"

"Huh?"

Mia is clearly waiting for a response. She sticks out her lower lip like a much younger kid.

"Tomorrow?" she repeats. "Promise you'll come say hi?"

"Of course." I grin and press the up button to call the elevator. "We're going to have plenty of hang time on this trip." I pull her into my side and she squeals as the elevator dings and the doors glide open.

3

ADDISON

The Maravilla Resort staff are friendly—too friendly. Between the moment our van pulls up to the curb and our departure from Guest Services, key cards in hand, I have to fend off three separate eager beavers in white polo shirts, reaching for my luggage handle. No one puts up a fight when I say I prefer to wheel my suitcase to my room myself, thank you very much, but eyebrows are raised. Clearly, it's not how things are done here. This is a place where life's minor inconveniences are handled for you, where no request is any trouble at all.

Mason gives me some serious side eye as we step into the elevator with Mom. I pretend not to notice, but it's too late. I've screwed up. That sniffer dog homing in on my suitcase was bad luck, out of my control, but just now, my cost-benefit analysis was off. I should have surrendered my luggage to the first guy with a cart. Instead, by keeping it close I've drawn way too much attention to its contents. I grip the handle and keep my eyes fixed on the numbers blinking above our heads as the elevator climbs to the fifth floor.

"Dinner's at six," Mom reminds us as the doors open. "Should Austin and I stop by—"

"I'll meet you at the restaurant," Mason cuts in. He's already out of the elevator and heading down the hall at an almost-jog toward the room he's sharing with Theo.

"El Mar," Mom calls after him. "On the first floor!"

"I'll meet you there too," I tell her. I feel a little bad, after Mason's abrupt departure, but Mom will be fine. She'll be with Austin. "I'm going to unpack and then maybe explore a bit."

"Okay," Mom says, obviously disappointed. "If you need some company, you know where to find us."

I flash her a weak smile. Mom is desperate for us to "spend quality time" with Austin and Theo on this trip, but she doesn't need to worry. There's going to be nothing but family bonding for the next seven days.

We walk together toward rooms 505—Mom and Austin— and 507, which I'm sharing with my cousins, Natalia and Mia. The resort has us all grouped together on the same floor. Only Uncle Corey's room is farther down the hall, because he didn't commit to the trip until last week. I entirely understand the impulse to duck out of a week of all Mayweathers, all the time, but it's not like Uncle Corey to pass up a free trip from Gigi and Pop-Pop. According to Mom, there was some sibling drama over whether or not he'd be bringing his new girlfriend, a woman named Holly that none of us have met.

"Go enjoy some alone time with Austin," I tell Mom when we arrive to her room. I give her a peck on the cheek. "I'll see you at dinner."

Then I wheel my suitcase two more doors down to 507, press my key card to the reader, and draw in a deep breath. The last time I saw Natalia and Mia was two summers ago, when Mom and I made a brief stop in Portland during a week-long trip up the Pacific Northwest coastline to Vancouver. Mason chose hockey camp over the vacation, which wasn't a big surprise. Beau, my oldest cousin from Aunt Kiersten's first marriage, was doing a summer internship in Boston, so it was just the six of us: Aunt Kiersten, Aunt Paola, Natalia, Mia, Mom, and me.

We got dinner at a trendy Vietnamese place, then stayed over at their house, but it was just one evening, and Natalia dodged the few chances we had to be alone. To really talk.

I'd been looking forward to seeing her, clearing the air, but the visit was awkward. Polite. When we were kids, growing up together in upstate New York, the three of us were inseparable—Mason, Natalia, and me. My brother and my cousin were my two best friends, and I thought that would never change. Then the Incident happened, three summers ago, and I thought the secret would bond us together forever, but that's not how it happened. Maybe we were closer because of it in those first few weeks, three guardians of a truth we'd never reveal, but then the reality of what had happened began to set in, and I could feel Mason's eyes on me, distrusting, feel Natalia pulling away. Then Aunt Kiersten got a new job in Portland, and Natalia moved to the other side of the country.

When I got into Tipton, and Mason stayed at our local school for the hockey program, the fissure was complete.

Now we're barely more than strangers. I hate that. I *get* it—I vividly remember how it felt to know then, how it still feels now. The heady buzz of the secret in our ears, then the descent of its weight across all three of our backs.

But it's been three years. Three and a half. Maybe, possibly, during this week of forced proximity in paradise, Natalia, Mason, and I can talk about what happened back then. The Incident, and the secret we vowed to keep. Maybe, finally, I can get my two best friends back.

The card reader flashes green, and I press the door open. Or, I try. It feels like there's a bed rammed up against the other side of the door.

"Hello?" I call, pressing harder. The door gives, grudgingly. Not a bed, just the air current from across the room, where sliding glass doors open onto a private balcony. I squeeze through, and the room door jerks shut behind me with a thunderous clap.

"Oh my *god*." Mia tumbles out of the hammock strung across the balcony, snatching earbuds from her ears. My little cousin must have shot up four inches since I saw her two summers ago; she's all arms and legs and dangly earrings, and she's wearing a classy, high-waisted two-piece that says twelve going on twenty. "You scared the crap out of me."

"Mia!" I flash her a grin and park my roller case against the wall. "Sorry, wind tunnel."

She runs over and wraps her arms around me, and it hits me that she's nearly the same age Natalia, Mason, and I were that summer three years ago. At not quite thirteen, Mia seems older than we were then, more sophisticated. Looking back, we were all such children. Or maybe it's just easier to remember us that way.

"Where's your sister?" I ask, shaking the memory off.

"Shower," Mia says. "We're about to go down to the pool, but she had to 'wash the airplane off' first. Come with?"

Before I can respond, the bathroom door swings open, and Natalia steps out wearing a plush, floor-length spa robe. Her short, wavy hair is pulled back in a thick fabric headband.

"Oh." Her face drops when she sees me standing with Mia, then quickly rearranges into a smile. "Addison, hi. So good to see you."

She takes two steps toward me, but doesn't offer me a hug. *So good to see you?* What are we, forty?

"Um, you too." My hand floats up into a little wave, and I can't remember the last time I felt so awkward.

"We were just about to check out the pool," Natalia says, walking over to the dresser and selecting a swimsuit from the top drawer. She doesn't invite me to come along.

"Get changed," Mia says, beaming down at me. She may be my little cousin, but she's got two or three inches on me now.

I glance at Natalia. She doesn't meet my eyes before slipping back into the bathroom to change. How many sleepovers did we have growing up? It never would have occurred to either of us to change in the bathroom.

"You two go down," I say, loud enough for Natalia to hear. "I need a minute to decompress and get unpacked."

"Okay." For a moment, disappointment registers on Mia's face, but then she's bouncing over to the dresser and opening the bottom drawer. "This one's for you, and they only gave us like three hangers in the closet, but Natalia already called down to the desk and they're bringing up more."

"No problem." I smile. "I didn't bring that much." I'm not worried about drawer or closet space, but this is my chance for some time in the room, alone. I need a good hiding spot for the box, which is burning a giant metaphorical hole through my roller case's hard shell. I brought it with me; there's no way to fix that mistake. Now I need to keep it safe.

THEO

By late afternoon, I've seen most of the resort. I hung in the room for an hour, scrubbing the sweat off my skin in the massive shower with an entire wall of bath gels and shampoos and two rainfall showerheads, then sitting on one of the two extremely plush queen beds and texting with Jay. He's kicking back in the lodge after putting in a few hours on the slopes, something we'd be doing together if I was home. I'm not worried about spending a week apart; our relationship is by far the most rock-solid thing I've ever had with anyone, boy or girl. I just miss him. And home. And winter.

And as much as I've been dreading a week as Mason's roommate after his low-key threats at Thanksgiving, I want to rip the Band-Aid off. But when Dad knocked on my door to say there was still no word from Elizabeth either, I gave up on politeness and set out to explore.

I have to admit, La Maravilla is extremely nice. Eight floors of guest rooms, each with an ocean view. A bunch of different restaurants, bars filled with wristband-clad adults sipping Coronas and slushy blue cocktails well before happy hour. I check out the ice cream parlor, the coffee shop, the one-room movie theater, and a room called the Teen Lounge filled with new Xbox and Nintendo consoles and a bunch of arcade games. Everything's included in the cost of your stay, which the Mayweather grandparents, Gloria and Gerald, are taking care of. I've never been in a place like this before, and it's a little weird to have these unseen benefactors bankrolling the trip, but Dad says they had a whole bunch of resort points that were set to expire, and with Gerald's health, it's hard for them to travel anymore.

The only part of the resort I haven't visited yet is outside. I take a seat at one of the open tables on the pool side of the lobby and stare out through the floor-to-ceiling glass windows. Objectively, the pool is gorgeous, a sprawling lagoon the length of the entire resort, with a waterfall and kiddie slide on one end and a swim-up bar and pool volleyball court on the other. On all sides, the water is surrounded by lounge chairs and covered cabanas, where waiters deliver drinks and snacks to sunbathing guests. Beyond the pool, several paths lead down to a white-sand beach with more lounge chairs and cabanas. Beyond that, the ocean stretches out forever, so blue it looks dyed.

Maybe later tonight, or in the morning, before it gets too hot, I'll take a walk along the beach and dip my toes in the water—which is about as deep in the ocean as I'll ever get. But not right now.

I pull out my phone and scroll through my contacts until I land on Mason's number. It's a quarter to five; dinner's in a little over an hour, and if I don't talk to him before then, it means our first interaction is going to be witnessed by his entire family plus my dad, and I'd really like to clear the air before that happens. Truly, Mason has nothing to worry about from me. He's going to be my stepbrother, and while we may have almost nothing in common, I have no reason to rat him out to his family. All of which I said at Thanksgiving, but I'll say it again. Maybe it will stick this time.

I take way too long composing a text, then finally settle on Hey, you at the hotel yet? When there's no response ten minutes later and I've drained two petite bottles of water delivered to my table by a smiling waiter in a white polo shirt, I open up our one-sided chat again.

> Can we talk before dinner? I just want to
> start over.

I hit send and wait for the three little dots to appear, but there's nothing. Either the Acker-Mayweathers still haven't made it to La Maravilla, or Mason's ignoring me. And my gut says it's the latter.

Maybe *I just want to start over* was too much. Nothing's going to erase the first time we met, and I know that as well as Mason. He probably thinks I'm incredibly naive as well as a threat to his privacy. I'm neither, but if he won't talk to me, I don't know how to make him see it.

At five, I shove up from my table and drop my phone back into my pocket. There's still an hour to kill before dinner, and it's cooling off outside. A little. I think. If Mason's here, he's probably out there—at the pool, on the beach. And if he's in the water, he's not checking his phone. Maybe he hasn't seen my texts. I resolve to head back up to the room to slather on some sunscreen. If I don't run into him there, or I still haven't heard back by the time I'm done, I'll brave the heat and do a loop around the pool deck before dinner. I have to try. And if nothing else, when Dad inevitably asks, I can honestly say I didn't spend the entirety of our first afternoon in Mexico hiding in the air-conditioning.

4

MASON

I'm twenty minutes into my run when my calves start to burn. For one thing, I'm out of shape. For another, running on sand is a beast.

I lean into the burn. For the first time since we crammed into the Lyft this morning, before the crack of dawn, I actually feel like I'm on vacation. Like maybe, this week off from school is going to be a real break. Fever 333 blares through my AirPods and sand slaps the soles of my feet, and the sun is hot on the back of my head. I'm a million miles from Rhyne Ridge and school and the team. There's nothing here to remind me about how epically I screwed everything up.

Except Theo.

The side of my foot comes down on something hard and flat, a rock, and I stumble, then grit my teeth and keep going. It wasn't sharp; I don't have to stop and look to figure out I'm not bleeding. Just a little bruise, nothing I haven't experienced times a hundred in the rink. Ice hockey isn't a pretty sport. Even at the high school level, where fighting is strictly forbidden and the refs toss down penalty flags with gusto, there's no shortage of pain. A little bruising is nothing I can't run through.

On my right, the ocean stretches out for miles. On my left, I pass resort after resort after resort, their open-air bars and giant striped umbrellas and canopy-draped cabana beds overflowing onto the sand. I've barely spent any time inside La Maravilla, but it's obvious it's one of the nicest on the strip. For one, it's built closer to the water than most of the others; from the balcony in my room, there's this optical illusion of the pool draining straight into the ocean. For another, there are bouncers stationed at each of the paths connecting the pool deck to the beach, blocking interlopers from other resorts from trying to sneak in, use the pool, or grab a free drink at the swim-up bar. Most of the other hotels don't have the same kind of security, at least from the beach side.

It tracks that Gigi and Pop-Pop would have a credit card with one of the top Caribbean resort groups, even though Pop-Pop says air travel is too exhausting for him now. It's weird being on this trip without them. We haven't done a big family vacation in six or seven years, but Gigi always planned out the *best* and *most comprehensive* itineraries with the iron hand of a beneficent dictator, and Pop-Pop was there to crack jokes and keep us all in the vacation mood. That's always been Pop-Pop's style: keep things light and lively, even when maybe it would have been good for us to take a hard look at ourselves, to acknowledge that the Mayweather Way isn't always the best way, that we are obsessed with our money and who will inherit what, that we are not a perfect family.

But why would any Mayweather want to do that?

On this trip, there's no itinerary save for family dinner tonight and Mom and Austin's engagement party at the end of the week. But there is Mom's mandate to "spend lots of quality time" with the Hunts, a sticky obligation I haven't quite figured out how to dodge. Hopefully, I can rely on Addison to pick up the slack. My sister's more science nerd than social butterfly, but she's always been the family diplomat—going out of her way to make sure everyone's happy, no one's fighting, everything's *fine, totally fine*. Even when it's definitely not. But if her passion for Mayweather diplomacy can keep Mom happy and get me out of a weeklong family bonding session, I'll take it.

At a curve in the shoreline, I slow to a stop and pull out my phone to check the time. It's getting late. I need to get back and shower before dinner. Cutting between hotels and up to the road would be faster, but I didn't bring my shoes, so I bump up the volume on my AirPods and break into a sprint. It took me half an hour to jog out here, but even though I'm far from my physical peak, I bet I can still make it back in ten if I push myself.

I'm maybe a mile from the resort when something I'd missed on the first leg of the jog catches my eye: a small thatched hut with a dozen surfboards lined up in a rack outside. Three deeply tan Mexican guys sit in lawn chairs out front; two play dominoes while the tallest taps at an iPad. I slow down to read the sign, painted letters carved into a wooden surfboard stuck in the sand: LA ESCUELA DE SWELL. If I had more time before dinner, I'd rent a board right now, but I need to keep going.

I make it back to La Maravilla in eight minutes flat, then collapse against the stone wall of the outdoor shower on a strip of beach belonging to the resort, heaving. My eyes burn, sand or sweat or both trapped under my contacts, and I swipe at my face with my jersey. Two college girls washing sand off their feet shoot me weird looks as I suck in air and try not to lose my lunch. Whatever. With my mom, my sister, and all the other Mayweathers hanging around, my prospects of hooking up on this trip are probably nil anyway.

"You okay, dear?"

My head snaps up from between my knees. A middle-aged woman in a floral one-piece and a giant straw hat is frowning at me, concern etched across her face.

"Fine," I choke out. "Just pushed myself too hard."

I dig my phone out of my pocket and hope she'll go away. It connects to the resort Wi-Fi, and I open up my texts. Two new messages from Theo Hunt.

> Hey, you at the hotel yet?

> Can we talk before dinner? I just
> want to start over.

When I look up, the woman is gone. I swipe out of my messages and shove my phone back into my pocket. Sorry, Theo. I already—stupidly—told you way too much, and there's no starting over from that. Besides, it's almost five thirty, and I have just enough time to hit the shower and change before we're all due at dinner.

NATALIA

This is, one hundred percent, the nicest pool I've ever been to. These cabanas must get snapped up fast in the morning, but this late in the day, Mia and I had no trouble claiming one in a prime spot out of the sun and close to the waterfall. In front of us, the pool undulates from a roped-off shallow end into a wide center where guests lounge on inflatable pool rings and sip cocktails out of plastic cups. The seasoned resort-goers sport brightly colored tumblers with their names etched on the sides. At the far end, more guests congregate at a swim-up bar or bat around a beach ball. Behind us, the ocean spools out forever like a giant ombré sheet, aqua to sapphire to midnight blue.

Mia and I took a dip when we first got out here; now we're drip-drying in the still-warm, velvety evening air. I lean my head back and close my eyes, letting my whole body melt into the cushions. The cabana is essentially a waterproof bed—a plush mattress and pillows beneath a wooden frame draped with a soft white canopy. In the hour we've been down here, Mia's ordered two Shirley Temples from the constantly circulating servers, and we've demolished a heaping plate of nachos.

I could get used to this.

And so far, the only Spanish I've encountered has been the basic kind of pleasantries most English-speaking Americans know. Hola; buenas tardes; sí, señorita. The staff is obviously used to toggling back and forth between languages, and they're probably very tuned into whatever the guests are speaking. Maybe I'll survive the week without any awkwardness after all, the kinds of exchanges that leave me feeling inadequate, not quite Latina enough.

"That boy is not dressed for Cancún," Mia snorts. She sits up, transforming from a carefully staged tableau of relaxation—arms behind her head, legs crossed at the ankles to show off their length—into a giggling kid. At twelve going on thirteen, my sister can oscillate between practiced sophistication and unabashed immaturity in a matter of seconds.

She grabs my wrist with one hand and points with the other to a skinny guy about my age, maybe a little older, with short brown hair and the kind of skin so white it's almost pink. He's wearing jeans with a little bit of slouch in the hips, black-and-white Converse high-tops, and a formfitting gray tee with an old-school I WANT MY MTV logo. Mia's right. He looks totally out of place among a sea of bathing suits, beach covers, and flip-flops, but he has a definite style. I admire that.

He's standing at the top of the stairs leading from one of the lobby entrances down to the pool, turning in a slow semicircle, hand shielding his eyes. He drops it from his face, clearly not finding what he's looking for, and—oh.

"I think that's Theo Hunt." In the photos Aunt Elizabeth sent from Thanksgiving, he looks pretty different—hair longer and curly, dyed blond at the tips, wearing slim-fit khakis and a green grandpa cardigan. But everyone looks different dressed for family holidays.

"Maddison's new stepbrother?" Mia says.

"Yeah. And I don't think they want to be called Maddison anymore." When we were little kids, the portmanteau was adorable—Mason and Addison—but that was a long time ago. According to Addison's emails, which she sends at least quarterly whether or not I get it together to respond, she and Mason don't see much of each other ever since she's been at boarding school and he's away at hockey camp every summer.

Without acknowledging what I've said, Mia shoots up from our cabana and hops up and down, hands waving in the air. "Theo," she shouts at the top of her lungs, voice definitely loud enough to carry across the pool, even over the Nelly blasting from the swim-up bar.

His head jerks toward us, but so do the heads of half the guests at the pool.

"Take it down a notch," I hiss, eyebrows arching skyward. I love my sister to death, but sometimes she's so embarrassing.

Mia stops jumping long enough to give me a withering glance, then gets back on her tiptoes and silently beckons Theo over to our cabana. Hands still shoved in his pockets, he gives us a slight nod with his chin, then starts to walk toward one of the bridges spanning the pool.

"Guess it's really him," Mia says, flopping back down on the bed.

I shake my head and reach for my water. "Looks like."

A minute later, Theo is standing at our cabana, rocking slightly on his heels.

"Natalia and Mia?" he asks.

I give him a smile and small wave from my seat, while Mia jumps back up and sticks out her hand. He stares at it for a second, obviously taken off guard, then extracts one hand from his pocket to take hers in his.

I like him immediately. He's as awkward on the outside as I feel on the inside, all the time. Trusting new people doesn't come easily to me, but I think I could let my guard down with Theo. It would be nice to have someone my age to talk to on this trip, someone who, unlike my cousins, doesn't come with three years' worth of uncomfortable baggage.

"Come sit," I say, grabbing a towel and giving the mattress a quick wipe-down. "Welcome to A Week of Mayweathers. We can be kind of a lot."

"Um, thanks." Theo takes a seat on the very edge of the bed, then twists to face me.

"Not a beach person?" Mia asks, sitting back down and pulling her knees to her chin.

"Not exactly," he says. "I don't really swim."

"Huh." I don't mean to sound judgey, but the grunt slips out automatically. The Mayweathers are excellent swimmers, adults and kids, without exception. We've been "like fishes," as Pop-Pop says with pride, since practically infancy. He's made sure of it. When Gigi and Pop-Pop still lived in the Hudson Valley, before they retired down to Naples in southern Florida, their house was on this sprawling wooded property with a big lake out back. Pop-Pop made sure his kids, and then his grand-kids, got swimming lessons as soon as we could walk. *Safety first,* he'd say every time we came to visit, before ushering us outside to play.

Swimming is like breathing to the Mayweathers. Uncle Corey was a lifeguard in high school, Mom competed on her school's swim team, and Mia is a Marlin, the second-highest level in the community aqua club. I can't imagine not being at home in the water, and I feel a little bad for Theo on this very water-centric trip.

"You'll be fine in the pool," Mia says without missing a beat. "There's no deep end, I checked, and we have floats up in our room."

Theo grins; he has a nice smile. Then he lifts his hand to his eyes again and looks around the deck. "Have you seen Mason? We're sharing a room, and his stuff is up there now, but he's been MIA."

I shake my head. "Not yet, sorry." I glance down at my phone; it's 5:40. I have a new message from Seth, but I force myself to flip my phone back over. I'd rather save it to read when I'm alone.

My eyes find Theo's. "See you at dinner? We've got to get changed."

"Yeah." He nods, standing when we do and slipping his hands into his pockets once again. "Family dinner. See you soon."

5

ADDISON

The servers have to shove the two largest tables together to fit our group at El Mar, a surf-and-turf restaurant on the resort's first floor. Three sides of the restaurant are enclosed in a bank of windows, giving off the impression of eating directly on the beach—but with all the comforts of plush chairs, air-conditioning, and electricity.

La Maravilla is shaped like an L. Eight floors of guest rooms stretch along the long arm of the L, windows facing the pool, then the ocean beyond. Facing the street are Guest Services, the gym, the spa, and the resort's other amenities.

Most of the restaurants are located inside the boot of the L, which juts out toward the ocean. The pool stretches out to our left; on the floors above us are a casual Mexican place, a fancy Mexican place, a Japanese restaurant, and a few more I can't remember. By the end of the week, I'm sure the Mayweathers will have tried them all. On the very top floor, overlooking the ocean, is the Vista Hermosa terrace, the private entertainment deck that Mom and Austin have booked for their engagement party on our last night in Cancún.

The moment the tables are in position, Aunt Kiersten takes charge, directing us to our seats as if this is a formal dinner. As if chaos might break out if we are left to choose our own chairs. Technically there's no kids' table, but Mason, Natalia, Mia, Theo, and I are all ushered to one end while the six adults settle on the other, in pairs. To my left are Mom and Austin, then Aunt Kiersten sits at the head of the table with Aunt Paola on her left, followed by Uncle Corey and his girlfriend, a much younger woman with unnaturally white-blond hair who looks like she models Victoria's Secret for a living.

She turns immediately to Mason, who is seated on her other side. "I'm Holly."

Her voice is plush around the edges, and I wonder if that's the way she talks or if she's fishing for attention. I wrinkle my nose, then swipe at my face with my napkin, hoping she didn't see. Holly Bird—what kind of name is that anyway?—is nowhere close to Uncle Corey's age, but she has to be out of college. Early twenties, I'd guess. Young for my uncle, but way too old for Mason, even if she wasn't already attached.

My brother takes her outstretched hand in his with a big, doofy grin. "Mason."

She nods, wheels turning. "Elizabeth's son. I hear you play varsity hockey in a very competitive league."

Mason's neck and face burn red. Oh my god, how

embarrassing for him. Could his interest in her be any more obvious? He mumbles something about Division 1 and reaches for his water.

Two servers position themselves on either end of our table, each bearing wooden stands that look like miniature coatracks.

"For your bags," the server on our end explains.

I tell him thank you, then lift my purse from my lap and pass it to Natalia, who slings the strap over one of the pegs. She follows suit, and Holly, whose seat is dead center between the "kids' side" and the "grown-ups' side," hands her tiny clutch with a delicate gold chain to Mason and says, "Would you mind?"

Instead of passing it down to Theo, Mason nods seriously and pushes back his chair. He walks over and hangs Holly's bag with the reverence of a child placing a delicate glass bauble on top of a Christmas tree.

On the other side of the table, only Aunt Paola has hung up her purse, while Mom and Aunt Kiersten keep their bags clutched in their laps. It's so typically Mayweather. After the family's "history of invasions," as Gigi likes to say, there's a general twitchiness among the adults about keeping a close eye on valuables. Given my missteps with my suitcase earlier, maybe it's rubbed off on me. But no one's going to steal our bags from directly beside our table at El Mar.

The servers take our drink orders and try to sell Aunt Kiersten on a pricey bottle of wine not covered by the resort's "all-inclusive" package. She is the oldest Mayweather sibling, but it's strange to see her at the head of the table, murmuring with the server like Gigi used to do. Uncle Corey's ears perk up at the name of whatever fancy bottle has been suggested, and so do Mom's, but Aunt Kiersten orders sauvignon blanc and pinot noir from the regular wine list and folds her hands firmly on the table. If Gigi and Pop-Pop were here, they would have sprung for the spendy stuff.

I turn to Natalia, who is gazing into her water glass and hasn't said two words to me so far. Even when she hung up my purse earlier, she did it with a polite smile, nothing more.

On the flight, I'd let myself hope things might somehow be instantly different the moment we stepped off the plane and breathed in the warm Caribbean air. That the picture-perfect backdrop would somehow erase the past. But instead, I'm going to need to initiate an attempt to restore some semblance of normal. Otherwise the three of us—Mason, Natalia, and me—will spend the entire week in three separate bubbles, encapsulated in the silence that's festered for the last three and a half years.

"It's great you and Mia could come this week," I say with a smile that I hope looks warm and genuine. "We missed you at Gigi's seventy-fifth."

Natalia returns my smile with a small uptick of her lips. "Oh right. I don't think Mami could get off work. Or maybe it was Mom."

I shrug. Gigi turned seventy-five three years ago, and it's not my intention to rehash the party—the last real Mayweather reunion—that Natalia's side of the family missed. The point is we're all together now.

"It's cool we're in the same room," I offer. *Cool* is not the right word, and it sounds childish sliding off my tongue, but I barrel on. "Remember all the sleepovers we used to have? It'll be like old times."

Natalia winces; I'm trying too hard. Already, I'm failing. I dig my nails into my thigh.

"I remember!" Mia leans across Natalia from the foot of the table, her face lit up in a megawatt grin. "One time we tried to dye my hair blond, but it didn't work."

Natalia rolls her eyes, coming to life now that her little sister has joined the conversation. "I remember that. Because we didn't bleach it first, which, in retrospect, thank god. You were only six. Mami would have murdered us both."

"I wanted to look like Addison," Mia says.

I run my fingers through my hair, which is a dark ash-blond. It used to be a lot lighter, when we were kids.

"Maybe later," I start to say, but the servers are back, delivering our drinks and brandishing tablets, ready to take our dinner order.

THEO

The thing about a table for eleven is it's nearly impossible to carry on a conversation with anyone but the people seated right around you. Which in my case is Mason, who grunted a quick hello, then quickly turned his entire focus to Corey's very pretty, very attached girlfriend Holly. Across from me, Natalia is engaged in a quiet conversation with Addison. Natalia was friendly at the pool earlier, but now she's speaking so softly, it would be awkward to try to jump in.

Which leaves me with Mia, who thankfully likes to talk. A

lot. From her spot at the foot of the table, she shifts effortlessly between Addison and Natalia, and me.

"Do you have a girlfriend?" she asks.

"Nope. I have a boyfriend, Jayden."

"That's cool. Can I see a picture?"

"Sure." I smile and pull out my phone, scrolling to find a shot from two weeks ago, Jay and me on the New Courtsburg slopes. My still-longish, still-curly hair spills out from beneath my hat. My eyes travel over to Jay, and my heart squeezes. Dark brown skin, close-cropped brown hair, pale brown eyes with amber flecks. He grins back at me from the photo, wide lips parted to reveal bright white, slightly crooked teeth.

"He's cute," Mia says. "Have you ever had a girlfriend, or did you always know you liked guys?"

It's the kind of personal question that would be rude coming from most near-strangers older than twelve, but honestly, I don't mind. It's a thousand times better than being ignored by Mason.

"I like both girls and guys," I tell her. "I've had a couple girlfriends in the past. But Jay and I have been together for almost six months." Which still blows me away, especially given that he's not out at school, a choice I understand but that hasn't made our relationship easy. But I'm not getting into all that with Mia.

When our food comes, the waiters deliver plates of steak, stuffed salmon, grilled swordfish, and mixed-grill kebabs. Dante, the waiter at our end, sets down my plate of linguini with jumbo shrimp and asks if I'd like anything else.

"Another Coke?" I ask, and he nods.

When everyone has received their entrees, Elizabeth taps the rim of her water glass with a knife. We all turn to look at her.

She clears her throat, and Dad slips his hand over hers. "I want to thank everyone for being here this week," she begins. "It means a lot to Austin and me. And to Theo." She twists in her seat to beam at me, and I give nine sets of Mayweather eyes an awkward smile. As far as I'm concerned, we could have waited until the wedding this summer to do the meet-the-entire-family thing, but this is important to Dad. So I'm trying to make it important to me.

"Theo and I have been a party of two for a very long time," Dad says.

Ten years and two months, to be exact. Since we lost Mom to breast cancer.

"We're so grateful to be joining such a big family," Dad continues. "I'm sorry Gerald and Gloria couldn't be here with us."

There are murmurs of agreement from the Mayweather adults. Apparently Gerald, who the twins call Pop-Pop, isn't very mobile anymore. I can't begin to imagine how many credit card points it takes to fund a resort vacation for eleven, but they're obviously loaded, and as much as the beach isn't my scene, I have to admit it was very generous of them to hook this up.

"Remember Christmas in Nyack?" Corey asks. He's obviously speaking to his older sisters, but we're all still hushed from Dad and Elizabeth's brief thank-you speech, and everyone's listening in.

"I'm surprised you do," Kiersten says. Her voice isn't unkind, but there's a slight edge to it.

Corey laughs. "Jesus. I'm not *that* young."

Kiersten raises her eyes to the ceiling and her wineglass to her lips, and I wonder if that's what she meant.

I study the youngest Mayweather sibling's face. I know from Dad that Corey is thirty-eight, a full ten years younger than Kiersten and eight years behind Elizabeth. But he looks even younger than that; he clearly knows his way around a pot of face cream. Makes sense. On the flight, Dad said Corey worked as an actor in NYC. I wonder if he's been in anything I've seen.

"Anyway," he says, "Mum's seventy-fifth aside, that Christmas in Nyack was the last time we were all together." Nyack is another Hudson Valley town, farther south than New Courtsburg and Rhyne Ridge. Must be where Gerald and Gloria lived before they retired to Florida.

Corey leans across his girlfriend. "Remember caroling in the village, Mase? You couldn't get enough."

Beside me, the tips of Mason's ears turn pink. "I think that was Beau."

"I am sorry Beau couldn't be here," Elizabeth says, turning her focus to Kiersten. "Mason had such a good time visiting him in the city over Labor Day."

For a moment, I have no idea who she's talking about, but then it clicks. Mia and Natalia's older brother—Mason's cousin. Beau is at college in New York, Columbia or NYU. Dad mentioned he wouldn't be here this week, something about an internship in the city.

Kiersten smiles. "It's hard having Beau so far away for school, but I'm glad the boys have remained close."

Her eyes land on Mason, then Natalia, who is very interested in her napkin all of a sudden. Before I can spend too much time wondering what that's all about, the conversation has already surged ahead.

"What I remember about Mayweather holidays," Addison says, "is Gigi's snowball cookies. I miss those."

"Oh my god, and Pop-Pop's Christmas village in the solarium," Natalia says. "That was so awesome when we were little. The little string band?"

"What I remember," Kiersten says, the edge returning to her voice, "is Corey taking the children into a *pub* on Christmas Eve, and everyone sniping over Dad's holiday checks, every single year. Frankly, I'm glad Dad and Gloria are settled in Florida, and that everyone has kept Christmas local this past decade. Large Mayweather gatherings have always brought out the worst in us."

Paola rests her hand softly on top of her wife's, and Kiersten's face melts, just a little.

For a moment, the table is silent. No one's eating, and the food is getting cold. But I'm starving. I lift my fork and twirl some linguini, careful not to let the tines scrape the plate.

"Well," Elizabeth says softly, "this week is going to be different. I'm sure having Austin and Theo here will keep us all on our best behavior, and everyone can use some sunshine at this time of year."

"Right on," Corey says, lifting his wineglass. "To family, sunshine, and good food in beautiful Cancún."

Elizabeth smiles at him gratefully.

Like that, the spell is broken, and everyone starts eating. I shove a giant bite of pasta and shrimp into my mouth, thankful this not-so-rosy stroll down someone else's memory lane seems to have come to an end. When I glance over at Mason, he's very pointedly angled away from me, engaged in conversation with his uncle and Holly.

I exhale through my nose and reach for my Coke, which has been refilled at some point. I didn't even notice. We're here for a whole week. I try to take some comfort in the fact that Mason can't ignore me forever, but Kiersten's words are still loud in my ears. *Large Mayweather gatherings have always brought out the worst in us.* There's nothing comforting about that.

2

THE SURFERS

Wednesday, January 3
From: Resort Management
To: All Guests

We write this morning to thank you for your great patience while La Maravilla's work with local authorities continues. I know many of you have questions!

The search for the guest who has gone missing from a private engagement party on the Vista Hermosa terrace is now into its second day. Because false and exaggerated reports have begun to circulate on the news and online, the Policía Federal Ministerial has released to the public these facts, which we now share with you: the missing person is an American minor under the age of eighteen, and the search is still ongoing. This is the only factual information that has been made public at this time, and we implore you to keep in mind that anything else you might see posted to news sites or the internet is not necessarily reliable.

Today, as a show of our gratitude, attached to this memo is a family VIP pass to Señor Pollo Especial, just half a kilometer down the street from La Maravilla! You'll receive half off frozen drinks, and the kiddies will have a blast at the playland. Don't forget to ride the Giant Chicken before you go!

As always, we also welcome you to remain right here at the resort and enjoy our pools, spa, and other amenities. We are afraid the section of beach belonging to our resort has been roped off during the search, but you will find beautiful white sands next door, and we're pleased to announce that the staff at the Wyndham will be honoring La Maravilla wrist bands on the beach today.

We appreciate your curiosity and willingness to help during this trying time, but truly we are not at liberty to share any further details, as search efforts remain very active. We continue to hope for a swift and happy resolution! If you have any information that could assist in the search for the missing American minor, please head right away to Guest Services. Yessica and Marta are at the desks today, and will be very happy to speak with you.

With our sincere thanks,

Your friends at La Maravilla

6

Five Days Until the Engagement Party

NATALIA

Eight o'clock is hours earlier than I planned to get out of bed on this trip, but since we forgot to pull the curtains across the balcony doors last night, the sun is a natural alarm clock. It's been in my eyes since seven thirty, but I've been too lazy to get up and fix the curtains. Finally I peel the comforter back from my face and roll over to find Addison's bed neatly made up and her purse gone from the table by the door. I didn't even hear her get up.

Mia starts Kids Kamp at nine, so when she asks me to come to breakfast with her, I drag myself into the shower and throw on some shorts and a top.

Breakfast is in El Buffet de Oro, one of the only restaurants not located in the section of the resort that juts out toward the ocean. The buffet is on the first level, off the lobby, and in addition to the tables inside, it has a large open-air porch that runs along the far side of the pool deck.

Mia heads straight for the waffle station, and I get in line behind a middle-aged American couple waiting for eggs to order.

"Look at this." The woman passes her phone to the man I assume is her husband. "This happened right here in the Cancún Hotel Zone, just down the beach."

He glances at whatever she wants him to read. "Good thing Eric didn't come on this trip," he says. "He would have been the first to sign up for surf lessons."

The woman shakes her head, frosted hair whipping against her ears. "This article says they're still operating, even after those two girls disappeared last month. Shouldn't someone shut them down?"

The chef behind the egg station beckons the couple forward to take their order, and I slip out my phone to google "Cancún," "surfers," and "missing girls." There are a bunch of hits, some from around a month ago, and a lot of new ones from today. I click on the first article, titled "Missing Minnesota Teens Found with Suspected SoCal Cult Group."

The article begins with photos of two smiling white girls.

Sophie Fletcher (17) and Julie Fletcher (19), from St. Paul, Minnesota, were located yesterday evening on a beachside commune several miles outside Southern California's Laguna Canyon, where the young women had reportedly been living with members of a suspected eco cult for the past month. The Fletcher sisters

disappeared in late November from the beach along
Cancún, Mexico's resort-dotted "Hotel Zone," where
they had been vacationing with their parents. They were
last seen taking an early morning lesson at Escuela de
Swell, a local surfing outpost. Escuela de Swell is now
being investigated for possible ties to the SoCal group;
authorities suspect the surf school may have been
operating as a recruitment front for the alleged cult.

Sophie Fletcher, a minor, has been reunited with
her parents, but Julie has not left the commune. At the
present time, the young women have declined to be
interviewed by St. Paul police about their experience.

"Buenos días, señorita. ¿Qué le gustaría?"

"Miss? Your order?"

My head snaps up. The man in the white chef's smock gives
me a patient smile. I shove my phone into my pocket.

"Sorry. Omelet, por favor. Veggies y queso."

He doesn't flinch when I break into the same Spanglish I'd
use with Mami at home, and when he reaches for the eggs and
a bowl of pre-chopped peppers, onions, and mushrooms, I dig
my phone back out. This time, I look up "Escuela de Swell."

Google tells me the surf school is about a kilometer down
the beach from La Maravilla, back in the direction we came
from the airport. There are a bunch of rumors online about
why California police *might* think its owners have ties to the
cult group—something about a shared last name and evidence
of a land deed a few miles from the commune—but aside from
the fact that the surf school was the last place the two girls were

seen before they turned up in a cult a month later, there's nothing concrete, and of course the police aren't talking because it's an "active investigation," and they are "cooperating with local authorities."

I wait while the chef loads up my omelet with sautéed veggies and cheese and wonder if anyone would be looking at the Mexican surfers so closely if they were white.

Regardless, I have no desire to test out the police's theory. I accept my plate from the chef and head over to the platters of sliced mango, papaya, pineapple, and grapefruit at another buffet station. My eyes skate around the room until they lock on Mia. She's balancing a glass of juice, a plate with a whipped-cream-doused waffle, and a second plate heaped with bacon and potatoes and heading outside, toward the patio tables.

I grab the tongs and pile some fruit onto my plate, not paying attention to what I'm getting. My eyes stay fixed on Mia. Suddenly I don't want to let her out of my sight.

MASON

When I carry my plate out onto the porch, Natalia and Mia are the only two people seated at a table meant for six. I'd planned on inhaling my eggs alone and getting out of here, but Mia spots me instantly and sticks her arm in the air, waving it back and forth like a possessed person.

There's no ignoring that, so I pivot and plunk my plate at an open seat at their table.

"Hey." I give them both a quick nod and shove a forkful of scrambled eggs into my mouth.

Natalia is reading something on her phone and twirling a perfect cube of pineapple on her fork. She gives me a small smile, then her eyes go back to her screen. Fine by me.

"What's your plan for today?" Mia asks. "I have camp until five, and it better not suck. Isn't it so weird that I'm signed up for camp and the rest of you don't have any activities?"

I shrug. "You're a kid."

Mia slumps back in her chair, looking wounded. I wasn't trying to offend her; it's just a fact. When Addison and Natalia and I were kids, our parents would sign us up for whatever structured activities were offered on vacation too. But this is the first time the Mayweathers have done a group thing like this when we've all aged out of "Kids Kamp" except Mia.

Natalia raises her eyes from her screen long enough to shoot me a glare. Then she turns to her sister. "It's definitely a little weird, but you're going to meet other kids your age, which will be vastly better than hanging with us for a whole week. And we'll still do stuff every night. Promise."

Mia smiles, soothed. Jesus. Remind me never to have kids; they're so *sensitive*.

"This seat taken?" Addison stands suddenly next to me, holding coffee and a giant bowl of oatmeal heaped with dried fruit and nuts.

"Sit here," Mia commands, patting the open chair next to her instead. Addison smiles and complies.

"You actually have to get moving," Natalia says, spinning her phone toward her sister to show her the time. "Mami's meeting you at our room to walk over to camp, remember?"

"Oh yeah." Mia turns to Addison. "Can we hang out later?"

"Sure." My sister gives her a big smile. "Bonfire's tonight, right? See you on the beach."

A moment later, Mia is gone, and Addison, Natalia, and I are alone at the table.

"This is perfect timing," Addison says, dropping her voice, "because I've been wanting to talk, just the three of us. It's going to be a long week, and—"

"Kids. There you are." We're saved from my sister's misguided attempt to dredge up the past by Mom, who is followed closely by Aunt Kiersten, both women speed-walking toward our table like the hotel's on fire. I wonder where Austin is.

The second they reach us, Mom's hand grasps my shoulder in a five-finger vise.

"Hi?" I look up at her, eyebrows raised. "That kind of hurts."

"Sorry." She relaxes her grip, but her hand stays put. "Aunt Kiersten and I just heard the news. Have you seen it?"

Addison looks as puzzled as I feel, but Natalia says, "About the missing girls? People were talking about it inside. The article I read says they were found safe, though."

"Missing girls?" my sister squeaks.

Natalia opens her mouth to say more, but Aunt Kiersten cuts in.

"Apparently two American girls were *lured away* from a hotel down the beach last month to join a cult in California. The police think a surfing school might be recruiting vulnerable kids here on vacation."

"Whoa." I fork another bite of eggs into my mouth and snap off a piece of bacon.

"We don't know they were *lured*," Natalia says. "Escuela de

Swell was the last place they were seen, but the surfers might not have anything to do with it. Just because they're Mexican . . ."

"You're right," Mom says. "Absolutely. It's an open investigation, and we don't know if the girls were recruited by someone at the surf school or somewhere else here in Cancún. There could be any number of explanations for how they wound up with that cult, but regardless, they were taken from this very beach."

"And your aunt Elizabeth and I just want you to be cautious. The resort is very safe, I'm sure, but if you go out on the beach, you need to be with a buddy."

"Fine," Addison says quickly, ever the peacekeeper, even though Mom and Aunt Kiersten's rule is stupid. For one thing, they just said *two* girls disappeared. Together. But if I point out the obvious, they'll start instituting curfews and hand-holding, so I keep my mouth shut.

"Did Mami meet up with Mia?" Natalia asks.

"Yes," Aunt Kiersten says. "And she's speaking to the counselors right now about their safety protocols. Honestly, I feel better knowing Mia's going to be in a supervised setting while we're here. It's you three I'm worried about."

"And Theo," Mom adds. "Has he come down to breakfast?"

She looks to me for a response. Again, I wonder where Austin is. How did I become his son's keeper?

I sigh. "He was still sleeping when I left the room."

"But we'll fill him in when we see him," Addison adds quickly. "Don't worry."

For a moment, both Mom and Aunt Kiersten linger, hovering over us.

"Maybe we shouldn't have come here," Mom says quietly. "We're staying at a very high-end hotel in a highly populated tourist area. I never thought . . ."

"Bad things happen everywhere," Addison says.

She's right, and Mom should know it. Run-of-the-mill bad stuff is by far the greater danger—not kidnapping and cults. My thoughts flash to Dad, who Addison and I used to see only through supervised visits after he nearly killed us all driving drunk when Adds and I were ten. We got lucky; Mom came out of it with a broken wrist, and Addison and I had some bad scrapes and bruises, but no one was seriously injured.

It could have been so different. Dad narrowly missed drifting into a semi on the highway, overcorrected the wheel, and we plowed into the guardrail instead. It was the last straw for Mom, after years of Dad's angry outbursts, poor judgment, and refusal to get treatment for alcoholism. They divorced as soon as Mom could file the papers.

When we turned thirteen, it was up to Addison and me if we wanted the supervised visits to continue, and we both opted out. Dad had cleaned up, but there were too many bad memories. Until recently, I've barely been in touch with Dad for years.

"But I'm sure whatever happened to those girls was just a freak thing," Addison is saying, her voice drawing me back to the sunny restaurant porch. "And we'll stick together."

Speak for yourself. I don't say it out loud. Natalia nods gamely.

Addison shoos Mom and Aunt Kiersten inside, toward the buffet. Satisfied for now, they go.

When we're alone again, Addison rolls her eyes, effortlessly toggling between appeasing the parents and aligning with us. "Note to self, don't join a surf cult on this trip."

"You think Mia will be okay?" Natalia asks. There's genuine concern in her voice.

"She definitely will." My sister leans across the table, toward our cousin. "Remember that day camp on the cruise when we were ten? They watched us like hawks. No way they're going anywhere near that surf school or letting the kids wander off."

"Right." Natalia nods, chin bobbing fast. "Totally."

Pretty sure Escuela de Swell was the name of the little board rental hut I jogged past yesterday. Checking it out was already on my agenda, and if they want to ship me off to some commune in southern California, fine by me. Anything would be better than going back to school next week. I shove back my chair, but my sister's fingers wrap around my wrist.

"Wait. We still need to talk. Just the three of us."

"Not now, Adds." I extract my wrist from her claws. "I'm going for a run."

"Natalia?" She turns to our cousin, her usually level voice pitching into a whine.

"Maybe another time," Natalia says quietly. "We're here all week."

"But—" Addison starts to protest, but I'm already on my feet. Natalia buries her head in her phone once again.

"Later." Instead of going back inside the restaurant, I walk across the porch, toward the pool deck.

I need some time away from the resort. Alone.

7

THEO

Addison brushes past me as I step through the sliding glass doors onto the restaurant's porch. She mumbles something that sounds like "good morning" or maybe "get moving," dark blond hair fluttering behind her, before disappearing inside.

"Morning?" I glance at my plate of breakfast tacos, which is jostled but fine, then out across the patio to the pool deck. My eyes land on Mason's back, retreating down a set of stairs leading to the beach. It's only nine thirty; guess the Mayweathers are early risers.

"Hey."

My head snaps toward Natalia's voice. She's sitting alone at a table meant for six, surrounded by a collection of dirty plates.

I flash her a grateful smile. "Mind if I sit?"

"Sure." She gestures toward the seat across from her. "No one should eat alone."

I put my plate down and pull out a chair. "Looks like that's exactly what the others left you to do."

"It's fine, I was done anyway." She fiddles with an empty white cup, and it clatters against the saucer. "Where's your dad?"

I shrug. "Working, probably."

I spotted Elizabeth and Kiersten sipping mugs of tea at a window table on my way through the restaurant, but Dad wasn't with them. Which most likely means he's already breaking his promise to keep his laptop locked up in the safe during this trip. Getting to know Elizabeth's family is clearly important to him, but Dad's a freelancer without any paid vacation, and he has a hard time taking a real break from work under any circumstances. Being around all these rich people is probably just as uncomfortable for him as it is for me, and working is an excuse to hibernate and bring in some more cash. It feels a little hypocritical after the hard sell he gave this trip, but at the same time, I get it.

"I could use some coffee," Natalia says, and my gaze returns to her.

As if on cue, or perhaps because he heard her, a waiter appears at our table with a fancy silver carafe. We both nod and slide our cups toward him.

"What's up with Addison this morning?" I ask around a mouthful of tortilla.

Natalia frowns, and her gaze drops to her phone. Either there's something very interesting on her screen, or she's deliberately not meeting my eyes when she responds. "Nothing. Our moms stopped by to warn us about the surf school and those two girls who joined a cult, and it put everyone in kind of a weird mood."

My eyebrows arch. "Huh?"

She pulls up something on her phone and slides it toward me. "Missing Minnesota Teens Found with Suspected SoCal Cult Group." I give it a quick read.

"That's wild."

"Uh-huh. They don't want us out on the beach alone. Buddy system."

Heading out on the beach alone is exactly what I just saw Mason doing. But I'm not about to rat him out; he already doesn't trust me.

"Sure, whatever." I'm not planning on spending much time on the beach during this trip anyway.

A notification pops up on Natalia's screen, a new message from someone named Seth with the text preview, I wish we could fast-forward to . . .

"Sorry." I slide her phone back across the table. "I didn't mean to read that."

"It's fine," she says, but her eyes are locked on her phone. She taps the message open and breaks into a grin, then types something back. I return to my tacos, feeling like a third wheel.

"I'm being rude," she says after a minute, making a show of dropping her phone into her bag. "I invite you to sit, then I'm texting."

I wash down a bite of taco with a gulp of really good coffee. "It's okay," I say. "Boyfriend?"

Her cheeks turn pink. "Sorta? It's new. His name's Seth."

"I saw."

"Mia said you have a boyfriend too?"

I nod. "Jayden. I just saw him two days ago, but I miss him already."

She gives me a bright smile. "I get that. I can't say I really miss Seth more than normal, because I live in Portland and he's in Spokane, but I guess I low-key miss him all the time?"

"Long distance is hard," I agree. "At the end of sophomore year, I started dating this girl Priya. It was a first relationship for both of us. Over the summer, her family moved up to Albany. It's only an hour and a half away, but we were both too young to drive, so it may as well have been Canada."

"And what happened?"

"We were broken up by the end of July."

Her face crumples.

"I'm not saying that's going to happen to you and Seth," I rush to add. "Priya and I probably weren't a great fit anyway."

Natalia stares down into her coffee. "I think Seth and I are a good fit. It's only been a few weeks, but I want this to work. This is probably TMI, but I've never dated anyone before."

"Not TMI," I say, giving her an encouraging nod.

She smiles, then continues. "When we moved to Portland, I was really shy. Meeting new people is okay, but getting close? That's different. It took me forever just to make a couple friends. Let alone trust someone enough to date them."

A warm feeling spreads across my chest. It's nice that Natalia feels comfortable opening up to me, given her self-described shyness. "Jay's the third person I've dated," I tell her, eager to keep the conversation going, "but I'm a senior. You're all juniors, right?"

She nods.

"And Addison and Mason don't have boyfriends or girlfriends."

"Not as far as I know."

"So." I shrug. "Those teen shows make it look like everyone's hooking up and going out all the time, but come on. Priya and I were together for three weeks, and then we spent a month breaking up. Last year I went out with a girl named Lexa for three and a half months before she dumped me for a basketball player. That sucked a lot. I was really into her. I'm still pinching myself that Jay and I have been together for six months."

"That's really awesome," she says. "Not about the basketball player thing. But you and Jay."

"Yeah. It is."

It hits me that we've both drained our coffee, and the sun is beating down on my back where my chair used to be in the shade. We've been talking for a while, which is definitely more than I can say for the progress I've made with my future stepsiblings on this trip. At dinner last night, Natalia seemed to shut down around her cousins, but one-on-one, she's friendly.

Addison's nice enough, but she seems distracted, like she has a lot more on her mind than getting to know Dad and me. And despite the fact that we're sharing a room, Mason has succeeded in thoroughly ignoring me so far. He can't avoid me for the entire week, but the dude has a temper, and as much as I want to set the record straight about this fall, I'm not trying to push his buttons.

"You're looking a little crisp," Natalia says, stacking up her plates for the waiter.

I touch my hand to the back of my neck and wince. "Yeah, I need to get back inside. I'm in the sun five minutes and I burn."

She laughs. "You need one of those giant floppy hats they sell in the gift shop."

I push back from the table, and when I stand, the sun is fully in my eyes. I feel a little nauseous. "Not a terrible idea."

ADDISON

I expected more from Natalia, although now, I don't know why. Maybe it's my naturally optimistic nature, or maybe I'm hopelessly naive. She doesn't return my emails at least half the time, and when she does, they're not the kind of note you send to your cousin, someone who used to be your *best friend*. They're short, polite, all surface. She's worse over text; I've tried.

Ever since she moved, I've told myself she's just bad at keeping in touch. But now that we're here, it's impossible to ignore the truth: we're broken.

I just want to fix us.

Early on, in the first year after the Incident, when Mason and I were both still at home, still in the same middle school together, my brother and I used to talk about the secret we were keeping, how it made us feel. But even before I left for Tipton, he pulled away. Shut down. He's been an emotional desert for over two years now.

I thought with all three of us together, it might be different. That we'd *have* to face the past and find a way to be us again.

But I figured wrong. Instead of leading the candid heart-to-heart we should be having, guiding us back to a place where we can all finally be close again, I'm standing in the center of the hotel lobby, at a total loss for what to do next.

It's Wednesday. The better part of a week in Cancún stretches before me, and what? I'm supposed to pretend I'm fine with how things have changed between the three of us, pretend I don't miss my two best friends? I like data, facts, research that leads to results. My brain does not operate in the land of make-believe, and besides—don't they miss me, too? I can't funnel all my energy into hockey like Mason or stick to the surface, like Natalia in her emails. How's school, what are you reading, seen any good shows lately?

I stamp my foot, hard, against the lobby floor, and the sole of my flip-flop makes a pathetic little *thwap*. The lobby is full of guests, but no one around me notices. If I was still a little kid, I would throw myself down on this hard marble floor and scream and scream until someone paid attention to me, came to tell me everything was going to be okay. But I'm not, and it's not. I'm Addison Acker-Mayweather, of the Hudson Valley Mayweathers, I am sixteen years old, and a tantrum isn't going to solve anything. Finding a solution is on me and me alone, and I'm just going to have to keep thinking.

In the meantime, I have another problem to tackle. Our room, while spacious and well-appointed with a Jacuzzi tub, a hammock, and a boozeless minibar, is entirely lacking in good hiding spots. At the moment, the box—nine by five inches of wood that once housed Cuban cigars—is shoved in the back of the closet, inside my laundry bag. But it can't stay there; it's too exposed. I need to find a better hiding spot, somewhere outside the room but very secure. . . .

My eyes skate around the lobby, searching for inspiration. They land on the palm arch leading to Guest Services, where we checked in yesterday. Two minutes later, I'm standing before one of the desks, smoothing down my skirt with my hands and speaking to a young woman with wavy brown hair named Marta.

"I'm looking for a rental locker," I explain. "Or a safe. Does the resort offer those?"

"Of course," she says, voice buttery, and my heart lifts. I should have thought to ask yesterday. "Right in your room, there is a personal safe large enough to hold a laptop computer, your passport, your jewelry, and so on. Theft is extremely uncommon at La Maravilla, but we recommend you store your valuables for your own peace of mind."

And my heart sinks right back to my gut. I did, of course, find the safe. It's on a shelf in the closet; Mia and Natalia and I already have our passports and electronics in there. And of course, we all share the same access code.

"What I need is something in addition to that, actually. My cousins have *a lot* of stuff." I flash her a smile. "I'm looking for a locker I could rent. At the gym, or the spa, maybe?"

Marta frowns. "There are day lockers available for both the gym and the spa, free of charge. You will also find lockers next to the restrooms at the beach. But these lockers are for day use only. They are cleaned and inspected by the staff each night."

I twist my lips, thinking. "Is there a bank on the premises?"

She slides open her desk drawer and pulls out a map. "Not at La Maravilla, but there is a bank located in our sister hotel about a kilometer down the beach." She circles it with a pen. "But I should tell you that if you are looking to rent a safe-deposit box, you will need an adult present to cosign on the account."

"Right," I say, and I must sound as discouraged as I feel, because Marta's face lights up again.

"You are staying in a room with your cousins? The Mayweather party?"

I nod.

"There is also a safe in room 505, Ms. Acker-Mayweather's room. Your mother?"

I stifle a sigh. This is going exactly nowhere, and if I say I can't share with my mom, she's going to start to get suspicious.

"Totally," I say brightly. "I should have thought of that. Thanks for your help."

"Anytime," she says. "There is someone available at Guest Services from eight to five daily. Please come see us whenever you have a question during the course of your stay."

I thank her again, then turn toward the doors. Beyond the palm arch, Mason is standing in the lobby, shoulder propped against a wide stone pillar. I freeze, heart stuttering in my chest. He's on his phone, typing, not paying attention to me, but the Guest Services doors were flung wide this whole time. He is, without a doubt, within earshot.

I walk briskly into the lobby and make a quick left, away from Mason and toward the restrooms. Without looking back to see if he's noticed me, I push through the door to the women's room and shut myself into a stall. How long was he standing there? And what did he hear?

8

NATALIA

Mia is at camp, Addison is off doing whatever Addison is off doing, and I have the room to myself, so I stretch out on the hammock on our balcony and make sure Wi-Fi calling is enabled so Mom and Mami don't kill me when they get this month's phone bill. Then I wait until our agreed-upon time and video-call Seth.

"Hey, beautiful."

I grin, a big toothy smile from ear to ear. I can't help it. From the moment we first messaged last month, I've been absolutely incapable of keeping my chill.

The story of how we met is so random. Twitter isn't a platform I use personally, but at school, I'm the social media chair for Hamilton Wind Ensemble, which means I'm responsible for posting about our events and maintaining "a lighthearted and whimsical presence" (the words of my conductor) on our channels once or twice a week. It basically involves posting a lot of classical music memes. You'd be surprised how many are out there. *To understand the future, we have to go Bach in time. Da club can't even Handel me right now.*

Seth Bates (@sethybgoode) had recently started following our account. We don't have that many followers who don't go to Hamilton, so I'd noticed when he liked a bunch of my memes. Then, a few weeks ago, I posted this joke about piping a classical playlist through the loudspeakers to lull our teachers into giving us a night off, asking Twitter for track suggestions. The post was totally tanking. It got two likes, one girl from my school suggested Chopin (so obvious), and no one else replied. I'll admit, it was a little juvenile. Not up to the caliber of my typical witty content. But then, four hours later, when I was about to delete it, Seth wrote, How about some Branca to wake them up instead?

You like Branca? I wrote back from the wind ensemble account.

Only when I want to break things, he wrote, but some of my teachers have been asleep since his death in 2018.

It was such a weird coincidence. I'd never even heard of Glenn Branca until the week before, when our conductor was late to rehearsal and Derrick Gaff, our first alto sax player, was blasting Branca's Symphony No. 13 (Hallucination City) for 100 Guitars on his phone. Derrick is this wiry, scenester kid from the East Coast—close to where I used to live in Nyack, actually—who transferred to Hamilton last year and doesn't really fit in with the rest of Wind Ensemble socially. But he's super talented on sax, and he's always trying to get the rest of us to play edgier stuff—like Branca.

Anyway, I DMed Seth, and we started messaging back and forth. It turned out he plays drums in his high school's concert band in Spokane. He also plays soccer in the fall, baseball in the spring, and does theater, peer tutoring, and Amnesty International year-round on top of six APs. We text every day, but with his schedule, we usually only video-chat about once a week.

"It's good to see your face," I tell him. It's a dorky thing to say, but Seth never makes me feel dorky. He loves that I'm so serious about flute. This spring, when we—hopefully—meet in person, we're going to collaborate on a composition for flute and drums. No one does flute and percussion duets; I already have a lot of ideas for things we can try.

"You too." He matches my grin. I love the way his cheeks crease into smile lines and how his reddish-brown hair falls across his forehead and almost, but not quite, into his eyes. Which are brown flecked with a bit of green.

"So tell me about Cancún. Met any hot surfers on the beach?"

"Hardly." I laugh. "Are you worried?"

"Maybe a little. You're there a whole week. It took me less time to fall for you."

My cheeks are a deep red, and I hope it looks like sunburn on the screen. "Well, don't be. I'm with my family. Like, *aaaall* my family. I think this is the first time I've been alone since we touched down."

Seth flashes me another smile. "You know I'm just teasing.

It shouldn't feel any different, since you're always a state away, but I guess I miss you extra."

"Me too." My cheeks are even redder, if that's possible. "But funny you should mention surfers, because there's a whole thing here with this surf school being accused of recruiting for a cult. Did you hear about this?"

Seth's hazel eyes go wide, and he shakes his head. His hair dances across his forehead.

I fill him in on the missing girls, the cult, the probably racist California police, and finally the parental mandate to stick together outside the resort. "And I get it, because I definitely wouldn't want Mia wandering off down the beach alone, but I'm almost seventeen."

"Not until March," Seth reminds me. It's a bit of a sensitive subject between us. I'm only five months older, but because of how our birthdays fall, I'm a junior and he's a sophomore. Sometimes he jokes about it, calling me his "foxy older woman," but I can tell he's a little insecure about the age difference. Not that he needs to be. It doesn't bother me at all.

We moved to Portland in the middle of eighth grade, which is a terrible time to change schools. I barely remember the rest of that year, except that I dreaded going to school each day and made exactly zero friends. Things got a little better when I started high school the next fall; Hamilton combines students from three middle schools, so I wasn't the de facto new girl anymore. But making friends didn't come much easier. Back at home, in Nyack, I had all the same friends I'd known since kindergarten. And until the Incident made things weird between us, I had my cousins—my closest friends—a short drive away.

At Hamilton, everyone had friends already, and on the rare occasion someone did invite me to do something, I'd freeze up. Did they really like me, or were they just being polite? Or, worse, trying to trick me into letting down my guard, only to burn me later?

After the Incident, I was paranoid. I didn't know who to trust. It was easier to keep my head down and make it through the school day, then go home and chat with my friends back in Nyack for hours.

Concert band helped. I met Lila (clarinet) and Charlie (percussion), and then we all made wind ensemble this September. We're a pretty tight-knit group. I finally have "my people," but it took three full years of living in Portland to get here.

Point being, I know how hard it is to meet new people and let them in and let them let you in. I'd never judge someone for being a few months younger than I am or discount them because they lived somewhere else. I wish Seth was a junior at Hamilton, that he played in wind ensemble with me, that I got to see him, in person, every day. But so what if he's five months younger and lives a state away? I think we might be perfect for each other. That's all I care about.

"I have to go," he says way too soon. "I'm tutoring Lexi in fifteen."

"Over break?" I can't keep the disappointment out of my voice.

"Yeah, we're meeting up over Zoom. She's still super struggling with chem."

"Talk soon?" I say, giving him a big smile even though part of me wants to beg him to stay on the phone five more minutes. But that would be so needy. I'm not like that.

"Yeah. I'll text you later."

And then he's gone.

MASON

The last thing I need today is another ambush appeal from my sister, so instead of hitting up one of the restaurants for lunch, I grab a plate of chicken tacos from the grill by the pool, then head up to the second floor, to something called the Teen Lounge. On the website, it looks like a loud, kind of dorky arcade. Which means Addison won't be there.

After a long run on the beach, I stopped in the lobby to catch my breath and check my texts, and there was my sister, talking to someone in Guest Services about renting a locker. Everything she brought fit inside one carry-on; what the hell does she need a locker for? Either Natalia and Mia are hogging all the hangers or Addison is getting more and more like the elder Mayweathers every day. Paranoid about material possessions, fiercely guarding their stuff as if at any moment, a thief might arrive on the scene to fleece them.

Even after the Incident, Addison was never like that. I don't know what changed, but it's not a good look on her.

Inside the Teen Lounge, the same club music from the swim-up bar is playing, at a reduced volume, but instead of droves of people pounding neon-green cocktails and knocking around a volleyball, in here I'm greeted by a lone staffer behind a reception desk. She asks for my room number, then tells me to make myself at home. Two boys who look around fourteen are deeply absorbed in a first-person shooter game in one corner, and a bored-looking girl with long black hair perches on the seat of a racing machine, knees propped against the wheel, ignoring the screen and stabbing angrily at something on her tablet. Other than that, the place is empty.

I put my lunch down on a small round table and take a seat on the bright blue couch beside it. I'm not sure if it's waking up with the sun, avoiding Addison, or my morning run, but suddenly I'm wiped. I sink my teeth into a taco and scroll through the game menu on the flat-screen in front of me. I'd rather be on the beach, but I'll hide out in here for the whole week if I have to. So far, between Theo's attempts to be my bud and my sister's sudden fixation on taking a stroll down Bad Memory Lane with Natalia and me, I'm surrounded by people hell-bent on making this week in Cancún the opposite of chill. And I need chill. I won't let my anger get the better of me, yet again.

To my point, I don't want to think about the Incident, but damn it, Addison, it's the only thing that's been on my mind all morning, and even the low-thumping bass in here and the promise of *Grand Theft Auto V* at my fingertips can't shake it out of my head.

It was almost exactly three and a half years ago, the summer we were thirteen, the summer before eighth grade. Addison still lived at home with Mom and me, still went to public school in Rhyne Ridge, and our cousins—Natalia, Mia, and their older half brother Beau—lived close by in Nyack.

Close. Addison, Natalia, and I were all so close then. But we were also just kids who didn't know how to cope when something rocked our precious baby world. How do you stay joined at the hip when you're put to the test, and everyone fails?

Natalia never should have dragged Addison and me into it, spilled a secret *she* went digging for, a secret that should have stayed locked away. But she couldn't keep her freaking mouth shut. For a moment, anger gleams red at the corners of my eyes, and I squeeze them shut. It's better I don't talk to my cousin on this trip. Addison should know that.

I suck in a lungful of air, then breathe slowly out. Of course the three of us aren't close anymore. Yes, they used to be my best friends, but that was all about to change anyway, even without the Incident. Natalia's family moved a few months later—Beau to the city for college, and everyone else across the country to Portland soon after that. And then Addison started researching boarding schools. Rehashing what happened—what Natalia discovered, what she stupidly shared with us—isn't going to help anything. Yeah, I'm angry, but the last thing I want to do is talk about it.

A concept my sister does not seem to understand.

If you asked Addison to list off her five best qualities, somewhere between a college-level talent for math and science and the ability to have a civil phone conversation with our dad, she'd tell you she's an excellent mediator. She's used to being able to fix things, but I'm sorry, this isn't something she, or any one of us, can fix. Not three and a half years ago, not now, not ever.

Even as late as eighth grade, some of our friends would still call us Maddison, as if we were still the cute little blond twins holding hands on the playground and making up synchronized swim routines in the pool, as if they couldn't see the distance widening between us. It made me cringe. When

Addison announced that she'd applied to some elite Hudson Valley academy with a stellar bio program, I'd never been more relieved. Pop-Pop stepped right up to foot the tuition bill; Mom has always been his favorite daughter, something he shows with his money, for better or worse. Mom asked if I wanted to go to Tipton too, even though I'd never have gotten in with my grades. I didn't. Without Natalia or Addison around, Rhyne Ridge meant no more daily reminders of the Incident. And besides, the hockey program at Tipton sucks.

I cram the last taco into my mouth and select the Banshee from the vehicle menu, because that's the kind of mood I'm in. As the game starts and my nerves begin to settle, I try to think positive about the days ahead: Mia's too young to remember anything, too young to know what we know. And thank god Beau's not on this trip, something about an internship orientation, per my sister. He's a senior at NYU now, always doing some new professional development thing. If I can spend the next six days avoiding Addison and Natalia, maybe there's a chance I won't rage out. Maybe there's still some hope of salvaging this vacation.

THEO

Tonight most of the restaurants are closed, and the resort staff is throwing a huge open-air cookout. At seven, I meet up with Dad and Elizabeth to walk down to the beach. It's the first time I've seen Dad all day; he's been shuttered in their room, working, and I wonder if Elizabeth was okay with that. But now they're both grinning from ear to ear, holding hands, giggling. I fight down the urge to tell them to get a room, because the truth is, it's cute. They remind me of Jay and me in private, how I wish we could be at school. How I hope we'll be in the future, in college.

My eyes linger on my dad's smile. It's been ten years since we lost Mom to cancer. Dad's dated a little, but nothing was ever serious. When I was younger, he worried a lot about me. That I'd think he was trying to replace Mom. But we both know no one will ever replace her, and I want Dad to be happy.

Something that, truthfully, he wasn't always before, even when Mom was around.

Dad has a tendency to let things get under his skin and then lose his shit. Nothing violent, nothing ever directed at Mom or me, but work stuff has been known to set him off. Once, when he thought I was out, I caught him listening to his voice mail on speaker and shouting all sorts of filthy shit back at his phone, as if the recorded voices could hear him. Or maybe because they couldn't.

But ever since he started dating Elizabeth, he's been much better at keeping his emotions under control. She must have a calming effect on him. He seems content. Happy.

And if happiness means joining forces with the Mayweathers, so be it. I keep reminding myself it won't be a huge deal, not much will really change. They're not getting married until June, and then I'll graduate and leave for college. I'm never going to live with my stepsiblings on a full-time basis or anything. Honestly, if the three of us can survive this week of forced proximity in paradise, I'm sure we'll be fine.

When we get down to the beach, Corey and Holly are there already, drinking beers and talking to another couple around Holly's age. It strikes me again how young she is—only a few years older than me. Dad and Elizabeth walk over to join them, and I look around for Mason, who has managed to make himself incredibly scarce since we got here, despite the fact that we're sharing a room. Mason's nowhere to be found, but my eyes land on Natalia and Mia, who are perched on a log near the bonfire. Beside them, a couple with two little kids are roasting marshmallows.

"Okay if I join you?" I ask Natalia for the second time today.

Mia grins and scoots toward her sister on the log to make room, but it looks a little tight, so I sit on the sand in front of them instead, my back to the fire.

"No floppy hat," Natalia observes.

"Nah. I stuck to the indoor hot tub this afternoon. Had the place to myself."

Natalia laughs. "I bet."

"What about you?"

"Ugh." Mia flings her long brown hair dramatically behind one shoulder, exposing a gold hoop earring. "I'm too old for Kids Kamp. I was literally the only twelve-year-old in the tens-to-twelves group. And I'm almost thirteen! I could be their counselor."

"That sucks," I say at the same time Natalia says, "That's going to change tomorrow. Marisol said that boy from New Jersey is arriving tonight." Marisol is, I gather, their actual counselor.

"And I'm sure he'll be my new bestie." Mia scowls.

I cast her a sympathetic smile, then turn to Natalia. "What about you? Pool day?"

"Mostly." She fiddles with a button on her phone, turning it absently on and off. "I talked to Seth after breakfast. Is it weird that we don't see each other when I'm home either, but I still wish he was here?"

"Not weird," I start to say, but Mia intervenes.

"The whole thing's weird. You haven't even met him yet. He could be *literally anybody*."

My eyes snap to Natalia's. She told me this morning that

they were long distance, but I assumed they'd met in person at some point.

"That is not true," she says. "We met online, but we video-chat every week. He's obviously the same person."

Mia turns to me, eyebrows arched. "Once a week. And *he* always sets the time."

Natalia's face is turning pink, either the flames reflecting off her cheeks or an angry flush, or both. "Because he has a lot going on," she explains. "Seth has a really regimented schedule with sports, APs, concert band, and all his other activities."

"Sure." I give her an understanding nod. "You don't have to explain it to me."

But maybe Mia's right. Something about the whole thing *does* seem a little off. Jay's an overachiever too—sports, theater, concert choir, volunteer work—but he still finds time to talk every day, usually several times a day. Then again, with Jay not out at school, our relationship's hardly what most people would consider "normal." So who am I to judge?

"We need another opinion," Mia says.

"Don't—" Natalia starts to say, but Mia is already waving Addison and Mason toward us.

"Would you date someone you met online?" she asks.

Addison squeezes onto the log with them and Mason squats down on the sand, keeping a good amount of distance between us.

"Maybe," Addison says. "It would depend."

Mason's eyes flick across the four of us. "Who's dating an internet rando?"

"Seth's *not* a stranger," Natalia blurts out. "Technically, we met online, but not on a dating app. We started talking on Twitter, about wind ensemble stuff. And the only reason we haven't met in person yet is because he lives in Spokane. That's a really long drive, and neither of us has a car. But I'm going out there this spring. We're already planning it."

"I guess that seems fine," Addison says, a hint of worry in her voice. "People meet through apps all the time. Like Mom and Austin."

"That's a little different, though." I don't want to offend Natalia, but it's *not* quite the same. "They sent a couple messages back and forth, then went out on a date."

Natalia gives me a wounded look, and I grasp for a handful of sand, let it trickle through my fingers.

"Mason?" Mia asks.

"Seems whatever," he says, obviously bored. "I'm hungry."

"Me too." I push myself up and step away from our little circle to dust the sand off the back of my jeans. My eyes travel to a row of grills, where a team of black-aproned staff are filling plates for a line of resort guests. "I'm going to grab a couple hot dogs. Anyone want one?"

"No hot dogs," Natalia says. She stands and shoves her phone into the pocket of her shorts. "But I'll see what else they have."

"We'll all go together," Addison says, also standing.

"Are you vegetarian?" I ask Natalia as we join the end of the grill line.

"The Mayweathers don't eat hot dogs," Mia announces before her sister can answer. "Because of Pop-Pop."

My gaze bounces among the four of them. "I don't get it."

Mason sighs. "Our grandfather can't stand the smell. It's no big deal."

"It *is* a big deal," Natalia argues. She turns to me. "Has anyone told you about Grandma Serena yet?"

I shake my head slowly, confused. I thought their grandmother's name was Gloria.

"Serena Mayweather is our biological grandmother," Addison explains. "Pop-Pop's first wife, before Gigi. Story goes, she disappeared on a camping trip with Pop-Pop and another couple back in 1977, when Mom and Aunt Kiersten were still babies."

Mason picks it up. "It's not a story, it's real life. Grandma Serena went hiking into the woods alone. Never a good idea. Seems like she was looking for more kindling, and got lost, because they found her backpack and a bundle of sticks at the top of a steep cliff over three miles from the campsite."

"Animals got her body," Mia says, voice hushed.

"Anyway," Natalia breaks in, "they were all grilling hot dogs on sticks at the campsite that night, Pop-Pop and Grandma Serena and their friends. Right before she died. They turn his stomach now, so we don't eat them, out of respect."

"Maybe it seems weird," Mason says, "but it's a family thing we do. We didn't grow up eating them, and burgers are the superior grilled meat anyway."

"I might try a hot dog tonight," Addison announces as we shuffle up in the grill line. Mason's, Natalia's, and Mia's heads swivel toward her.

"What?" she says, shrugging. "Pop-Pop's not here, is he?"

"I guess not. . . ." Mia grinds her toe into the sand, sounding unsure.

It's finally my turn, and I step up to the first grill and ask for two hot dogs and a burger. I'm starving. As I take my plate down to the next station to get an ear of corn, I can't help but wonder what kind of sick hold their grandfather has over this family. Not eating something a person has a bad association with in front of them is one thing; that's just being polite. But the others looked like Addison had sprouted a second head when she announced she was going to buck tradition tonight, when their Pop-Pop is a five-hour plane ride away.

That's not normal.

ADDISON

When we're settled back by the fire with our food, my phone chimes. I set aside my plate of contraband hot dogs—a particularly aggravating Mayweather family custom that everyone regards with near-religious reverence—and dig it out of my bag.

> Are you alone yet? You and I need to
>
> talk.

Definitely not alone, and this is not what I need right now. I glance around the circle at my brother, my soon-to-be stepbrother, and my cousins, eyes lingering on Mason and Natalia. Ironically, the two people I've been desperate to talk to are right here, and they've made it clear they're not interested in the kind of open conversation that could—I hope—end the awkwardness and resentment between us.

My eyes drop back to my screen. If I don't respond, the

texts will keep coming. But what should I say?

"Not so into hot dogs after all?" Mason eyes my untouched plate with a hint of triumph on his face.

I close out of my messages without responding and grab a hot dog, cramming half of it into my mouth.

"Mmmm." I lock my eyes with my brother's. He shakes his head.

The Mayweathers have lots of traditions, many of them stemming from Pop-Pop. Some make abundant sense, regardless of their origins. Of course we should all be comfortable in the water; swimming is a good life skill. When Mia mentioned to me earlier that Theo didn't know how to swim, she delivered the news with a hushed kind of horror.

But while living my life without hot dogs certainly wouldn't kill me, swearing them off doesn't sit right anymore, now that I know there's much more to that story than Pop-Pop has ever let on. . . .

My phone chimes again, and I tilt the screen toward me before anyone else can see.

> You know how important this is,
> Addison. I'm counting on you.

You don't have to worry, I start to type back, then stop. Maybe you *should* worry, I want to type instead. Hot dog rebellion aside, I've always been such a good little soldier, playing peacekeeper, toeing the Mayweather family line. But it's an exhausting act to keep up, and these past thirty-six hours in Cancún have revealed nothing to indicate our baked-in dynamics are going to change. Can we go on like this forever? I shove the other half of my hot dog into my mouth and chew.

"Who're you texting?"

Natalia is peering toward my screen. Startled, I switch my phone off and toss it back into my bag. When we eventually sit down to talk, if we can start to patch things up, then I'll share the texts with my cousin and brother. But Mia's right here, and Theo. This is not the time or place.

"No one," I say quickly, which is of course the exact wrong thing to say.

"Didn't look like no one," Mia says, face breaking into a wide grin. "Do you have a boyfriend, Addison?"

"No," I say, a bit too loud, and everyone is looking at me now. Mia's grin has stretched even wider, and Mason's eyebrows are arched skeptically skyward.

"Or girlfriend?" Theo adds, voice kind, clearly giving me space to push against heteronormative assumptions if I want, which is great and all, but everyone is way off base.

"It's nothing remotely that interesting." I scoop a large bite of potato salad into my mouth, buying some time. Everyone is still looking at me. I'm not romantically involved with anyone; aside from a monthlong period last year when I was hooking up with this guy Josh from the advanced genetics seminar I talked my way into as a sophomore, I've never done anything resembling dating. School keeps me really busy, and I have a lot of other stuff going on. It's fine.

But if they think I have a boyfriend, maybe that's exactly what I need to get them off my back. . . .

I swallow and plaster on a smile. "But if I *was* involved with someone, that would be my business." I hope I sound coy and mysterious.

It works.

"I bet it's someone she met on an app," Mason says. "Like Natalia and what's-his-name."

"Seth. And we did *not* meet on an app." She sounds exasperated. Perfect. And like that, the heat's off me.

"Well, *technically* . . . ," Mia pipes up, and then Mason asks to see a picture of Seth, and I take a small bite of my second hot dog, breathing a sigh of relief. For now.

LA
MARAVILLA
HOTEL RESORT

Thursday, January 4
From: Resort Management
To: All Guests

We write with great sadness in our hearts to inform you that the missing American minor has been found dead. The body was discovered by a dog walker early this morning, washed up on the beach approximately 1.5 kilometers from La Maravilla. The public access area between the Hyatt and Sandals—including Fred's Steakhouse and Raw Bar, La Piscina *Splash!*, and Escuela de Swell—is currently closed while a full investigation is conducted by the Policía Federal Ministerial. The preliminary cause of death has been listed as accidental drowning.

We are aware that many of you have, by this time, been in contact with family members of the deceased here at La Maravilla and may have informally gained access to information including the minor's identity. Please remember that this information has not been released to the public by local authorities. We ask you to please respect the family's privacy by not speaking to any media you may encounter in the vicinity of the resort, or who may try to contact you.

The safety of our guests is paramount. We wish to take this opportunity to remind you that lifeguards are on duty both in the pool area and along the beach between the hours of six a.m. and nine p.m. daily. Swimming in the resort pool after hours is not permitted, and La Maravilla strongly discourages swimming in the ocean outside roped-off areas or when lifeguards are not on duty.

The Policía Federal Ministerial will be conducting interviews in La Maravilla's fourth-floor conference room this week. We do not anticipate the need for law enforcement to speak to resort guests outside of immediate family. However, if you are asked to speak to a member of the police, we request your cooperation so they may successfully and quickly conclude their investigation into this tragic occurrence.

With our sincere thanks,

Your friends at La Maravilla

10

ONE WEEK AGO
THURSDAY, DECEMBER 28

Four Days Until the Engagement Party

NATALIA

"You're muted, Gigi Gloria." I point to the bottom of Mom's iPad screen. "See the little microphone button? Click on that."

It's midmorning. Mia is at Kids Kamp, and Mom, Mami, and I are down at the beach, posted up on cushioned loungers beneath tall white umbrellas. If anyone else is up, they're not at the beach. I lean back into the plush cushion while Gigi Gloria and Pop-Pop futz with their Zoom settings and Mom props the iPad up against Mami's beach bag.

"Now we're in business." Pop-Pop's voice is deep and warm, even through the tinny speaker. He gives us his familiar rakish grin. "My ladies. Is everyone enjoying paradise?"

"We truly are," Mami says, matching his smile. Mami and Pop-Pop have always gotten along.

"Everyone wishes you were here," I add, and it's not just a

line. Vacation might be a little easier without Gigi Gloria over-
seeing every inch of the trip, but we all miss the way Pop-Pop
makes the Mayweathers feel like more than a collection of dis-
parate parts unused to running as one. It may sound cheesy, but
he's the heart of the family.

"Did Corey bring . . ." Gigi Gloria's coral-red lips twist to
the side, and she makes a small flapping motion with one hand,
four rings glinting in the sunlight on their Naples veranda. "The
blond?"

"Holly," Mom supplies. "And yes, they're down the hall
from us. She seems . . ."

"Nice," I cut in before Mom can say something that will
set Gigi off. Biologically, only Uncle Corey is Gigi Gloria's son,
and she reserves her deepest scrutiny for him. Aunt Elizabeth
and Mom were born to Pop-Pop and Grandma Serena just a
year or two, respectively, before her tragic death on the notori-
ous camping trip.

Gigi Gloria has always held strong opinions about how the
Mayweather money is spent, especially by those who are "not
true Mayweathers." She may be Pop-Pop's second wife, but it's
impossible to see her as anything other than the family matri-
arch. I've always wondered if her attitudes about wealth, and
her need to assert a healthy amount of control over family deal-
ings, grew out of her insecurities about marrying into Pop-Pop's
money. But I'm no shrink.

"Holly's very grateful to be here," I add, although I've barely
talked to her and don't actually know if that's true.

"Well, that's wonderful." Pop-Pop gives me a wink, and
I know it was the right thing to say. Addison is the family

diplomat, but I have my moments. When it comes to money, this family has always needed plenty of defusing.

Pop-Pop is the kind of rich that most people only encounter via reality TV, but there are no trust funds among the Mayweathers. My grandfather is very generous, but he'd rather dole out cash on an as-needed basis, and after what happened when he turned twenty-one, it's hard to blame him.

Gerald Mayweather, our Pop-Pop, was raised by his aunt and uncle after the first wave of tragedy struck the Mayweathers: my great-grandmother died during the 1943 flu epidemic only months after Pop-Pop was born, and then my great-grandfather was killed in a home invasion when Pop-Pop was eight. The family's very profitable chemical and polymer company went to Pop-Pop's uncle, and the rest of the family money went to Pop-Pop in the form of a trust he could access at twenty-one.

It was only a few years before Uncle Ambrose ran the family business into the ground, but Pop-Pop's trust fund was shielded from the collapse. With the company shuttered and all the income dried up, Uncle Ambrose and Aunt Blanche grew resentful of the trust, which held the last of the family money. They repeatedly tried to tap into the account, but it was impenetrable until Pop-Pop turned twenty-one.

As an adult, Pop-Pop did send money regularly to his uncle and aunt, but the years the trust was off-limits had driven a permanent wedge between them.

So Pop-Pop's dislike of trust accounts is understandable, but his belief in simply being generous as the occasion arises has led to no shortage of bickering and judgment among his three children, which is hard to ignore, even when they make some attempt to hide it from us kids.

I expect Gigi Gloria to bring up Austin and Theo next, the other not-yet-fully-minted Mayweathers benefiting from their resort points this week, but she goes in a darker direction.

"Natalia." With one coral-tipped finger, she beckons me in. I squirm on the cushion to lean close to the screen, and she lowers her voice, in case someone on a nearby lounger might be paying the slightest bit of attention to what she has to say.

"You must be exceptionally careful with outsiders, once they find out what you have. I don't need to remind you of the fate that befell your great-grandfather Maurice."

Funny that I'd just been thinking of our family history. I know the basics of the story; it was the early 1950s when an invader broke into my great-grandparents' vast New York home. Pop-Pop was safely at school during the robbery, but on that day, Maurice was home in the middle of the afternoon— possibly because, as the head of Mayweather Polymers, he kept a flexible schedule.

In any event, my great-grandfather startled the robber, who must have thought he was breaking into an empty house, and he shot Maurice in his living room, killing him. He made off with the family safe, which contained some valuable jewelry, but it was probably a disappointing haul, overall. I imagine he would have taken more had no one been home.

"Of course," I say to Gigi Gloria, matching her hushed tone. "We're all very careful."

Not that we need to be, not like Gigi and Pop-Pop. Mom and Mami make plenty of money, as far as I know, but we're not ostentatiously rich like my grandparents. And Mom has always resisted accepting gifts from Pop-Pop that she deems "too much"—either that, or she's just not his favorite. It's hard to know what's true. But either way, Mom definitely looks down on her younger siblings a bit; Pop-Pop funds Uncle Corey's often out-of-work-actor lifestyle in NYC, and it's his money keeping Aunt Elizabeth's shop afloat and paying for Addison's tuition at boarding school. Who gets what—and who accepts what they're given—has always been a big point of tension within our family.

"Or when your Pop-Pop and I were robbed," she continues, hand landing dramatically in the center of her chest. Her rings flash against her papery skin. "You can't trust just anyone, especially outsiders."

"Enough of that talk for one day," Pop-Pop intervenes, taking her hand in his. "Kiersten, sweetie, tell me about the food. Let an old man live vicariously through you."

Clearly relieved at the change in topic, Mom launches into a description of the brunch buffet, and Pop-Pop weighs in on what's changed since the last time they came to La Maravilla, when he could still travel with ease. While they talk, my mind stays on Gigi Gloria's words. Neither robbery has been solved—the home invasion that killed my great-grandfather back in the fifties or the more recent theft of several of Pop-Pop and Gigi's most valuable antiques from the vault in the back of their home in Florida. Fortunately for my grandparents, most of the family money is secured in investments and the bank, but apparently they'd been lax about renewing the insurance policies on the antiques stored in their home. It's a sore point for Gigi Gloria, who is typically exceptionally on top of such things. Pop-Pop would prefer not to dwell on the loss, but it's only cemented Gigi's distrust of "outsiders."

"I want everyone to have the most incredible time this week," Pop-Pop is saying. "Paola, you make sure Kiersten orders the nice wine at dinner. Put it on our tab."

"What exactly did Elizabeth say about the wine?" Mom asks, brow furrowing, and my mind flashes to family dinner on our first night in Cancún, how Mom had balked at paying extra for a bottle not covered by the all-inclusive package. Somehow, this has already gotten back to Pop-Pop, and Mom's probably not wrong about the source.

Pop-Pop holds up his hand, the sugar to his wife's vinegar, and sometimes, his daughter's. "I don't want to stir up trouble between you girls. Please enjoy yourselves this week. You're on vacation, right, Kierstie?"

Mom scowls, but she doesn't protest, and Paola is smiling and nodding gamely. The wine isn't really the issue, of course. Pop-Pop is paying for the engagement party this week and then Aunt Elizabeth and Austin's wedding next summer, and why not? Austin can't rake in the big bucks as a magazine copyeditor, and Aunt Elizabeth's shop in Rhyne Ridge is cute—she sells cards, stationery, and pottery by local artisans—but I doubt it's very lucrative.

Ever since our grandparents' plan to finance the wedding came out, Mom has muttered again and again that she "didn't ask for a dime" for her second wedding, to Mami. It's something I always thought was a point of pride, but now I wonder if it's actually a sore spot.

I love my family, but sometimes they can be a lot. I smile broadly at Mami's description of the pool deck, which has apparently been updated since Gigi and Pop-Pop last came here, but I'm already counting down the minutes until this Zoom ends and I can go into the water, float for a while, and forget all this bickering.

My gaze drifts from the screen, down the beach, toward the Hyatt. A tall, broad-shouldered kid around my age is emerging from the ocean in a black-and-neon-green wet suit, a longboard tucked beneath his arm.

Mason.

MASON

The waves here are fucking awesome. The water is choppy enough to keep most swimmers constrained to the roped-off area in an alcove farther down the beach, but it's perfect for catching waves. It's been a while since I've surfed. Not much opportunity in the middle of New York State. I forgot what a rush it can be; finally, I am getting the release—and time away from my family—I've been craving since we touched down in Mexico.

When it's getting close to lunchtime, and I'll have to start making excuses if I stay out any longer, I drop off the board I rented at Escuela de Swell. The three guys working the little hut are a little older than me, college-aged, and they appear to be enjoying an optimal beach-bum existence—renting boards, teaching the occasional lesson, chilling beside brown paper bags stuffed with bottles of blue Powerade and cans of Pringles while a steady stream of Mexican rap spills from the old-school boom box in the sand at their feet. It's hard to believe anyone really thinks these dudes could be part of a cult trafficking operation, or whatever they supposedly did to those girls who wound up on the commune in California.

"Gracias," I say to the tallest, and tannest, of the three, who takes my board and points me toward a wooden stall around back where I can rinse off and change out of my wet suit. I grab my stuff from the little locker where I left it earlier this morning and head toward the stall.

I'm toweling off when I hear a kid's voice ask, in English, if he can sign up for a surf lesson.

"Not here," a woman's voice answers, her reply a hiss. I press my face to the slats and peer through. A mom with big sunglasses and an even bigger straw hat has a vise grip around her son's skinny arm; he looks around twelve or thirteen. She's pulling him away from Escuela de Swell as if any second now, the hut might erupt into flames and swallow them whole.

"Mierda," the tall surf instructor mutters when they're gone. He spits into the sand.

I don't know much Spanish, but I'm fluent in cursing.

The three guys break into a heated conversation. I can't follow much, but I get "el culto," which is obviously cult, "policía," another unmistakable cognate, and "las chicas Americanas," which everyone knows is the American girls.

"We're going to go to fucking jail," the quietest of the three breaks in, in barely accented English. He's short and wiry, and he wears a clear pink visor, turned sideways, and four chains of puka shells around his neck.

The third guy, a stocky, muscular dude with blond-tipped hair, gives him a shove. "Shut the fuck up. Nadie *something something something* a la cárcel."

I'm pretty sure cárcel is jail.

"Hey, excuse me?" All three turn toward the speaker, a petite woman in her early twenties, I'd guess, who's leaning against the wooden signpost at the front of the hut. "My boyfriend and I want to take a lesson. Can you take us out this afternoon?"

"Sí, señorita." Everyone is smiling now, and the tallest instructor grabs a beat-up-looking iPad off the white plastic table inside the hut. "What time is good?"

I fasten my swim trunks and pull my T-shirt over my head, then slip out of the stall, hoping no one remembers I've been here, in earshot, this whole time. I still don't think these three beach bums did anything to those girls, but the skin along the back of my neck itches, and I suddenly want to get out of here.

11

THEO

After lunch, Dad retreats to his room to answer emails, and I don't see Natalia or the twins around anywhere, so I slather myself in sunscreen and find one of those canopy-covered bed things down by the pool.

Soon it's clear why this spot was abandoned by its morning occupants—now that the sun is high in the sky, the area around me has transformed into the "party side" of the pool. Dance tracks blare from the speakers, a shrieking crowd of day-drunk twentysomethings shuttle neon drinks between the swim-up bar and a raucous game of water volleyball, and my bed is in the splash zone.

It's fine. This is far better than frying on a towel on the quiet side of the pool deck, where all the canopy beds are taken. I promised Dad I'd "spend more time outdoors" on this trip, so

I pull out my phone and snap a selfie. Proof. Not that he's following his own advice; I should have known Dad would spend the whole vacation working.

Photographic evidence of my efforts to enjoy paradise turn out to be unnecessary, because one chapter into *Aristotle and Dante*, Elizabeth is waving from a few feet away and asking if she can join me.

"Yeah, absolutely." I pat the cushion beside me. "If you don't mind bad Rihanna remixes and the occasional shower."

My future stepmom is wearing a linen beach cover over a stylish black one-piece, and she has her long brown hair pulled back in an ivory clip. She definitely doesn't belong here on the "party side" of the pool any more than I do, but ever since Thanksgiving, she's been very committed to getting to know me, which is cool. I'm not sure I'll ever fit in with the Mayweathers, but Elizabeth gets an A for effort.

She smiles and climbs onto the cushion, dropping a massive cream-and-black-striped beach bag onto the deck beside her. "I'll take *uns-uns-uns* over burning to a crisp on the chill side of the pool." She makes a dorky attempt to fist-bump to the music, and we both laugh.

"Same," I agree.

A waiter stops by to take our drink order; I get a bottle of water and a Coke, and Elizabeth orders a glass of white wine.

"I know it's not five o'clock yet," she says when the waiter has gone, "but it is vacation."

"Oh sure," I say. "I'm not judging." My eyes travel back to the pool; plenty of our fellow resort guests are clearly on their third or fourth or sixth drink of the day. Classy

Elizabeth Acker-Mayweather and her one indulgent midafternoon Chardonnay will be fine.

"Oh." Elizabeth frowns, and I follow her gaze to the land side of the swim-up bar, where Corey is seated on a wooden swing suspended from the bar's roof, Holly snuggled on his lap. She's wearing one of those white, triangle-cut bikinis that typically only look good on *Sports Illustrated* models, but it's natural on her. Corey is likewise in great shape, and I'm again struck by the thought that he looks very youthful for thirty-eight, which I'm sure serves him well in the NYC acting scene. They're both holding frozen drinks, and Corey is nuzzling into her neck.

They're cute in a very hetero, photo-ready way, and immediately, I miss Jay.

"Has Corey spent any time with you this week, Teddy?" Elizabeth asks.

Should I remind her that I prefer—*strongly* prefer—Theo? I fiddle with my bookmark.

"Shoot," she says before I decide if it's worth bringing up. "*Theo.* I swear, I'm not doing it on purpose. Your dad got me in the habit, but I'm really going to try to do better."

"It's okay," I tell her. "And not really, but it's only Thursday."

Four more full days among the Mayweathers to go.

"Well." She adjusts the pouffy white pillow behind her back and slides her sunglasses onto the top of her head. "This is a family vacation, not a couples retreat. When Kiersten didn't want Corey to bring a date, I told her it would be fine. This trip is a celebration of your father's and my engagement, after all; it seemed wrong to tell my little brother he couldn't bring his girlfriend. But this week is about family time, everyone getting to know you and Austin. I don't like *this*." She waves dismissively toward Corey and Holly, still intertwined on the swing. "And where are my kids this afternoon? Why are you out here alone?"

I tuck my book behind me, away from the splash zone, and scratch uncomfortably at the back of my neck. "I'm not sure what they're up to right now."

"Of course." Elizabeth's face softens. "I'm sorry; I didn't mean to imply it was your job to keep tabs on them. The opposite. With you, Addison, and Mason all enrolled in different high schools, I suppose I've been putting a lot of pressure on this week. And then your dad wound up having to work, which I understand entirely, it's just disappointing. I want everyone to get to know each other."

I open my mouth, the urge to make an excuse for Dad bubbling on my tongue, but I'm saved the effort by the volleyball, which lands in the water directly in front of our spot. Two thick dudes dive for it, sending a wall of water our way. Elizabeth lets out a small yelp as our legs get drenched.

"Sorry, ma'am," one of the guys says, voice sheepish, and then they're gone, back to the game.

"Here." I grab a couple of towels from the deck beside me and hand one to Elizabeth. With the other, I start mopping up the puddles on the mattress.

"Mason!"

My head snaps up, following Elizabeth's gaze once again. She's on her feet now, beckoning widely toward Mason, who has just come through the sliding glass doors from the lobby to the opposite side of the pool deck. A bridge arches over the pool to our side, and Elizabeth is gesturing for him to cross over to us.

Mason's wearing shades, and he's too far away for me to make out his facial expression anyway, but I would bet the cost of my stay here that he's not smiling. Nonetheless, Elizabeth is impossible to ignore, and he sets off across the bridge.

"I'm going to take a dip and find some more towels," she says when Mason has arrived and grunted hello. "Why don't you boys go join Uncle Corey and Holly?"

It's not really a suggestion. Mason drops his stuff down with his mom's and scans the pool until his eyes land on the golden couple, who have untangled themselves from the swing and are now seated on concrete stools lining the water side of the swim-up bar, ordering another round.

"Yeah, sure," he says, and without waiting for me to get up, he's plunging into the pool and swimming toward them.

"Mase—" Elizabeth starts to call after him, but it's too late.

"It's fine, really." I shove up to my feet and reluctantly pull off my T-shirt. Like Mia said on our first day here, the water doesn't go above four feet, so I'm not worried about getting in. The sun is my far greater enemy.

I grab a bottle of SPF 55 from my bag. "I'm going to put on another layer first anyway. I'll join them in a sec."

"Okay," Elizabeth says reluctantly. Then she unfastens her ivory clip and slips off her beach cover. "I'm headed to the quiet side. See you in a bit?"

I nod and give her a toothy smile. "I'll be fine. Promise."

Five minutes later, I'm wading awkwardly over to Mason, Corey, and Holly, who have left the bar and are hanging out in

109

the water, out of range of the volleyball game. Holly has found a bright pink inner tube to float in, and with her white-blond hair, white bikini, pink drink, and a tan she clearly began building pre-Cancún, she looks like she should be part of the photo gallery for this resort.

"Hey, man." Corey greets me with a toothpaste-ad grin and a clap on the shoulder, and I flinch. It's not like it hurt; it's just instinct.

"Oh, sorry." His manicured brows narrow, taking in my startle reflex. "You sunburned already?"

"Yeah, a little." I don't exactly want to get into a discussion of my defaults around alpha guys like Mason and his uncle.

"Let me get you a drink," Corey says. He holds up his wristband and flashes his teeth again.

"Oh, no thanks," I say quickly, eyes traveling to the plastic cup in Mason's hand. A lime floats in amber liquid, which I realize now is probably beer.

"It's cool, promise. Pick your poison." Corey takes one hop-step backward in the water, then another, toward the bar. It clicks then that he's loaded.

I'm not straight-edge or anything, but this is so not my scene, and risking the world of trouble I'd get in if Dad found out is seriously not worth knocking back a piña colada in the pool.

"Nah, pass," I say. "Just a Coke."

"One rum and Coke, coming up. Viva la Mexico!" Corey spins around, waving his drink in the air.

Then three things happen at once. Mason snorts and raises his beer to his lips. Holly slides off her inner tube, a frown on her face, and starts to say something to Corey that I can't hear, because all my impulse control evaporates, and I spit out, "Seriously, man? I said I didn't want any fucking booze!"

It comes out much louder than I'd intended.

Fortunately, no amount of shouting could rival the dance music piping from the speakers, and no one else is paying any attention, but all the color drains from Corey's face. He raises his hands up defensively. "Whoa, okay then."

Mason shakes his head at me. "Dude. Be cool."

"No," Holly says, wading over to Corey. "*You* need to be cool. What the hell?" Her voice is steely.

"I'm sorry. I thought . . ." He scowls, unable to finish the sentence, apparently.

Shit. Mason's uncle was definitely out of line, but would it have killed me to say sure and dump it out later? Now Mason thinks even less of me than he did two days ago, and I'm causing tension between Corey and Holly, too. Perfect.

"You know what?" I say. "I think I've had a little too much sun. See you all later?"

Without waiting for anyone to respond, I turn and wade as fast as I can back toward the edge of the pool, keeping everything crossed that Elizabeth is still in the water and I can collect my stuff quietly and escape to the room.

ADDISON

Two and a half days in, and already my hopes for this vacation are wavering. Natalia and Mason have succeeded in making themselves remarkably scarce, which is absolutely no coincidence. And no offense to anyone else, but without things back the way they used to be with my brother and cousin, family bonding seems kind of pointless.

After lunch, I ignore the buddy system mandate that no one else seems to be following either and take a long walk on the beach, past the roped-off swimming alcove and the dozens of other resorts lining the sand. My gaze lingers on the three young guys working the hut at Escuela de Swell. I'm not sure what cult recruiters are supposed to look like, but it's hard to picture these puka-shell-wearing surfers kidnapping those girls. Regardless, I give the hut a wide berth.

By three, I'm tired and sweaty, but I don't feel like going back to the pool, where I can see Mason chilling with Uncle Corey and Holly near the swim-up bar. The blaring bass, the boozy volleyball game, the thick bouquet of tanning oil—it's not exactly conducive to Real Talk. Instead, I take a quick shower in the room, grab my bio text, and head down to the coffee shop.

It's quiet in here. Across the lobby, there's a line out the door of the ice cream parlor, but the coffee shop is nearly deserted, and I pick out a small corner table where I can post up. Cappuccino and bio reading spread out in front of me, I can almost pretend I'm back at Tipton, hanging out at Manny's Joint, the grab-and-go campus eatery. I slip in my AirPods and turn on "mountain sounds," my favorite white noise app for studying. Think babbling brook, birdcalls, and wind rustling through fir trees. Very not resort vacation. Very home, and given the too-frequent "check-in" texts, my complete lack of success in gaining any ground with Mason and Natalia, and my ever-increasing anxiety over not finding a permanent storage solution for the box, home is where I'd much rather be right now. Rhyne Ridge, or preferably Tipton, where I could be at Manny's Joint for real, or curled up on a library beanbag chair, or hibernating in my dorm.

Except that's not an option, for myriad reasons, not the least of which is the Hudson Valley Student Leadership Conference we're hosting, and the two student leaders from other schools currently sleeping in my room.

So. I take a sip of my cappuccino, disrupting the little cat face the barista drew in the foam, and distract myself with cellular respiration and metabolic pathways. If Mom caught me doing my bio reading instead of "enjoying paradise" and bonding with Theo, I'd be on the receiving end of one of her disappointed frowns, but honestly, this is the least stressed I've felt since touchdown. Biology and caffeine at a quiet café table is my happy place, and no one can be expected to clock 168 hours of uninterrupted family time.

By four, I'm beyond homesick, an unintended consequence of this little retreat from the fam. I switch off "mountain sounds" and scroll through my contacts until I find Rebecca Joy. Then I hit call.

"Addison." Her voice is a bright balm in my ears. "I didn't expect to hear from you this week!"

"I know," I tell her. Is it peak nerd to call your dorm faculty over break? Absolutely. But do Ms. Joy—Rebecca—and I have that kind of relationship? We do. "Vacation is great and all, but I really miss school. How's Anders?"

"Logan and I are holding down the fort at the dorm. I made

sure you got the quietest pair of the bunch assigned to your room. These girls are lights-out by nine, no parties."

"Good looking out." I smile, even though she can't see me. "How's Logan?"

"Delighted to have a new audience for his stories. This week, he's decided the first floor of Anders is 'the palace grounds,' which is guarded by Pink Palace Unicorn, Manny's cousin."

Logan is Ms. Joy's highly imaginative four-year-old, who I babysit regularly. Manny the winged stallion is the school mascot.

"Love it. Can't wait to meet Pink Palace Unicorn when I get back."

"By then, I'm sure she'll have a full complement of mythical friends. But right now, shouldn't you be at the beach? Or, I don't know, spending some quality time with your brother?"

"Ugh. You sound like my mom."

"Well. We parents share a common wisdom." She laughs. "But seriously, I'm hanging up now. Go enjoy Mexico. Logan and I will see you in a few days."

Too soon, she's gone, and I'm left sitting in the coffee shop, now-empty cappuccino in front of me, the week's anxieties settling back in. Mia will be back from Kids Kamp in under an hour, and I forgot to check the box when I went to the room to shower. Maybe I'm being paranoid, but I won't be able to sit still through dinner unless I set eyes on it first. I close my bio text and grab my phone, then head up to the room.

12

NATALIA

After dinner and two trips to the dessert buffet with Mia, I drift out to the pool and sit on the edge, down by the slide, feet dangling in the water. The lifeguards are packing up for the night, but I'm not planning to go for a swim. It's quiet out here, the complete opposite of the daytime crush, and with the sun tucked away there's a pleasant ease to the air, a relief against my skin after the amped-up air-conditioning.

I dip my feet and cue up Poulenc's Sonata for Flute and Piano, sending it to my earbuds and letting my thoughts drift. Ten minutes later, I'm lost to this morning's call with Gigi Gloria and Pop-Pop, Gigi's firm conviction that "outsiders" are coming for the Mayweather money, when a dark shadow falls over me, blocking out the bright pool lights. My head jerks up.

The shadow begins to descend, backlit against the resort, and I squeal.

"Shit, sorry." The figure takes two steps back.

I scrub my hand across my eyes. *Theo.*

So silly.

"No, it's totally fine." I shake it off and pat the deck beside me.

"Didn't mean to sneak up on you." He kicks off his sneakers and plops down cross-legged on the ground.

"You didn't. My mind was who knows where."

With the *outsiders*. Which Theo either is or is not, depending on how Gigi deigns to think of her future step-grandkid.

"Everyone else is inside," he says. "Watching the entertainment."

"Yeah." I dip my hand into the pool, let the water trail around my fingers. "I can't quite put my finger on it, but there was something a little exploitative about the 'traditional dancers.'"

"Like their costumes are from Walmart, and you know they're not really into putting on a show for all these white people?" Theo says.

"Exactly."

"What were you watching?" He gestures toward my phone, which is open to YouTube.

"Listening, really. It's a classical playlist, compositions featuring the flute." I pop out one earbud and offer it to Theo. "Want to listen?"

He nods. "Sure."

I raise my eyebrows, sure he's just being polite, but for the next five minutes we sit in silence while Theo listens attentively to Bach.

Eventually the piece ends, and we both slip our earbuds out.

"I'm sorry about the cookout last night," he says, out of nowhere.

I cast him a confused glance. "What do you mean?"

"Everyone was kind of ragging on how you and Seth haven't met in person yet, and I made it worse, saying that how Dad and Elizabeth got together wasn't the same thing."

"Oh. It's fine." I shrug. "Mia's just trying to fit in with the big kids, and I guess my cousins are worried about me. They don't need to be, to be clear, but they weren't trying to be assholes."

"Okay," he says, staring hard at the pool deck and rotating the earbud between his thumb and index finger. "But still, I owe you an apology. The thing is, Jay's only out to his family and close friends, so we're not public at school. A lot of people would have Strong Opinions about that if they knew. Like it's not okay to be partially closeted, even though Jayden has his reasons, which I respect."

"I'm not judging," I tell him.

"Thanks. And neither should anyone, about your relationship with Seth. I hope you can meet up soon, but it's cool that you found each other. That's the main thing."

My grin splits my face in two. "Thanks, Theo."

MASON

The show is fine, but there has to be something better to do around here at night than congregate in the hotel lobby with my entire family, watching five dancers perform in headdresses and body paint.

Actually, not my entire family. Natalia is missing, as are Uncle Corey and Holly. Which means family bonding is over for the evening, and I don't have to hang around here either. I cast a quick glance at Mom, but she and Austin have their arms wrapped around each other's waists, totally absorbed in the performance.

Watching the two of them together, a queasy fist takes hold of my guts. Mom seems happy, but for years, she put on a show of being happy with Dad while he slowly destroyed their marriage. And as much as she insists the two men are nothing alike, I can't forget the fight I overheard last summer, the night Mom and Austin came home from that magazine launch party. Nothing like that has happened again, as far as I know, but there's something about Austin I don't like. I've been trying to shove the feeling down, for Mom's sake, but a part of me is waiting for him to screw up again and justify my instincts.

Mom nuzzles into his neck and I push my doubts aside, for now.

I slip through the sliding glass doors and out onto the pool deck. The swim-up bar is closed, but there are at least three bars inside that will be open for hours. If I can find Uncle Corey, he'll definitely hook me up with a beer. I start a lap around the pool, which is all but deserted with the lifeguards off duty. A lone security guard paces between the end with the volleyball net and the end with the waterslide, patrolling for intruders, or more likely, wasted guests struck with the brilliant idea to take a night swim. Given the hard partying that goes on during the

daylight, I'm sure resorts like these are desperate to avoid float-
ers, and the accompanying lawsuits.

They have nothing to worry about from either generation
of Mayweathers. Pop-Pop trained us well: become an excellent
swimmer, and never go into the water drunk or high.

I pass by three gray-haired ladies kicking back in lounge
chairs with glasses of wine, a couple making out in a cabana bed,
and a group of millennials presumably here on a girls' trip, sitting around the fire pit that separates the beach from the pool
deck. I look all around, but Uncle Corey and Holly are nowhere
to be seen. Then my eyes land on two familiar forms talking by
the waterslide, a man and a woman, and I head over.

"Hey, Mason."

Shit. It's Natalia and Theo, not Holly and Uncle Corey.

I look down at my cousin. "What's up?"

"Just talking," Theo says. "Want to join?"

I'm about to respectfully decline, but Natalia pats the deck
beside her with her hand. Christ. Not exactly the two people I
was hoping to run into out here, but I'm not quite a big enough
asshole to say "nah" and head back inside.

I sit.

"I'm glad you're here," she says, "because I have to go make
a call, and I didn't want to abandon Theo. Now you two can
hang."

She gives me a bright smile and jumps to her feet. Fucking
fuck. I hold back a glare—I'm not about to explain to Natalia
why I don't particularly want to chill solo with Theo—and
mumble, "See ya."

Then Theo and I are alone.

I can see it written all over his face: Theo is hungry to launch into the conversation he's been trying to have with me since we got to Cancún. Not gonna happen.

"So you and Natalia, huh?" I ask. "You know she's about to be your *cousin*."

Theo's brows shoot up. "What? No, definitely not."

"You sure about that?" I ask, even though I don't actually think something's going on between them. Theo's into both guys and girls, as far as I know, but he has a boyfriend, and Natalia has her online thing going. Awesome that they're bonding, or whatever, but I do not trust Theo, and even though buddying up might be the smart play, I can't bring myself to do it.

"Totally sure. But fortunately she's cool, given that you and Addison have barely been around on this trip. I was thinking maybe tomorrow—"

"Mia!" My little cousin is hovering on the deck a few yards away from us, right beneath a light post, probably hoping we'll notice her. Perfect timing, kiddo. I give her a big wave, and she breaks into a run.

"No running by the pool, idiot," I tell her, and she slows to a walk, then plops down beside us.

"Not into the performance?" Theo asks.

"It's okay," Mia says. "But I was looking for Natalia."

"She was out here, but she went in a little bit ago," Theo says. "She's probably back in your room."

Mia rolls her eyes dramatically. "Talking to *Seth*, I'm sure."

"Probably," I say. "So hang with us for a while. How's the camp thing going?"

"Ugh. So boring." She fills us in on the past two days of activities, which do sound pretty babyish, and on the only other twelve-year-old in the group, a boy from New Jersey who spent the entire day sulking when the counselor took away his video game system.

"How about tomorrow, when Kids Kamp lets out, we get some ice cream?" Theo suggests.

"I have the afternoon off!" Mia squeals. "Marisol is taking the little kids somewhere up the beach, but it's optional for the tens to twelves."

While they make a plan to meet up, I shove up from the deck and give them a small wave, hoping they won't try to follow me inside. They don't.

Uncle Corey's probably at one of the bars; I shoot him a text as I walk back toward the sliding glass doors, and soon, three little dots appear on my screen.

"SUSPICIOUS CIRCUMSTANCES" UNCOVERED IN DEATH OF AMERICAN MINOR ALONG CANCÚN'S HOTEL ZONE, POLICE SAY

Miami Herald staff

Friday, January 5, 8:22 a.m.

On Monday, a vacation turned tragic for one American family staying at Cancún's La Maravilla, a luxury resort in the popular tourist region of Mexico, when a minor disappeared from a private engagement party being held at the resort. Following a search, a body was discovered yesterday morning on the beach nearby, and while Mexican authorities have not yet released the minor's identity, they have confirmed that the remains found were those of the missing hotel guest.

Now, police are saying that what initially appeared to be an accidental drowning may in fact be much more sinister. "The victim's body shows signs of a physical altercation," said Romina Salazar, spokeswoman for the Policía Federal Ministerial, early Friday morning. According to Salazar, while the body was found washed up on the beach, preliminary autopsy results revealed broken bones and lacerations consistent with a struggle prior to the victim's death. "We believe the perpetrator of this heinous crime disposed of the body in the water, or that the body was pulled into the ocean by the tide," Salazar added.

Police are now treating the American minor's death as a homicide. A full-scale criminal investigation is underway in Cancún.

13

ONE WEEK AGO
FRIDAY, DECEMBER 29

Three Days Until the Engagement Party

ADDISON

I don't know why Mom had to schedule our spa appointments for nine o'clock sharp, but now that I've dragged myself out of bed, I have to admit, this is pretty sweet. Mom, Aunt Paola, Holly, and I are seated in a row of pedicure thrones, sipping brunch beverages—iced coffee for me and mimosas for everyone else—and listening to rain-forest sounds while our feet are soaked, exfoliated, and massaged by four young women chattering busily in Spanish.

In a separate room, Mia is getting a "rejuvenating facial," something I'm not sure anyone needs at the advanced age of twelve, but when we arrived twenty minutes ago, I overheard my little cousin whispering back and forth with her mom, something about having gotten her toenails done right before the trip. Aunt Paola didn't look particularly happy, but she sent

Mia off for her treatment and settled into her pedicure throne with a smile.

Aunt Kiersten and Natalia are conspicuously absent from the morning's festivities. I want to ask Mom what's up with that, but she's on her second mimosa and laughing loudly with Holly, something about a New York City boutique specializing exclusively in bedazzled flip-flops, and I don't want to put a damper on her good mood. This morning is for her, after all.

Which is why it's so weird that Aunt Kiersten and Natalia aren't here. Spa treatments are a pricey add-on to La Maravilla's all-inclusive package, but surely all four of them could have come this morning, for Mom's sake. Mom says she doesn't want a bridal shower or bachelorette party or anything like that. She had all the trappings for her first wedding, to Dad. Before they split up, before Dad started struggling with alcohol and stopped being anything close to a good husband to Mom, I used to love looking through their old photos—the early days of their relationship, the engagement, the wedding.

Anyway, this trip is like a shower and girls' night out and engagement party all rolled into one, and when Mom sent out an email a few weeks ago suggesting the Mayweather ladies book fancy spa treatments together one morning, I assumed everyone would say yes.

The thought that Natalia is avoiding me, that her absence this morning is *because* of me, flits through my mind, and once it's landed, I can't shake it off. It's our third full day at the resort, and I've still made zero progress with my brother and cousin. In fact, the opposite. After my attempt at breakfast on Wednesday, I've barely seen them outside of meals or the occasional run-in at the pool. In my fantasies leading up to this trip, we hashed everything out the first day here, then spent the rest of our time in Cancún sharing stories and laughing and having fun like the three best friends we used to be. In reality, it's like we're on three separate vacations, and everyone but me seems perfectly happy to keep it that way.

Some reunion.

I glance across Holly, over to Mom, who is talking to Aunt Paola now. At the mention of the name Serena, my ears perk up.

"When David and I got engaged all those years ago," Mom is saying, "the realization that my mother wouldn't be there to see me walk down the aisle hit hard. Her absence had been a part of me for my entire life, but something about the engagement brought new, ugly feelings to the surface. There was the usual dull sadness, but beneath that, I was *angry*. If only she hadn't gone camping with Dad, if only she hadn't gone off alone, if only someone had gone to look for her sooner . . . There I was, all grown up, starting a new chapter of my life, and my mother would never get to see any of it."

Aunt Paola nods sympathetically. "And now?"

Mom shakes her head, thick brown hair dancing across her cheeks. She smiles. "Things are very different the second time around. I will always miss the idea of my mother, but I've been at peace with her death for a long time now. When I stopped casting around for someone or something to blame— Dad, their friends, the universe, sometimes my mom herself— things got a lot easier. It was a tragedy, plain and simple, and finger-pointing didn't make me feel any better." She laughs, and the look of relief on her face is lovely. "Anger takes a lot of energy. I learned that from my first marriage. I'm starting fresh this time, with Austin. No anger, no blame."

From the chair beside mine, Holly clears her throat. I startle, turning to her.

"This is so nice," she says, giving me a wide smile. "Your family's been so kind, inviting me on this trip."

"Oh, of course." Part of me is still listening to Mom talk, but the discussion of Grandma Serena seems to be over, and now Mom is pulling up something on her phone to show Aunt Paola.

"I appreciate being included," Holly says.

"Mom really wanted you here." I return her smile with my own. It was Aunt Kiersten who didn't want my uncle bringing his girlfriend of only a couple of months on a trip that is, ostensibly, a family reunion. Is Holly the reason Aunt Kiersten isn't here this morning?

"I don't think your aunt is too happy with my presence," Holly says, as if reading my mind. "The truth is, I've always had trouble making female friends. I just give some people the wrong impression." Her pink-glossed lips form a little pout.

Pretty face, big boobs, perma-tan, white-blond hair, tiny waist. Yeah, I can see how some women might be threatened by Holly, but I'm pretty sure her appearance has nothing to do with Aunt Kiersten's reservations. More likely, my aunt has been taking a page out of Gigi Gloria's playbook—her distrust of "outsiders," her suspicion that anyone new is only after the Mayweather money, of which Uncle Corey has a steady stream, supporting his not-so-successful acting career.

"I don't think it's that," I tell her. "Aunt Kiersten can take a while to warm up to new people. She'll come around."

Probably not on this trip, but I keep that to myself.

Felicidad, my pedicurist, is applying a layer of quick-dry top coat over my lilac polish when Mia bounds into the nail spa, face glowing.

"That was *incredible*," she declares, brushing her fingertips delicately against one cheek. I stifle a laugh; she's incredibly cute, but I doubt she'd appreciate me finding humor in her attempts to act older than her age. "My face is one hundred percent impurity-free. And my esthetician applied all these antioxidants, which bring out my natural glow."

I bite down on my lower lip, not sure if I can keep the grin off my face, but I'm saved by Holly, who takes my little cousin's proclamations in stride.

"Aren't antioxidants amazing? I have this face serum back in my room that you'd totally love. Why don't you stop by after lunch?"

"Really?" Mia's face lights up even brighter. "I'm getting ice cream with Theo after lunch, but I could come over after that?"

"Sure." Holly grins. "Anytime."

"All done," Felicidad tells me, guiding my feet gently off the chair and onto the floor. "This way for drying."

Mia follows me over to the heaters. "Want to come with us?" she asks.

"That's okay. I don't think I need any antioxidant serum."

"No, silly, with me and *Theo*. For *ice cream*."

"Oh, maybe," I tell her. I should spend more time with Theo, like Mom's been pushing. Just because we haven't hit it off yet doesn't mean we won't. He seems nice enough; I've just been distracted.

"Please, please, please," Mia says, tugging my hand. It's amazing how she can go from adult-in-training to little kid in two seconds flat.

"Maybe," I say again. "Let's see how I feel in a couple hours, okay?" The truth is, if I have another opportunity to talk to Natalia and Mason alone this afternoon, I'm going to jump on that. With Mia and Theo occupied, my odds of making that happen are slightly improved.

"Fine," she says, tucking a lock of long brown hair behind her ear. "We're meeting in the lobby at one. Come find us."

THEO

At twelve forty-five, I'm leaving the room and headed down the hall toward the elevators when the door to room 506 swings open and Paola steps out.

"Theo," she says brightly. "I was hoping I might run into you today."

"Yeah?" I give her a smile. Natalia's other mom is a little scary, but Paola seems nice.

"Care to take a walk with me? There's a nice shady overhang out on the terrace, and I was hoping we could talk." She says it like she's looking to bond, not like I'm in some kind of trouble. She has a few decades on me, but bonding would be kind of nice.

I glance at my phone, even though I know what time it is. I'm supposed to be meeting Mia for ice cream in a few minutes.

"Not a good time?" she asks.

"No, it's fine. Let me just . . ." I trail off, sending Natalia a text. I don't have Mia's number, if she even has a phone, but Natalia can tell her little sister I have to push our ice cream date to a little later this afternoon. I'm sure it's no big deal; it's not like any of us have busy schedules this week, and I really want to get to know Paola. As far as I know, she and Kiersten are the only other queer people in this family, and Paola is a fellow "Mayweather outsider." Mason's still avoiding me, and Addison hasn't exactly been much of a welcoming committee, but I like Natalia a lot, and I've barely talked to Paola this week.

"Okay," I say when I've hit send. "Where's the terrace?"

Five minutes later, Paola and I are emerging from the elevator in the part of the resort with all the restaurants, the arm that juts out toward the ocean. The Vista Hermosa terrace is on the top level, above the Japanese steakhouse. It's a large space, spanning an entire floor, and it's decked out in all-weather furniture, large planters, and lanterns that I bet look really pretty when lit up at night. In the center of the deck is a babbling stone fountain.

Like Paola promised, half the terrace is shaded by an overhang, from which long, leafy vines drape down. A small white ladder on the wall leads up to a roof above us. The sign beside it is partially obscured by hanging vines, but I can see it says something about restricted access.

Aside from Paola and me, the terrace is entirely empty.

"Are you sure we're supposed to be here?" I ask, remembering now that Dad said something about booking a private deck for the engagement party.

Paola takes a seat on a wide wicker couch with citrusy-colored cushions and gestures to an identical couch across from her, a matching wicker table between them. "No one else is using it, are they? If someone comes to tell us to move, we'll move."

Right. It's probably just the roof that's off-limits. It's not like I'm some sort of ardent rule-follower, but I realize as I sink into the surprisingly deep cushions that I haven't really been myself since we got to Cancún. I'm not exactly walking on eggshells around the Mayweathers, but I'm not relaxed here either. It's partly that I don't feel at home around my future stepsiblings, and partly the heat, but it's also that this place is extremely hetero. New Courtsburg is hardly an LGBTQIA+ haven, but at home I have Jay. I have my out theater friends and the kids in queer youth alliance.

"Good call," I say, settling into my spot in the shade. "So how long have you been hooked up with the Mayweathers?"

She smiles. "That's a good way to put it. Let's see, Kiersten and I met nineteen years ago, and we got married two years after that. She had a toddler when we met—Natalia and Mia's half brother, Beau—and she was in the middle of getting a divorce from Beau's dad. It was a terrible time to start a relationship." She laughs.

"Because of the divorce?"

"Yes, and the reason for the divorce. I'd been out since college, but Kiersten was a baby lesbian. She was just figuring out who she was at twenty-nine, and I'd sworn to myself I'd never again date someone who wasn't already fully out and part of the community."

"Is she bi, though?" I ask. Maybe I shouldn't be asking Paola to divulge the details of her wife's identity, but there's a lot of hate for bi folks among "the community," as Paola put it. Queer people who don't think we're queer enough, or who judge bi folks who choose an opposite-sex partner. I want to connect with Paola, but not if she's that kind of close-minded gay.

"She's not," Paola says. "Kiersten was with Keith—Beau's dad—partly because getting married felt expected after they'd been together since halfway through college, and partly because she just hadn't figured out who she was yet, in no small part because she'd been in the wrong relationship for so long. Some people are late bloomers when it comes to identity, especially us olds." She laughs. "Now it seems like everyone has it figured out by middle school. But it wasn't always that way."

"It's still not. We don't," I assure her. My mind travels automatically to Jay, who definitely knows who he is, but who probably won't come out to anyone aside from close friends and immediate family until college, or beyond. And to my friend Trish, whose specific labels used to change monthly until they decided labels were for suckers.

Paola nods. "Seems like your generation has things easier than we did, but I know that's not really true, or at least only in certain ways. Anyway, I'm glad you're here, Theo. On this trip, and joining the family. I don't know where you're thinking of for college, but if you wind up on the West Coast by any chance, please don't be a stranger to Kiersten and me."

"Oh, thanks. Yeah, I don't know yet. I applied to Reed, but it's still a couple months until notifications go out."

My phone dings, and I open up the text. It's Natalia.

> Sorry just saw this. Pretty sure Mia's at
> camp tho!

"Crap," I say, closing out of my messages.

"Something wrong?"

"I was supposed to meet Mia for ice cream, and I guess she didn't get the message that I was going to be late. I should probably go find her."

Paola frowns. "Mia's still at camp. Kiersten signed her out this morning, so she could come to the spa with her aunt Elizabeth and me, but she went back this afternoon."

"Oh." Now it's my turn to frown. "I thought she had the afternoon off, but sounds like she had the times mixed up. Guess I didn't miss our ice cream date after all."

"I'm sure she'll be thrilled to take you up on ice cream after dinner," Paola says.

I nod, and she begins to fill me in on the must-know Mayweather family history, something about a chemical and polymer plant and a feud between the kids' Pop-Pop and his uncle, over a family trust account. I'm half listening, but the other half of my brain is still on Mia. Maybe she did have the times mixed up, or maybe she was intentionally messing with me. The thought that something could be wrong crosses my mind, but we're at a posh resort surrounded by equally posh guests. I brush it aside.

14

NATALIA

"Okay, fess up."

I'm in our room, sitting crisscross on the bed next to Mia, while everyone else is at dinner. My little sister sulks against the cushioned headboard.

"Seriously," I say, scooting around to face her. "I stayed here with you, didn't I? You owe me."

"Can we order room service?" she asks.

"Obviously." I pluck the little tablet from the nightstand and pull up the menu. "If you had to get grounded for the night, at least we're at a resort. But don't think you're getting out of a full explanation."

Mia and I scroll through the menu and enter our order. When it's gone through, I put the tablet back in its holster and stare her down.

"Fine," she relents. "It was Mom's fault, really."

"Tell me."

Mia sniffs. "I know you don't care about this stuff, but everyone else was getting pedicures, and I wanted to go."

"You and Mom got pedicures the day before we flew out here," I remind her gently.

"Yeah, but that's only because Mom said it was 'ridiculous' to spend three times as much as the salon at home charges to get one here. She said Mami could do what she wanted, but she and I weren't 'wasting money' at the resort, and I'd be at Kids Kamp anyway." She puts exaggerated air quotes around the snippets of Mom's dialogue.

"So you ditched camp?" I ask.

Mia sinks farther into the headboard. "Mom doesn't get it. Camp is stupid, and everyone else was going to the spa, except you and Mom. So I texted Marisol from Mom's phone, saying I was sick, and I told Mami that Mom had signed me out. She let me get a facial, since I'd just gotten my toes done."

My brows arch toward the ceiling. Pretty slick.

"I'm surprised Mami didn't check your story right away." Mia's spa treatment scheme is hardly a high crime, but faking a text to her counselor, then playing one parent off the other, is definitely grounds for punishment.

"She'd already put her phone in the spa locker, and she said she trusted me. I feel bad about lying, but Mom should have let me go in the first place."

"Maybe." It's clear that Mia's feeling left out on this trip, but I kind of agree with Mom that paying $105 for a pedicure is ridiculous. I might be biased, though; I don't like people touching my feet.

"Holly was really nice to me," Mia says quietly, fiddling with the comforter. "This afternoon, she let me use her antioxidant serum, and she gave me this." She reaches over to the whirlpool tub, which sits between our bed and the sliding glass doors leading out to the balcony, and plucks a travel-sized bottle of some European bubble bath from the rim.

I shake my head slowly back and forth. "So you didn't go to camp this afternoon, either?"

"Not exactly. Marisol already thought I was sick, and I was supposed to get ice cream with Theo, but I guess he forgot. Addison too." Her lips curve down at the edges, and I think she might burst into tears. She sniffs and places the bubble bath back on the rim of the whirlpool tub. "So I hung out with Holly for a while."

I open my mouth to tell her how Theo did try to get in touch with her earlier, but just then, the service light beside our door switches on, and the moment passes.

"Food's here!" Mia leaps from the bed and runs over to the little cubby the hotel staff uses for delivering room service. It's pretty cool; you open a small door in the wall on your side of the room, and the food is inside.

We take our dinner out to the balcony. I sit at the small glass-topped table, and Mia takes her burger and fries into the hammock.

"Look, I'm sorry you got in trouble, but no more lying to Mom and Mami, okay? We've got three more days to get through here."

Mia shoves a fry into her mouth and frowns. "Three more days of stupid camp."

"I'm sorry. At least you got out of going today, right?" I give her a small smile, then start on my wrap.

"I guess."

For a few minutes, we eat in silence. When we're done, we go back inside and switch on the TV, and Mia finds some show she likes. Eventually, I hear the door to the room beside us unlatch, and the *thwap, thwap* of Mami's sandals against the tile. I expect the click of Mom's heels to follow, but she must still be downstairs.

Which, honestly, is where I'd rather be. It *is* Friday night, and it's not even eight o'clock yet. I'm getting bored.

I shoot Theo a text.

> Figured out what happened with Mia
> this afternoon—she ditched camp.

He texts me back right away.

> Whoa, what a rebel. Sorry about the ice
> cream thing.

> Don't worry about it. What are you up to?

> Everyone's in the hot tub out on the
> pool deck. It's chill, actually, you should
> come hang.

Be right down.

I slip off the bed and grab a dry suit from the drawer.

Mia's eyes light up. "Want to try out Holly's bubble bath?"

"Sorry, kiddo." I step into the bathroom to change, but leave the door open. "I'm going out to the pool deck for a while."

"That's not fair," she says. "You said you'd stay here with me!"

I shimmy out of my clothes and into my suit, then grab a beach wrap from the back of the closet door. "Which I have been. But I'm sorry, I'm not the one who's grounded."

"I hate you," she says, voice flat.

I walk back into the bedroom. "No, you don't. And Mami's back; go next door and watch a movie with her."

"Mami's mad at me," Mia whines.

"Not really," I tell her. "She's just disappointed you lied. Go make up with her."

"Fine." She grabs a key card and stalks into the hall. I wait until I hear Mami open her door and the sound of their voices. Then I grab my phone, slip my feet into my sandals, and head off to find Theo and the others.

MASON

Hanging in a hot tub with my sister, my cousin, and my future stepbrother is hardly the stuff of Cancún dreams, but Holly's out here too, and her presence seems to be keeping the mood light and everyone firmly anchored in the present. Thank you, Holly.

Until Natalia speaks up. "What do you think they're talking about?"

She means Mom, Aunt Kiersten, and Uncle Corey, who are off in someone's room for a "Mayweather sibling meeting."

Addison shrugs. "Mom called the meeting. Probably just engagement party stuff."

"No way. Mom's pissed we haven't spent more time bonding with the Hunts." I glance at Theo. "No offense, but you can't force that shit. And what are we doing right now?"

"If that's what it's about, she'd be talking to you and me"—Addison gestures between the two of us—"not Aunt Kiersten and Uncle Corey."

"It's not a big deal," Theo mumbles, looking uncomfortable.

"Maybe she's upset about this morning," Natalia suggests. "Mom and I didn't go to the spa, and it turned into a whole thing. We should have just gotten pedicures. Mia snuck out of camp to get a facial, and now she's grounded."

I snort, and four heads turn toward me. "What? That's funny, right? If the biggest drama of Mayweather Family Reunion Cancún is Mia getting in trouble over some fancy spa thing, I'd say we're killing it."

Holly bites her lip. God, she's gorgeous. Obviously totally off-limits, but damn, Uncle Corey is freaking lucky.

"I hope I didn't make things worse," she says to Natalia. "I didn't realize Mia was supposed to be at camp today. We spent a couple hours doing makeovers this afternoon."

"Not your fault," Natalia says quickly. "You didn't know."

Holly shakes her head, and a piece of white-blond hair falls out of the knot thing on top of her head.

"I don't know what it is about me, but I've always been

better with kids than adults. Corey was all worried about ditching me for a couple hours tonight for this family meeting, but hanging out with you guys has been great."

Did she just lump us in with Mia? Burn. I must flinch or something, because Holly's eyes widen.

"Not that you're kids!" she exclaims. "I should have said young people."

Addison, ever the diplomat, gives Holly a big smile. "We get it. You're what, like twenty-two?"

"Twenty-four, yeah."

So that makes Holly closer in age to me than to Uncle Corey. By kind of a lot, actually.

"Well, you're definitely welcome to hang with us anytime," Addison says kindly.

Holly asks her about boarding school, and my sister launches into her usual spiel about the biology program and genetics lab on campus. I tune her out, thoughts still stuck on Holly Bird. I make a mental note to google her later; I don't think she's mentioned anything about her job on this trip, but she doesn't exactly strike me as a high-powered professional. Not to be shallow, but it's pretty obvious what my uncle sees in her. But why exactly is she with Uncle Corey? Sure, he's a good-looking dude for thirty-eight, but he's a struggling actor a full fourteen years her senior. Maybe it's shitty to assume she's in it for the Mayweather family fortune, but first thought, best thought, right?

I sink lower in the tub and decide not to care. I'm sure Uncle Corey knows what he's doing, and honestly, it's none of my business.

15

THEO

"If you'll excuse me," Holly is saying, "I'm going to grab a drink before they close the bar out here. See you all in a bit?"

She twists around to lift herself out of the water, and then it's just Mason, Addison, Natalia, and me. Mason's eyes follow Holly longingly, either for her, or a drink, or both, but then Addison asks me a question, and my head snaps back to the hot tub.

"So what's up with your dad anyway? Dinners aside, I've barely seen him all week."

"Yeah, that." I let my hand float to the surface, and the water threads through my fingers. "Some stuff came up at work, I think. He's permalance for the magazine, so he doesn't really get vacation time. And it's hard for him to turn down work, especially rush jobs that pay really well."

"Oh," Addison says. "I see."

Mason frowns. "I saw Austin on the beach earlier, shouting into his phone. Didn't look like copyediting or whatever he does."

Well, crap. It's true that Dad's never been good at leaving work at work, and he has been holed up in his room with a rush job of some sort, but it's also true that Dad's always had a bit of a temper, something that used to spike a lot more before Mom died. Now he keeps that side of himself behind closed doors most of the time. But clearly he slipped up.

Three sets of eyes are on me.

"He's usually very chill," I say reluctantly. What the hell was Dad flipping out about on the beach? I was really hoping we'd get through this trip without his temper flaring. "But sometimes work pushes his buttons. You'd think magazine publishing would be a pretty low-key industry, but there are a lot of quick turnarounds and tight deadlines and stuff. It just stresses him out sometimes."

Mason, Addison, and Natalia all exchange a look.

"What?" I ask, clearly on the outside.

Mason's lips are pressed together into one thin, bloodless line, and Addison sighs deeply.

"Their dad has some anger management issues," Natalia says softly.

"He's an alcoholic," Addison says, voice flat. "An angry drunk. Mom swore she'd never date another man with a hot temper."

"It's nothing like that." The words spill out in a defensive rush. "Dad doesn't drink, not anything abnormal anyway, and he loses his cool sometimes, but never at me. Never at Mom, when she was alive."

"Excuse us if that's not super reassuring," Mason says.

"It's true," I insist.

No one looks convinced in the slightest.

"Okay." I draw in a deep breath. I have to make them understand. "The last time he lost his temper, dumb work stuff aside, I was seven. It was ten whole years ago."

Addison nods. "And?"

Well, shit. Now I'm going to have to tell the story. My point was just how long it had been, but that's clearly not going to satisfy anyone.

"It was the day Mom made the decision to move to hospice care," I say carefully. The implication had hit Dad like a blow, how the move to hospice would mean Mom definitely wasn't getting better. "Dad was at the absolute lowest I've ever seen him—pushed to the emotional brink."

I let the stream of water from the hot-tub jet gush through my fingers, hoping that will be enough for them.

It's not.

"So what happened?" Mason asks. "Specifically."

I withdraw my hand from the jet stream and run my fingers through my hair, stalling.

"He took it out on Mom's care staff," I say after a moment, trying to keep my voice casual. "There were some choice words tossed around in the hospital room. He may have punched a wall. It was a long time ago, I can't quite remember the details."

Dad definitely punched the wall. I can still see the plaster flaking to the floor, the shocked looks on the faces of the hospital workers, the bruising across Dad's knuckles that took days to fade away. But those aren't details I'm about to share with my future stepsiblings.

Addison's eyes are wide. "Jesus."

"That was an entire decade ago," I rush to say. *That's* the point. "And it took *so much* to push him over the edge. His wife was dying. No one would be their best self in that moment. And even then, he just hit a wall. He'd never hurt anyone."

Not on purpose, anyway. Dad's good at managing his emotions. Most of the time. Elizabeth and the twins have nothing to worry about.

"But that's a lie," Mason says. He's staring straight at me. "Or did your dad not tell you about the launch party?"

All the air escapes from my lungs. How does Mason know about that?

"That was a misunderstanding," I sputter.

Suddenly the water in here is too hot. I reach back and heave myself out, until I'm sitting on the pool deck. From across the way, Holly gives me a friendly wave from a hammock where she's posted up with a glass of wine. Maybe she'll come back over here and save me. I return her wave, but she doesn't make a move to get up.

"What happened?" Natalia is asking. Before I can get it together to respond, Mason launches into the story.

"It was at the end of the summer," he says. "Theo's dad's magazine had some sort of party at a restaurant in Rhyne Ridge. Mom was his date."

My brows fly up. Did Mason get this story from Elizabeth?

"The party was for the launch of their hundredth issue," I mumble. Not that it matters.

"Whatever," Mason says. "Austin completely lost his shit at the end of the night, who knows why. He smashed some waiter over the head with a rocks glass. The guy had to be rushed to the hospital."

"What the hell?" Natalia says, eyes darting between Mason and me.

"How did you not tell me this?" Addison's question is directed at her brother. Her voice is tight.

My heart thuds in my chest. This whole week, I've been thinking Mason was avoiding me because of the way we got off on the wrong foot this fall. And I'm sure that's part of it. But also—it's this story, which he's gotten twisted somehow. *Mason's* the hothead with anger issues and a taste for booze, both of which he probably inherited from his father. He has the wrong idea entirely about my dad.

"That is not what happened," I nearly shout. My face is hot, despite the light breeze on the pool deck. All three of them turn to look up at me. "I mean, yes, my dad dropped a glass, and yes, it smashed and a waiter got hurt. But it was an accident. He didn't *hit* him, for god's sake."

"Bullshit," Mason says. "I heard Mom and Austin talking about it when they got back to our house that night. Your dad didn't drop anything; he threw that glass. On purpose."

Is that true? My jaw hinges open. That can't be how it went down; Dad would have gotten fired. The restaurant would have sued.

But if Dad dropped the glass like he told me, how did

the waiter get cut bad enough to land in the hospital? I didn't think about that when it happened, but now the question needles at me.

"Then Mom sent Austin home," Mason adds. "She was pissed."

I remember Dad coming home late that night. He had been planning to stay over at Elizabeth's, but he'd made the drive back to New Courtsburg instead. He told me about what happened. That it was *an accident*. He was embarrassed, but then it never came up again, and he and Elizabeth were fine. Two months later, they got engaged.

It was nothing.

But the way Natalia and the twins are staring at me, it's clearly not nothing. They think Dad is dangerous.

ADDISON

"I think I'm fully cooked," I say a few minutes after Mason and Theo have quit going toe to toe about the details of a night none of us were there to witness, and we've all been sitting in awkward silence for too long.

I hoist myself out of the hot tub until I'm sitting beside Theo on the pool deck, then grab my phone from its resting spot on top of my flip-flops. Five new texts, just from the time I've been out here. I am so not in the mood.

If I don't read them, maybe they'll go away.

"See you all later," I say, drying off quickly, then slipping into my beach cover and wrapping the towel around my hair. For once, I hope Natalia doesn't try to follow me. She hasn't been out here nearly as long as the rest of us, and if Mia is still with Aunt Paola, that means I'll have our room to myself for a while.

I hurry across the deck toward the sliding glass doors to a chorus of mumbled "laters." Three minutes pass, and I'm tapping my key card against the sensor and shoving hard against the room door. Natalia and Mia must have left the balcony doors open again; this wind tunnel is no joke.

Our room is thankfully empty. From Aunt Kiersten and Aunt Paola's room next door, I can hear the soft murmur of the TV. Good. Mia's still over there.

I set my phone facedown on my nightstand; whatever's in those messages, it can wait. I'm still processing Mason's claims about Austin's violent temper and Theo's counterclaims that whatever happened that night, it was all an accident. Of course Theo would defend his dad, which doesn't make him the most reliable source, but my brother's not entirely trustworthy either. He can be quick to jump to conclusions, quick to judge, and ever since the divorce, he's been very protective of Mom. Bottom line, none of us saw what happened that night, and there haven't been any repeat instances of Austin losing his cool like that. As far as I know. I make a mental note to be on alert.

But right now, there's something more pressing on my mind. I need to take advantage of this solo time to check on the box and find a new hiding spot. It's been zipped up inside my otherwise empty roller case since yesterday, and I don't like it there any more than I liked it in my laundry bag the day before.

For what feels like the hundredth time, I scan my surroundings, but it's still the same lovely, modern hotel room. The exact opposite of a space equipped with loose floorboards or other useful nooks and crannies. Maybe it would be fine to keep it where it is, but as I roll my suitcase out of the closet, I can hear the box rattling suspiciously around inside. What if Mia got curious, decided to take a peek. . . .

I heft it onto my bed, and that's when something moves. Not inside the suitcase—*under my sheets*.

My hand flies to my mouth to stifle a shriek. Carefully, I grasp the comforter and top sheet and pull them slowly, slowly down. The rustling toward the bottom of the bed continues. I bite my lower lip and rip the sheets the rest of the way off. A blotchy brown lump about the size of my closed fist rests on top of the fitted sheet, at the foot of my bed.

Then it jumps, and I stagger back, hand still clamped to my mouth.

Not a lump. *A frog.*

Just a common Mexican tree frog. My hand falls to my side, and I laugh.

"How'd you get in here, little buddy?" I ask, eyes returning to the wide-open balcony doors. That's how.

Quickly, I unzip my suitcase and check the box—which is, thankfully, undisturbed—then jam it back down into my laundry bag at the back of the closet. At least it can't rattle around in there. Until a better hiding spot hits me, that's where it will have to stay.

Then I spend the next few minutes carefully ushering the little tree frog back toward the balcony doors and outside, where it belongs. I close the doors and latch them, then switch on the AC.

It's not until I've changed into my pajamas and settled in bed with the remote that it occurs to me to wonder how the frog got all the way beneath the sheets, which had been so carefully spread up by room service. I'm not scared of frogs; I think they're cute. But there was definitely a momentary freakout, before I realized what was moving. Was someone trying to scare me?

If so, it had to be one of my cousins. No one else has a key to this room.

Then again, anyone could have slipped a key card out of one of our beach bags and used it for a few minutes. The room's been empty since Mia went next door and Natalia went down to the hot tub, and before that, it was probably unoccupied for most of the afternoon.

My eyes travel to my phone, still facedown on my nightstand, then to the closet door, envisioning the laundry bag at the back, the wooden cigar box tucked inside. Has someone on this trip figured out that I'm hiding something? Is someone intentionally messing with me?

AMERICAN MINOR FOUND MURDERED IN CANCÚN NOW IDENTIFIED

Miami Herald staff

Saturday, January 6, 11:48 a.m.

According to multiple online sources, the missing American minor, whose body was found washed up on a Cancún beach early Thursday, has been identified as Mason Acker-Mayweather, 16, of Rhyne Ridge, New York.

Got an email from Mason's mom this morning, wrote Chase Henley via a public Instagram post earlier this morning. *It's him. Mason's dead. It's his body they found. At a loss for words. RIP my friend.* Henley is one of Acker-Mayweather's teammates on the high school varsity hockey team, where he was a forward. The post displayed a photo of the two boys on the ice, dressed in their team jerseys, arms across each other's shoulders.

Henley's post was one of many shared across social media platforms this morning by friends and family of the victim. Mexican authorities have not responded to a request for comment.

3

THE INCIDENT

16

ONE WEEK AGO
SATURDAY, DECEMBER 30

Two Days Until the Engagement Party

MASON

This morning I was the only person renting a board from Escuela de Swell. After Thursday, I wasn't sure if I'd go back, but these guys have the best prices on the beach—probably because they're desperate for customers—and despite the itchy feeling I got last time, it's still hard to believe a couple of laid-back surfer dudes are cult-affiliated thugs. Besides, if the cops had something real on them, they would have shut the surf hut down by now.

Probably.

Nonetheless, Mom would flip her shit if she knew I was out on the beach without a "buddy," at Escuela de Swell of all places. But catching a few waves early in the morning, no one pissing me off or hovering over me, is the best I've felt all trip, and I'm not trying to get caught. So by nine, I've toweled off and changed, and I'm careful to make sure there are no

Mayweather eyes on me as I climb the stairs back to the pool deck, then head toward the lobby.

I arrive to the breakfast place, El Buffet de Oro, to find Mom and Austin at a window table, a stack of plates beside them. They're chatting, nursing mugs of coffee. I make a bee-line for the hot trays of eggs and breakfast meats and hope they won't see me.

"Mason!" Austin's voice is bright, cutting through the chatter in the restaurant. Perfect.

Slowly, I spin around and give them a small wave. Mom gestures for me to come over to their table.

I lift a plate from the buffet station and hold it up, signaling *busy over here*. But my avoidance strategy is short-term. Once I've loaded up my plate, then dawdled by the toaster for an extra couple of minutes, I'm out of excuses. Reluctantly, I head toward their table.

"Well, don't just stand there." Mom flashes me a grin and gestures to an open chair. "Join us."

"I don't want to keep you," I say, nodding at their stack of empty plates and attempting to channel my sister's best diplomatic tone. I'm not sure it's working. "I was going to take this outside."

"Don't be silly," Mom says at the same time Austin clears his throat and begins to push back from the table. She shoots him a glance that makes him freeze mid-motion. "You can stay while Mason eats, can't you?" she asks.

"I'm sorry," Austin says sheepishly. He scratches at the back of his neck. "Can we do a late lunch instead? I really have to get back to it."

He doesn't specify, but I assume he means back to work, to the "rush job" Theo said he picked up during this vacation that's supposed to be all about family time. Not that I care. In fact, I'd be more than happy for him to hide out in his room for the rest of the week. But Mom cares, and that's what matters. Austin may have that dorky-handsome look—tall and trim, salt-and-pepper hair, wire-rimmed glasses—but underneath all that, he's just another disappointing prick with a bad temper, and Mom deserves so much better.

"Mason, you'll join the Hunts and me for lunch today?" she's asking. "Let's say two o'clock at Casa Armando. Tell your sister?"

I rack my brain for an excuse, but I have literally no agenda, and Mom knows it.

"Sure," I sigh. No way out of this one. At least Addison will be there as a buffer.

"Great." Austin flashes me a big smile and stands, collecting his key card and wallet from the table. He leans around to give Mom a kiss on the cheek. "I'll be at my desk."

Meaning the tiny hotel-issued desk with a matching white wicker chair in each room. I'm sure it's never before been used for anything other than charging a phone or housing a portable speaker system; this isn't the kind of resort that hosts conferences or business travelers. The more I learn about Austin, the less I like him. He's one of those guys with a boring, probably not very well-paying job who overcompensates by trying to make it seem *so important*. He may have fooled Mom, but he's not fooling me.

I watch his back retreat toward the lobby.

"So," I say when he's gone. I'm still standing at the table, holding my rapidly cooling brunch plate. "Guess I'll see you at two?"

Mom frowns. "No, stay. Sit with your mom? I'm still drinking my coffee."

I pull out the chair.

"Were you on the beach?" she asks, taking in my wet hair and the thin layer of sand I'm sure I've tracked inside.

"Just for a few minutes," I lie. "I slept in."

"Is Theo still in the room?"

I shrug. No idea, seeing as I haven't been back to the room since I left around six.

Mom sighs. "Have you been spending *any* time with him on this trip?"

"Yes," I say quickly, around a mouthful of toast. This guava jam isn't bad. "We all spent a couple hours in the hot tub last night."

Mostly arguing about Austin. And then Theo slunk back to the room after getting all defensive, and by the time I came in, he was sleeping, or at least pretending to be.

"We're bonding or whatever," I say.

Mom lifts her mug to her lips. "That's good."

I study her face. The urge to say how I really feel about her fiancé and his son is strong, but so is the voice at the back of my head insisting, *Don't ruin her trip.*

Austin's not the only one on this vacation with anger issues. I got mine from Dad, and I don't trust my ability to have a calm, rational conversation with Mom about this. It's why I didn't say anything after the launch party incident at the end of the summer. Why I still haven't all these months later. I kept thinking Mom would come around, that she'd ditch him like she's ditched everyone else who's come after Dad. But then they got engaged. And now, it feels like it's too late.

"You know you can talk to me," Mom says. She's always been too good at reading me, and I have been openly staring since I sat down.

"It's nothing," I mumble, shoveling a giant forkful of eggs and chorizo into my mouth.

Mom frowns. "Doesn't seem like nothing. Did something happen between you and Theo?"

I put down my fork. I could say no and leave it at that. It wouldn't be a lie; nothing has happened between me and Theo on this trip. And I'm not about to mention what happened this fall.

But I can't stop thinking about Austin. This vacation hardly seems like the right time to bring it up, but will there ever be a good time? If I keep saying nothing, when they get married this summer, then inevitably divorced one or three or five years later, I'll only blame myself.

"Not between me and Theo." I concentrate on keeping my voice soft. I can talk to her about this without getting all heated, without damaging my own credibility. "It's what happened last August, the night you and Austin went to that launch party for his magazine."

Mom runs the tip of a finger around the lip of her coffee mug. "Ah," she says. "You overheard that?"

I nod. "You sent him home that night. You were upset."

She reaches out and places her hand on top of my hand.

"You're right, I was. And I'm sorry you heard us fighting; we should have kept that conversation private."

"That's not the point," I say, struggling to keep my voice level. "He hit a waiter with a rocks glass. The guy had to go to the hospital. I heard you say it!" My voice pitches up, despite my best intentions.

"Oh, Mason." Mom gives my hand a small squeeze, and I jerk it away. I'm not looking to be comforted right now. "I wish you'd come to me sooner about this. I had no idea you've been carrying this around."

"Would it have made a difference?" I ask. "You're still with him."

She nods. "Because that's not who Austin is. He lost control that night, and I was very upset. But what happened was an accident, which the restaurant acknowledged, and fortunately, no one was seriously hurt."

"I don't believe you. That's not how it sounded when you and Austin came home from the party."

Mom sighs. "After your father, I've been very cautious about who I date. As you know. That night, Austin got into it with a coworker, something about his latest assignment for the magazine. He'd had a bit too much to drink, and he was shouting. A waiter came over to check on them at just the wrong moment. Austin flung out his arms, and he struck the waiter with his glass. He didn't see him approaching; it was a complete accident."

I sit with this for a moment, processing. "It didn't sound like a complete accident at the time," I say finally. "You said he smashed the waiter in the face."

Mom lifts her coffee mug, then sets it back down. It's

empty. "I probably did say that," she says after a moment. "I was rattled. But Austin is not a violent man. I wouldn't be with him otherwise, Mason. I promise you."

I want to trust Mom, I really do. She *has* been very selective about who she's dated after Dad; she's the opposite of impulsive or starry-eyed when it comes to guys. But I heard her that night. She was *scared* of Austin. And whether or not he hit that waiter intentionally, he got into a drunken shouting match with a colleague at a work party, which is absolutely something Dad would have done. And Theo admitted that his dad went postal on the hospital staff when Theo's mom was dying. The guy has a quick temper, any way you slice it. And I may have no right to talk, but I don't want Mom with a guy like that.

Mom's looking at me, eyes wide and pleading. She wants me to let this go. But nothing she's said this morning is particularly reassuring. For her sake, I'm not sure I can drop this.

NATALIA

After breakfast, Mom marches Mia over to Kids Kamp, and I turn down Mami's offer to join them on the beach. It's clear they're still stressed about yesterday, and I don't have any interest in getting in the middle of their parenting woes. Instead, I text Theo to see what he's up to, and when he says he's headed over to the Teen Lounge, I decide to check it out.

"Everything okay between you and Mason?" I ask when we're both settled on a big blue couch with sodas and a basket of tortilla chips, even though it's only ten a.m. It's hard to turn down all the free stuff around here.

"Sure, fine." Theo flips absently through the available game options on the large flat-screen in front of us. After a minute, he sets the controller down without choosing anything. "I mean, not really. I feel like he's already made up his mind about Dad and me, and he doesn't like what he sees. I'm not sure there's anything I can do to change his mind."

"I'm sorry," I say.

"Thanks. It's not that big of a deal if Mason hates me; I'm leaving for college in a few months. But when Dad and Elizabeth move in together, it's going to be the two of them and Mason for at least a year. I don't want him messing things up for Dad, and I'm not sure I can trust him not to do just that."

"That sucks," I tell him. And it does, although I'm not sure who I feel worse for, Austin or Mason. Maybe Elizabeth.

"Let's talk about something else," Theo says after a minute. "What's Seth up to today?"

I grin. "It's Saturday, so he has peer tutoring this afternoon, but right now he's out hiking with a couple friends. Here." I pull out my phone and pull up the photo Seth sent me a little bit ago. He's on a hiking trail, bundled up in winter gear, waving at the camera. A stunning, white-capped mountain range stretches behind him. "Isn't Washington State beautiful?"

Theo looks at the screen, then lifts the phone from my hand. For a moment, he's completely silent.

"What?" I ask. "You're making me nervous."

When he hands my phone back, his lips are curved down at the edges. "I'm sure Washington State is lovely, but that's New Courtsburg. I'd recognize those mountains anywhere; Seth's like ten minutes from my house."

My stomach clenches, and I stare hard at my phone screen. There's no sign, no trail marker, nothing to identify the mountains in the background. Theo is wrong.

"No," I say. "Seth's in Mount Spokane State Park, hiking with his friends."

Theo breaks off a piece of tortilla chip, then drops it back into the basket. "It's what, seven a.m. in Spokane right now?" he asks.

I nod. "Seth's a morning person. It's not weird."

"Sure, but look at the light in the photo. If this was taken early in the morning, the sun would be a whole lot lower."

I squint at the picture again. True, it doesn't look like it was taken at sunrise, but it could be the angle of the shot. Or a filter.

"I think you're reading too much into this." I click off my phone and set it facedown on the couch cushion. "Why would Seth lie about where he lives? That makes no sense."

"I have no idea," Theo says. "But I've hiked those trails a hundred times. Those are the Catskills."

I don't think Theo's intentionally trying to mess with me, but my stomach clenches harder. He seems *so certain*.

"Okay," I say after a minute. "I still think you're wrong, but let's say Seth is in New York. I'm sure there's a perfectly good explanation."

"Maybe," Theo mumbles.

"But you think, what, he's catfishing me or something?"

Theo looks pained. "I truly have no idea. But something's not right. I don't think Seth is the person he's been saying he is. Or at least, he's not being entirely honest."

I shake my head slowly. I opened up to Theo on this trip. Of everyone, he's supposed to have my back. This can't be happening.

"I used to live in the Hudson Valley," I say. "As you know. Why would someone from there pretend to live in Spokane now? Why would they lie to me?"

"Could Mason or Addison have something to do with this?" he asks. "Or, was there anyone you were on bad terms with when you moved to Portland? Someone who'd want to trick you?"

"No," I spit out, but that's not entirely true. By the time my family moved, my cousins and I were hardly as close as we once were. Not after the Incident. But that was three whole years ago, and my new boyfriend has absolutely nothing to do with what happened back then.

Theo gestures toward my phone, resting on the cushion between us. "Can I see one thing?"

"Fine." I pick it up, unlock it, and thrust it at him. "Be my guest."

He scrolls through my apps, then opens Twitter. "This is where you first started talking, right?"

I nod. "That's the wind ensemble account; I don't have a personal one. I'm the social media chair."

Theo clicks on our followers; we don't have that many.

"That's him," I say. "Seth Bates. @sethybgoode."

Theo opens up Seth's profile. "He only joined in September," he says after a moment. "When did you guys meet?"

"Early November," I say. "Almost two months ago."

"Hmm," Theo says, clicking around Seth's profile.

"What?" I ask, impatient. Yeah, we've only been talking for a few weeks, and yeah, Seth hasn't been on Twitter since infancy. None of this is new information.

"It's just he doesn't have that many followers, and none of the accounts he follows look like IRL friends. It's all national high school organizations and musicians and soccer players and stuff."

"Okay," I say. "But it's Twitter. So what if Seth doesn't use it to chat with his real-life friends? Neither do I."

"Don't you think it's a little weird, though? He'd just joined, he's barely on there, and then he meets you a few weeks later?"

"Not really," I say, bristling. "Like you said, he mostly follows musicians and high school organizations and stuff. He's in concert band at his school; he followed our wind ensemble account. It just happened to be me running it. Besides, people have lots of reasons to not be all over social media. Your boyfriend's not out at school, right? I'm sure he's not his 'most authentic self' on social either."

Theo winces at my air quotes, the bite in my tone. I thought we were getting close, but now I'm pissed. He has me doubting Seth, and for no good reason. *This* is why I have a hard time trusting people, why I'm slow to make friends. Letting Theo in so fast was a mistake.

"You're right," he says. "Jay's social accounts are private, and he doesn't use his real name. That's entirely different, though."

"I don't think it is." I shove up from the couch and stuff my phone into my pocket. "Mountains are mountains. And after those first DMs, Seth and I never even talked on Twitter. He's very real. And he's in Spokane."

Without giving Theo a chance to respond, I turn and walk fast toward the door.

17

THEO

I should go after her.

I half stand as Natalia's back retreats toward the door, but then I think better of it. True, her anger would be better directed toward her supposed boyfriend, not me, but what am I going to say to make things better? Seth—if that's even his real name—is not who he says he is.

Part of me wishes she'd never shown me that photo, but isn't it better she learns the truth now, before she's in too deep? That hiking trail is *not* in Spokane. Maybe to some people, all nature looks alike, but not to me. I hiked past that spot just last week, with Jay.

I sink back down onto the couch and pull out my phone, tap open my messages.

> Miss you. Still down to hang Tuesday
> night when I get home?

While I wait for Jay to respond, I lift one of the two untouched Cokes from the table beside me and take a long gulp. There's a reason why Jayden's profiles aren't under his real name, why he keeps his accounts set to private. Yes, it's because he isn't out at school, but there's more to it than that.

Natalia would understand if I told her, but it's Jay's business, not mine. I've already said too much to Mason, something I never would have done had I realized I was speaking to my future stepbrother.

We were officially introduced over Thanksgiving, Mason and me, when our families got together for the first time. But we'd already met in the stands, during a hockey game a few weeks before. We just didn't realize who we were talking to.

Jay's on varsity for New Courtsburg. I could not care less about hockey, but Jay cares a lot. None of my friends are sports people, but because I am a fantastic boyfriend, I go to the games for moral support. Alone.

Maybe that's why I took notice of the guy sitting alone in the opposing team's gear at New Courtsburg's scrimmages with Rhyne Ridge—always sitting high in the bleachers with an aqua beanie pulled down over his forehead and an unreadable expression on his face. At those practice games, I wondered what his deal was. Was he some kind of friendless superfan?

So when I spotted him again at the New Courtsburg arena watching the first game of the season and looking even more miserable than he'd looked at the scrimmages, I took a chance and climbed up the bleachers, stopping two rows down from where he was camped out.

"Hey, I'm Theo. Okay if I sit here?"

He shrugged. "Suit yourself."

"Rhyne Ridge fan?" I tried again.

"Something like that."

For the entire first period, then the second, we sat in silence, two rows apart. He clapped stoically when his team scored. I cheered loudly when Jay was on the ice, playing defense.

When the buzzer sounded to signal the second intermission, I stood up to stretch.

"You here alone?"

I spun around, surprised he was talking to me.

"Yeah. Just supporting a friend. You?"

He stood up then and clambered down to my row. "I should be out there. Playing center. But I fucked up big-time."

"You're benched?" I asked as he settled in on the bleacher, not exactly next to me, but within easy earshot in the same otherwise empty row.

"Worse than benched. Off the team, permanently."

"Oh shit," I said.

He stared at me, hard, clearly deciding how much to say to some stranger. "Fighting," he said finally. "You can get away with a lot in the NHL, but not on varsity. Which I fucking knew. But I had some family stuff going on, and then this prick from Hudson had been screwing with me all game. I lost it."

He lifted his glasses from his face and scrubbed one hand across his eyes, nudging the beanie up a bit. I might have recognized him then, but I didn't. I'd seen a few photos of the twins, and I'm sure he'd seen some of me, but he hadn't told me his name, and it didn't click.

"Shit," I said again, at a loss for something more intelligent to contribute to the conversation.

"Black eye, bruised jaw. I broke his fucking nose," he said. "I've never been so out of control. Anyway, I deserved what I got. Kicked off the team and a two-week suspension from school. My dad's an ass, but he signed the forms and promised not to tell Mom. Only solid he's ever done me."

I nodded. Either this kid's parents were divorced, or his family had serious communication problems.

"So as far as she knows, I'm still on the team. I go to every practice, every game. It sucks, but it's better than not going."

I steepled my fingers together and pressed them to my lips. This kid just spilled his guts to me. Guess he'd been carrying all this around with him, and sometimes it's easier to open up to a stranger. I felt like I owed him something in return.

"My boyfriend plays for New Courtsburg," I said. "I go to all the games too."

I waited for him to make a face or react in some way— hockey isn't exactly known for its diversity and acceptance as a sport—but he just nodded. "Cool."

"He's not out on the team, though," I said. "I'm usually here alone."

It's lonely enough being one of three Black kids in all of Division 1. Jay says if it wasn't for hockey, he might be ready to come out at school, and online, but he's just not there yet.

I was careful not to look down at the rink while we were talking, careful not to give this kid any idea who on the team I was talking about. In an ideal world, Jay would be out, but this isn't an ideal world. And I'm good at keeping secrets.

"That's rough," he said. "He should be able to just be himself, but not everyone's cool. I get it."

Then he stood and shoved his hands in his pockets. "I'm gonna head out before the third period starts. Good meeting you, Theo."

"Yeah, you too." He still hadn't told me his name.

He turned, and that's when I saw the back of his jersey for the first time. ACKER-MAYWEATHER.

As in Mason. My future stepbrother.

I should have shouted after him, or found him on social and messaged him, or something. But I didn't. *Maybe he knows who I am,* I thought. *I did introduce myself, after all. Maybe that's why he told me.*

But it was wishful thinking. I should have known Mason didn't realize the kid craning around in the stands and saying, "Hey, I'm Theo," was his future stepbrother Teddy Hunt, the nickname Dad can't shake, which has subsequently rubbed off on Elizabeth. I wasn't trying to hide my identity; the whole world, save for Dad, knows me as Theo.

Over Thanksgiving, my wishful thinking got a full-blown reality check. When Dad and I showed up at Elizabeth's house, Mason's jaw dropped open.

"You said your name was Theo," he hissed when we were alone, fingers cinched a little too tight around the arm of my forest-green grandpa sweater. "What the hell?"

"It *is* Theo," I insisted. "Only my dad calls me Teddy. It's a stupid childhood nickname. I had no idea you didn't know my real name, and in my defense, I had no idea who I was talking to either!"

Which had been true, until he stood to leave. But I left that part out.

"You can't tell anyone what I told you," Mason said. "Not Addison, not your dad, and definitely not my mom. Got it?"

"Why would I?" I sputtered. "I swear, your secret's safe with me." Although eventually, Elizabeth was going to find out that Mason had gotten kicked off the team. Whatever he was doing to convince her to stay away from his games, it wasn't going to last forever. But that was his problem to deal with—not mine. I was serious about not telling.

"I never should have said anything," he muttered, releasing the arm of my sweater. "I never would have, if I'd've known."

"I get that," I said, "But I have zero reason to tattle on you. And we both know stuff about each other. Let's chill."

Mason sneered. "Yeah, I know you have a boyfriend, but I don't know who he is, and you're not the one in the closet. That's not the same kind of secret. I don't trust you, Hunt."

That was the last thing he said to me all night, despite my best efforts to convince him I wasn't a snitch, that I had no intention of blowing up his spot. But nothing I did that night made any difference, and then he didn't respond to a single text I sent him between Thanksgiving and Christmas. And now here we are, in Cancún, and Mason still thinks I'm a little shit who's going to squeal on him at any moment.

Which I'm definitely not. But the fact is, he smashed up some kid's face, which makes his suspicions about my dad's capacity for anger management just a little ironic. I want to make things right with Mason—we're going to be stepbrothers, whether he likes it or not—but I'm also a little afraid of him. Not that I think he's going to beat me up, although maybe I should worry about that, too, but mostly that he's going to mess things up between Dad and Elizabeth over some perceived notion of who Dad is.

For the first time in a long time, Dad's truly happy. I want Mason to trust me, but more than anything, I need him to chill and leave this stuff with Dad well enough alone. My fist tightens around my phone.

ADDISON

I'm half dozing by the pool, stretched out in a cabana bed I claimed hours ago, Lana Del Rey flowing through my AirPods, when a shadow falls over me, blocking out the sun.

I pry one eye open. The figure above me leans hard against the cabana's wooden frame, arms raised overhead. I squeal.

"Adds." Mason drops his arms down by his side and lifts his sunglasses to his forehead. "Chill."

"Christ, Mase." I pop out my AirPods and shove myself up to a sitting position. "Way to be a creeper."

"Whatever. We're having lunch with Mom and the Hunts, two o'clock at the fancy Mexican place."

"Casa Armando?"

He nods.

"'Kay. Fine." That's hours from now. I pat the cushion beside me. "Care to join me?"

Ninety-five percent chance my brother will blow me off for whatever he's been doing on the beach all week, no "buddy," when he thinks he's being all sneaky. I bet he met some girl.

But Mason surprises me.

"Sure." He sits on the edge of the bed, kicks off his sandals, then leans back against the pillows. "These things are pretty sweet. They should get them for the pool at home."

I smile, trying to picture it. The Rhyne Ridge community pool is clean and well-maintained, and it has a fancy snack bar, but it's still a public pool with little kids in floaties and designated hours for seniors to swim laps. Our hometown is definitely upscale in a lot of ways, but the pool is not exactly a luxury destination.

Just then, my phone chimes. I reach into my beach bag and switch the ringer off.

"Aren't you going to check that?" Mason asks, clearly suspicious.

I freeze. I'm not addicted to my phone or anything, but it's not exactly like me to ignore a message either. And I've been doing that a lot on this trip. Clearly, Mason's not the only one failing to be sneaky.

"It's spam," I say quickly. "I keep blocking the numbers, but they won't stop. So annoying."

He frowns, not entirely sure if he should believe me. Which he shouldn't.

I *do* want to show him the texts. But not like this, Mason accusing me of hiding something and me confessing to him like I've done something wrong. If he's not in the right headspace, the texts will only set him off. So until Mason and Natalia will sit down with me for a real, open conversation, it's best to keep them to myself.

"Yeah, okay," he says. "But you've been acting weird all week."

"No, I haven't."

It's the exact wrong thing to say. Mason shakes his head, and his dusty blond hair falls over his forehead.

"You definitely have. That whole thing with your suitcase at the airport. And I saw you at Guest Services the morning after we got here, asking about renting a locker? What's that all about?"

My heart stops. Maybe not literally, but there's a very real pain in my chest, and I struggle to keep staring straight ahead, out toward the open ocean. The teals and aquas and navies, the not-quite-calm waves.

"Natalia and Mia brought so much stuff," I say, eyes still locked on the water. I force a laugh, which comes out sounding strangled. "There was literally no room in the closet. But Mia moved some of her clothes. Problem solved."

"Okay, weirdo." He sounds unconvinced.

"Oh my god, speaking of our room," I say, voice maybe a touch too bright. I place my hand on Mason's arm, and he arches his brows at me. "Last night, I found a tree frog *in my bed*. Like, under the covers, hopping around."

He snorts. "Good thing you like all that creepy-crawly stuff."

"Totally. If it was someone's idea of a joke, they had the wrong target. Or the wrong kind of prank." Although I *was* a little freaked out—for a second. Not that I'd admit that to Mason.

"Nah," he says, sinking deeper into the pillow and slipping his shades down over his eyes. "It's the Caribbean. I'm sure it just hopped in from the balcony."

Which is precisely the conclusion I'd come to last night, before I started overthinking things.

I slip my AirPods back in and decide my brother's probably right. No one suspects anything; no one's messing with me.

Everything's going to be fine.

18

MASON

Fifteen minutes into lunch with Mom, Addison, and Austin, things are unremarkable. Smooth.

Too smooth.

Austin tells a story about his brief stint as a science major before switching to English, and Addison seems entirely charmed. Mom orders all the appetizers on the menu, and I focus on loading up my plate with tiny empanadas, taquitos, and skewered shrimp while everyone else smiles wide and exchanges polite, surface-level banter.

I promised Mom I'd make an effort, but Chill Austin is not the real Austin, or at least not the *whole* Austin, and the further we get into this trip, the more obvious it's becoming that I can't let the week end with Mom still in the dark.

"Where's Theo?" I ask when there's a momentary lull in

conversation. The four of us are seated at a table for six, and he was supposed to be part of this lunch, wasn't he? Maybe there's tension between him and his dad; maybe bringing him up will make Austin bristle.

Instead, he sighs. "I entirely forgot to tell Teddy about lunch. After breakfast, I got so absorbed in work, I lost track of time. I meant to text him sooner, but by the time your mom came to collect me from the room, it was already five of two." He gives Mom a sheepish grin.

Which she falls for, hook, line, and sinker. She places her hand on his. "It's fine; I never explicitly said to invite him. I forgot too."

I glance at Addison, and she returns my look with an eyebrow raise. This is the exact kind of appeasing behavior Mom would engage in with Dad, when she could sense a flare-up on the horizon. Mom may be in denial, but Adds is starting to see it, even if she wasn't before.

"Anyway," Austin says, "turns out Teddy already ate, but he said he'd stop by in a bit. He knows we're here."

If this lunch were a lake, I've drawn some ripples along the surface, but it's not enough to prove anything. Time for a wave.

"Hope he's being safe," I say, lifting an empanada from my plate and dragging it through the small pot of creamy white sauce in the center of the table. "I haven't seen him around the resort that much, and what with those cult recruiters out on the beach . . ." I stuff the whole thing in my mouth, letting that hang in the air.

Mom twists sharply in her chair to face me. "I know a

buddy system must seem juvenile to you kids, but there's a very good reason for concern. Those two girls—"

"Mom," Addison cuts in. "It's fine. Mason's just being dramatic."

My sister cuts me a look and mouths, *What are you doing?*

Traitor. I thought she was on my side.

Austin laughs, but it sounds a bit strained. "Ted—*Theo*. Shoot." He clears his throat. "My son is not the sun-and-surf type. He's definitely found somewhere cool and shady at the resort to hibernate."

"Thank goodness," Mom says.

Austin turns to me. "I'm sorry he hasn't been very present, Mason. I'm going to speak to him about that. But there's really no cause to worry about Theo wandering down the beach."

Mom relaxes a bit in her chair. Not exactly the tidal wave I was hoping for, but if I keep chipping away at Austin's cool exterior, eventually he'll crack. I want Mom to be happy, truly I do, but falling for yet another guy with an anger problem is not the ticket to marital bliss. And shit, I know I have my own stuff to work on, but that doesn't mean Austin gets some kind of free pass.

Suddenly Mom straightens up, hand shooting into the air. I turn to look behind me, expecting to see Theo, but it's Uncle Corey and Holly at the hostess stand. He says something to her, and she nods, white-blond hair brushing her shoulders. The hostess leads Holly to a table on the other side of the restaurant, behind the small buffet station where guests can pack up boxes to go, and Uncle Corey walks over to the four of us. Just then, our waiter arrives with our entrees, and we all wait in awkward silence for him to clear the appetizer dishes and set our new plates down.

When he's gone, Mom says, "Would you and Holly like to join us? There's room." She gestures toward the two empty chairs at our table.

Uncle Corey shakes his head. "Just saying hi. You'll be done by the time we order."

I grin up at him. "Pool volleyball later?"

"Definitely." His eyes travel back to the two empty chairs. "No Theo?" he asks Mom.

"There was a bit of a miscommunication about lunch," she says. "He should be by in a bit."

Austin clears his throat and looks to Uncle Corey. "Theo's not very big on the pool, but perhaps you might invite him along for volleyball?"

"Ah." Uncle Corey shifts back and forth, looking uncomfortable. "Of course. Not sure how that'll go over, but happy to try."

I snicker, thinking back to Uncle Corey's last attempt to make Theo feel included down by the pool, which ended with Theo shouting that he "didn't want any fucking booze," then making a hasty exit. Oil and water, those two.

Austin's eyes narrow, first at me, then at my uncle. "Something I should know about?" he asks.

"Nope," I say fast. Should have kept that snicker to myself. I *do* want to get a rise out of Austin, but not at Uncle Corey's expense.

Austin fidgets, clearly agitated. Mom places her hand on his hand again.

"I'm serious," he says. "If there's something going on with my kid on this trip, I want to know about it."

"It was no big deal," I say quickly. "Seriously."

"Corey?" Mom says, voice sharp. Her eyes are laser-focused on his.

My uncle holds her gaze for a moment, then sighs in defeat. "Fine. I might have offered to get him a rum and Coke. Which he declined, I might add. You've got a good kid."

"You what?" Austin shoots up from the table, chair squealing against the tile, then toppling backward with a crash. His eyes are molten.

"Austin," Mom says, standing and reaching for his arm as a petite hostess in an orange-and-red sundress rushes over to right the toppled chair. Austin brushes Mom's hand away.

"We're fine," Mom assures the hostess, whose eyes dart back and forth between Austin and Uncle Corey. Then Mom turns to Austin again, this time placing her hand on his shoulder. "We're fine," she repeats, this time more firmly.

Austin turns to her. "He tried to give my son liquor," he growls. His eyes flash.

"Which is very not okay," Mom says softly, narrowing her eyes at her younger brother. "And which we will discuss, at length." She turns back to Austin. "But not here. Not during lunch."

Beside me, Addison hasn't moved. She's sitting bone straight in her chair, barely breathing. We've never had that "twin thing"—the ability to read each other's thoughts, or whatever—but it doesn't take some kind of genetic ESP to figure out she's finally thinking the same thing I am: Austin's anger issues are definitely real.

He's very bad news for Mom, and for us.

"You're right," Austin says finally, shoulders deflating as he sinks back into his chair. He nods toward the hostess, who gives us all a nervous smile, then retreats to the front of the restaurant.

"Won't happen again," Uncle Corey says, shoving his hands into his pockets. "My bad." Then he's retreating too, toward Holly and their table.

For a few minutes, we eat in silence. I've definitely lost my booze hookup for the rest of the trip, which is a bummer, but it's a small price to pay for seeing Austin Hunt's true colors on display in front of Mom and Addison and the whole restaurant. Maybe what Mom said at breakfast was true—what happened at the magazine launch party was an accident—but he was still arguing with a coworker that night. And the flash of anger in Austin's eyes just now was undeniable. If Mom hadn't been there to defuse the situation, he would have lashed out at Uncle Corey. No doubt.

Theo walks into the restaurant just as we're telling the waiter we'll skip dessert. No one's in the mood. Theo gives us a wave, then makes his way over to the to-go buffet to box up some snacks.

"I'll go tell him about volleyball," I offer, pushing my chair back.

"I'm not sure—" Austin starts to say.

"Don't worry," I cut him off. "Uncle Corey will be on his best behavior. I'll see to it."

Before he can say anything else, I make a beeline over to Theo. From their table behind the buffet station, Holly gives me a small wave. Uncle Corey is absorbed in something on his phone, or at least pretending to be. I wave back.

"Hey." Theo gives me a chin tilt, then continues lining his box with Mexican pastries.

"Heads-up," I say. "Uncle Corey confessed to trying to get you a drink the other day. It didn't go down well with your dad."

He freezes, pastry tongs in midair. All the color drains from his already pale face. "Oh shit."

"Don't worry, you're not in trouble. But your dad has some serious anger issues, man. He looked like he wanted to clock my uncle."

Theo swallows, hard. "But nothing happened?"

"Mom defused the situation, fortunately. But what about next time?"

He shuts the box's cardboard flaps and sets it down on the counter. For a moment, he doesn't say anything, and I study him. He's about my height—six feet, give or take an inch—but gangly where I'm broad and muscular. The thought that I could take him in a fight flashes through my mind, and I shove it away.

Theo looks me in the eye, voice dropping to a whisper-hiss. "What about you? You beat up that kid so bad you got permanently kicked off the team, but does that define who you are?"

"That was entirely different," I snarl. Although, if I'm honest, it really wasn't. I was mad, and I lost control. Just like Austin is clearly capable of doing. I lean in so only Theo can hear. My lips are an inch from his ear, and I can feel his hot breath on my neck. "This isn't about me. And I swear to god, if you ever bring that up around my family—"

He steps back and raises his hands defensively to his chest. "Your secret's safe with me, promise. We're good."

I glower at him. He'd better keep his mouth shut, or we will be the exact opposite of *good*.

NATALIA

I need some alone time—away from the beach, the pool, the hordes of resort guests, and my family, most of all. Yesterday or the day before, Mami mentioned that the deck where Aunt Elizabeth and Austin are holding their engagement party is usually empty unless it's in use for a private event, so I figure there's a good chance I can find my solitude there.

First, I suffer through lunch at the hibachi place with Mom and Mami, keeping a smile plastered to my face, but my thoughts keep cycling through my conversation with Theo in the Teen Lounge this morning.

I don't think Seth is the person he's been saying he is.

When lunch ends, I decline my moms' invite to join them on the beach. Instead, I head to the elevators.

It's only one floor up from the Japanese restaurant to the Vista Hermosa terrace. Inside the elevator, I respond to yet another text from my brother, Beau, who I've admittedly been ignoring all week, then I open my chat with Seth for the hundredth time today. The last message plainly says he's on a hike in Mount Spokane State Park. The harder I stare at the mountains in the background, the more they look like any mountains, anywhere. I don't think Theo was intentionally trying to meddle, but he's way off base.

I close the chat and shove my phone into the pocket of my shorts as the elevator doors slide open.

But as much as I want to, I can't shake Theo's words. A little voice in the back of my head asks: If Theo is so wrong, why can't I bring myself to message Seth back?

The terrace is lovely—tons of patio furniture with plush cushions in bright tropical colors, planters bursting with flowers and lush greenery, hanging lanterns strung from above, and a stone fountain in the middle. But it's not empty.

A rectangle of couches is occupied by a group of eight or ten older adults sipping sweating glasses of wine and chatting. It doesn't look like they're having a formal party, but they probably had the same idea I did—to come up here for a little privacy.

There are other couches; I could sit somewhere else. But I want to be truly alone. My eyes skate around the terrace. Large umbrellas shade the couches where the group is sitting in the sun. The other half of the terrace is shielded beneath an overhang draped with spiny vines and little white flowers. My gaze falls on a small white ladder leading up the wall to the roof above.

A little sign is posted beside the ladder, its words half-covered by vines. I brush them aside. NO ACCESO AL TECHO EXCEPTO POR EMPLEADOS AUTORIZADOS. NO ROOF ACCESS EXCEPT BY AUTHORIZED EMPLOYEES.

In other words, there almost definitely won't be anyone up there. The wine drinkers aren't paying any attention, and there's no one around to stop me, so I grab onto the ladder and climb up. It's only a half story, and when I peer over the top, it's clear someone comes here a lot. Probably hotel staff. A small stack of lounge cushions rests in one corner beneath a plastic tarp pinned down by heavy stones, and there's a smelly pail filled with sand and cigarette butts in the center of the rooftop.

The entire roof is surrounded by a low stone wall. I can see why they don't want guests—especially drunk guests—coming up here. The wall is knee-height, not really high enough to prevent someone from climbing over and falling off, but the white-painted cement beneath my feet is rock solid, and as long as you don't do anything stupid like turn cartwheels along the ledge, it's completely safe.

And, thankfully, deserted except for me.

I walk along the south side of the roof, overlooking the Vista Hermosa terrace, and peer down. Here, the vines originate in beds laid out along the top of the wall. If they were looking up, the wine drinkers could see me, but no one's paying any attention. I turn and keep walking around the perimeter.

Past the terrace, the west side of the wall overlooks the front of the resort, down to the street. The north side overlooks the pool. I scan the deck, then the water, for my family, eyes finally landing on Mason, Uncle Corey, and Holly on the "party side," playing pool volleyball.

Finally, the east side overlooks the beach below. It's low tide, but at night, the water must crawl up pretty close to this section of the resort, which juts out much farther into the sand than the long section with all the rooms. I hop up on the wall so I'm sitting and looking out, legs dangling over the edge. It's peaceful up here. The view is gorgeous—wide blue sky hung with the occasional puffy white cloud; white-sand beach dotted with cabanas and loungers and every-color umbrellas leading out to the ocean's many blues, the water capped white everywhere except the roped-off swimming area farther down the beach.

From my perch at the top of the eight-story resort, noise from the beach is blissfully muffled. Gulls cry overhead, low and longing, and I close my eyes, losing myself in the solitude.

After a moment, I slip my phone out of my pocket. I've been spotty about documenting this trip, but I definitely want to remember this view. I open my camera, but before I can center the perfect slice of sand and water in the shot, my eyes travel down to the latest image on my camera roll. Is that *Seth*?

I tap it open. The image is definitely of Seth—with his arm wrapped around another girl. He's grinning at the camera; her head is nuzzled into his neck.

What the hell?

I swipe back to the previous photo, which is also Seth, from the same series. In this one, he's peering sweetly into the girl's eyes.

I swipe again, but the next image is a selfie I took yesterday afternoon, followed by a photo of my fruit plate from brunch yesterday morning.

How did these photos of Seth and the girl get on my camera roll? I tap them open again. He definitely didn't send them to me, and I didn't download them from anywhere. I've never seen them before.

I zoom in on the first photo, closely examining Seth's face. It must be recent; he looks the age he is now, and his haircut is the same. Does he have some other girlfriend in Spokane?

On the other hand, we've only been chatting a few weeks. This could easily be from before we met.

Nonetheless, everything Theo said this morning rattles around my skull.

I'd recognize those mountains anywhere; Seth's like ten minutes from my house.

Look at the light in the photo. If this was taken early in the morning, the sun would be a whole lot lower.

He doesn't have that many followers, and none of the accounts he follows look like IRL friends.

Something's not right.

The sinking suspicion that Theo is onto something, that's Seth is *not* the person he says he is, settles like a rock in my gut.

Would I be wrong to trust Theo, or was I wrong to trust Seth?

I have no idea why he'd do it, or what exactly he's been lying about, but as I slip off the ledge and back onto the roof, wanting the solid concrete beneath my feet, the notion that Seth has been catfishing me takes hold, sending a chill rocketing up my spine.

19

THEO

It's "casino night" at La Maravilla, and the theme has inspired a weird mix of attire among the guests. Some people mill around the lobby in their regular resort clothes—sundresses and linen slacks and gauzy dresses that might actually be beach covers—but there are some experienced resort-goers who clearly packed for this. I spy one middle-aged woman wearing a deep red floor-length gown and copious amounts of gold jewelry at the black-jack table. One of the poker tables is populated entirely by men in suits and ties. I snap a few surreptitious photos to send Jay.

After fifteen minutes in the Under 18 section, playing one of the arcade games they've dragged down from the Teen Lounge, I'm officially bored. Addison, Natalia, and Mia are hanging out on one of the lobby couches, but I'm pretty sure Natalia's still pissed at me after the stuff about Seth this morning, so I give them space and wander over to the lobby bar for a Coke.

"Theo." Paola greets me with a wide smile. The bartender sets a plastic cup of pink wine down in front of her, and she slides a dollar across the bar. "Having fun?"

"Honestly? This isn't really my scene."

She takes a sip of her wine. "Me either. Want to take a walk down the beach?"

I nod. "Definitely."

Five minutes later, I've told Dad where I'm headed and Paola and I are strolling down the mostly deserted beach, drinks in hand. The sun set nearly two hours ago, and it's surprisingly dark out here despite all the lights from the seemingly endless string of resorts. Paola pulls a mini flashlight from her purse, and I switch on the flashlight app on my phone.

"I haven't seen you much since Thursday," she says, referencing our chat on the Vista Hermosa terrace that afternoon.

"I know. I'd say I've been busy, but that's not really true." I laugh. "I burn really easily, so I'm not out at the pool or down on the beach much."

She nods. "How are things going with the Mayweathers? Is everyone making you feel at home?"

I grimace, in spite of myself, and I hope she can't see in the dark.

"Theo?" she prods gently.

"There was this thing the other day, with Corey." I didn't mention it the last time Paola and I talked because I'm not a rat, but now that he's confessed to Dad and Elizabeth, I'm sure all the adults will find out soon enough, if they don't know already. "He was trying to be the cool uncle or whatever, offering to get me a drink at the pool bar, and I said no thanks. Actually I kind of shouted it, loudly, and there was maybe some swearing. It wasn't my finest hour."

"And also entirely not your fault," Paola says. She doesn't sound surprised by my revelation; clearly word has already spread. "Corey was behaving entirely inappropriately. I'm so sorry you had to deal with that."

I take a large swig of my Coke. "I felt like a baby. I don't even know what kind of impression I'm trying to make on this trip, but it's not that one."

"Don't beat yourself up," Paola says. "Corey put you in a bad position. Whatever you said to him, no one thinks it reflects poorly on you. Promise."

No one except Mason, but maybe that doesn't matter. He already hates me.

"That's not even the worst part, though," I say. "Today at lunch, Corey admitted to the whole drink thing. I wasn't there to see it, but sounds like my dad didn't take it very well. In the past, he used to get heated all the time, but that almost never happens anymore, outside of work, anyway. Everyone's getting the wrong impression, and I don't know what to do about it."

"Vacation can do strange things to people," Paola says. "It's supposed to be relaxing, but not everyone thrives outside their regular routine. He's probably feeling a lot of pressure to impress this week, just like you are."

It's weird to imagine Dad feeling the same social anxiety I've been feeling, but Paola's probably right. It explains why he picked up that extra copyediting job that's kept him locked in his room.

"Tomorrow evening," Paola continues, "there's some kind of street market at the resort. I'm going to suggest to the others that we all go. I think we need some low-key family time, before the engagement party." Which is on Monday, two days from now. And then this trip will finally be over, thank god.

"Sounds good," I say. "I'm worried Mason and Addison have already written my dad off. He's not violent, ever, and it's just stress that's bringing out his temper. He's not normally like this."

We're coming up on a trash bin. Paola gulps back the rest of her wine and extends her hand for my empty cup. "I know it's hard, but they'll come to see everything that's special about him, in time. No one's perfect. Including me." She gives me a meaningful glance, then pitches our cups in the trash.

"I'm sensing there's a story there?"

"Sure is. When Mia was in fourth grade, one of the kids in her class teased her mercilessly for having two moms. It was absolutely not okay, but my reaction wasn't great either."

"Yeah, that wouldn't fly with me."

"Mia's classroom teacher was great. But the administration, not so much. They claimed the girl's behavior didn't qualify as bullying, and when her parents insisted their daughter had been 'exercising free speech,' and that a discipline plan 'wasn't appropriate,' we pulled Mia out of that school. I don't know who I was angrier with—the principal, or the parents."

"Wow."

"Mia's in a much better school setting now. So maybe it all worked out the way it was supposed to. But I couldn't let it go. That family went on believing that bullying was okay, that sexual-orientation-based discrimination was okay. A more mature person than I would have gotten involved in community government or made a big donation to the Trevor Project or run for school board. But I was *angry*."

Ah. I think I see where this is going.

"I trawled the internet, searching for anything embarrassing. It's amazing what people will share online. Eventually, I found two posts in a local mommy's group of the girl's mother selling hand sanitizer and disinfecting wipes early in the pandemic. She blatantly advertised that she'd bought out Amazon and was reselling them to 'the right people' in her community. It was gross on multiple levels."

"These people sound like real winners."

Paola laughs. "True pinnacles of the community. I should have showed the posts to Kiersten, leaned into the satisfaction of being the better human being, and moved on."

"But you didn't?"

"Not exactly. I screenshot the posts and circulated them— anonymously, of course—to the parents' email list at Mia's old school. And I have to admit, it was deeply satisfying to witness the public shaming that followed."

My eyebrows fly up. It's hard to imagine her sourcing incriminating photos and anonymously hacking a school email list. But now that I think about it, I'm pretty sure she does something in tech, and I'm probably guilty of assuming most adults are as clueless as Dad when it comes to social media and "the interwebs."

"My point is," Paola continues, "your dad snapped at Corey because Corey behaved badly, and because he loves you a whole lot. It's parental instinct. We're all guilty of moments of poor judgment when we should be acting rationally and taking the high road."

"Thanks," I mumble.

She wraps her arm around my shoulder and steers us gently back toward the resort. "Cut your dad a little slack, and cut the twins a little slack too, if you can. Merging two families together—it's a tall order. There's bound to be a little friction before things settle."

A little friction is one thing. But my gut says things aren't going to settle before they get a whole lot worse.

ADDISON

We've been hanging out on one of the lobby couches and talking for over an hour. That is, Mia has been talking and I've been listening, at least part of the time. Natalia is glued to her phone, and when she takes a break from the screen, she's distracted by something going on at the blackjack table or zoned out watching new layers of perfectly puffed kernels rise behind the glass of the popcorn cart, which is being operated by a cute La Maravilla staffer who doesn't look much older than we are.

"Do you want some?" I ask when her eyes have been locked on the cart for a full five minutes. "Natalia?"

"Huh?" She jerks around to face me.

"Popcorn. Or are you eyeing the tasty snack operating the machine?"

"What?" Her eyes dart toward the cart again. "No, neither."

I let out a thin stream of breath. This is going nowhere.

"Mia, c'mon." Aunt Kiersten is hovering over us then, beckoning for Mia to get up off the couch. "Bedtime."

Mia scowls and crosses her arms over her chest. Very mature.

"Actually," Aunt Kiersten says calmly, "it was bedtime fifteen minutes ago. So say good night to the girls, and let's head up."

"It's vacation," Mia says, voice shifting into a whine. "No one else has a bedtime."

"And no one else here is twelve," Aunt Kiersten replies. She extends her hand and stares Mia down until Mia shoves off the couch, ignoring her mom's hand but resigned to the indignities of being the only preteen on the trip.

I feel bad for her. But mostly, I'm excited about this turn of events. With Mia and her constant, bright chatter removed from the equation, Natalia *has* to talk to me. I watch Aunt Kiersten's and Mia's disappearing backs for a moment, then turn to my cousin, but she's already standing, shoving her phone into her shorts pocket and collecting our empty plastic cups from the table.

"Where are you going?" I ask, shooting to my feet. "I'll come with you."

She frowns, and I know I sound overeager, but I can't help it. The week is almost over, and I miss my best friend.

"I'm tired, Adds," she says. "It's been a really long day."

"Tell me about it," I say, reaching for the hand not filled with cups. "Please. Let's go out to the pool deck and talk. I bet the cabana beds are all free now."

She gives me a weak smile, and for a moment my heart lifts. But then she says, "Rain check on the deck hang, okay? I'm heading back to the room."

Gently, she tugs her hand free. Disappointment is written all over my face, but I can't help it. It's nine fifteen on a Saturday night, and she's going to bed?

"Listen," she says, leaning in close. "I really am exhausted. But casino night is boring, and I found the best view from the whole resort this afternoon. Sorry I can't join you, but I'll tell you how to get there."

Five minutes later, Natalia is headed back to the room, if she isn't there already, and I'm scaling a small white ladder to the hotel roof, above the Vista Hermosa terrace.

Natalia was right. Up here, you can see sky for miles and miles. A light breeze tugs at my hair, and the air is a little damp, the way it always is right by the ocean when the sun has long ago set. I walk to the east side of the roof and take a seat behind the low wall, propping my elbows on the stone. From here, the ocean looks inky black and very, very close. It must be high tide.

What I wanted tonight was a real conversation with my cousin, the person who, along with my brother, I used to consider a best friend. But what I got instead was an ocean of time alone with my thoughts. They travel first to Mom—after lunch this afternoon, I'm not so sure she's making the right decision by marrying Austin. I want to like him, I really do. Mom seems so happy. But that flash of anger in his eyes when Uncle Corey admitted to trying to serve Theo alcohol? That was real. We might never know the details of what happened at that launch party last summer, but my brother wasn't way off base. This afternoon confirmed it: Austin has a temper, just like Dad.

My heart squeezes in my chest.

And then there's Mason. This morning at the pool, he

circled way too close to everything I've been trying to hide.

That whole thing with your suitcase at the airport. And I saw you at Guest Services the morning after we got here, asking about renting a locker.

Did he believe what I said about our cousins hogging the closet?

My hand travels automatically to my phone. It's nearly ten. Is that too late to call Rebecca? I pull up the photos she sent me earlier today—her four-year-old, Logan, dressed in the dinosaur costume I helped them make for Halloween this year, many strands of Mardi Gras beads draped around his neck, and a child-sized top hat angled on his head. He's clearly having a blast, hamming it up for the camera. My heart squeezes. Logan will have been in bed for hours already, but Rebecca might still be up. Then again, I know she's the only dorm faculty on call in Anders this week, which means she probably crashed early if she could.

Reluctantly, I keep scrolling through my camera roll and pick out a few of the many photos I've taken this week. Then I compose a text to Hailey and Lauren, my two closest friends at Tipton, instead. Our friendship is no replacement for what I used to have with Natalia and Mason, but they're not talking to me, not in any real way, and Hailey and Lauren are almost guaranteed to write me back.

Having the best time in Cancún! I write, attaching the photos. **Wish you were here.**

Witness: Addison Acker-Mayweather (minor accompanied by mother, Elizabeth Acker-Mayweather)
Statement Taken by Oficial Juan Parra
Sunday, January 7, 8:36 a.m.

Addison Acker-Mayweather: It started the night we were all in the hot tub after dinner. Thursday or Friday? The days are blending together.

Oficial Juan Parra: Austin Hunt was there?

A. A-M.: No, he wasn't in the hot tub with us. I don't remember exactly how it came up, but Mason and Theo got into it about Theo's dad. About Austin. Theo admitted his dad had a temper. He told us how he yelled at some nurses when his mom was in the hospital, but that was a long time ago. The main thing was an incident at a work party this summer, when Austin threw a glass at a waiter. Allegedly.

Oficial J. Parra: Allegedly?

A. A-M.: We weren't there. You'll have to ask my mom about it. [Glances at Elizabeth Acker-Mayweather.] She was at the party.

Oficial J. Parra: [Nods.] We'll speak separately. But back to this conversation in the hot tub. It led to tension between Mason and Mr. Hunt?

A. A-M.: It escalated at lunch the next day. I think it was the next day. My uncle Corey had done something stupid, which he admitted to Mom and Austin. Austin got angry. He got up from the table, like he wanted to hit Uncle Corey, and his chair fell over. The hostess came, and we got a lot of looks. But then Mom calmed Austin down. Nothing happened.

Oficial J. Parra: And what did this have to do with Mason?

A. A-M.: Mason and I were both there, at lunch. Mason's very protective of Mom, and he'd already been wary about her marrying Austin. After we saw Austin's temper on display, it really affected my brother. [Sniffles.] I'm sorry, are there tissues?

Oficial J. Parra: And then what happened?

A. A-M.: Then things got more strained. Mason laid down an ultimatum about the engagement.

20

ONE WEEK AGO
SUNDAY, DECEMBER 31

One Day Until the Engagement Party

MASON

It's almost nine, and my stomach is audibly growling in antici-
pation of the brunch buffet—waffles and huevos rancheros and
chorizo and orange juice—on the walk back from Escuela de
Swell. I'm about to take the steps up to the resort from the sand
when I hear my name.

"Mason! Hey!"

Caught. I freeze, scanning the rows of loungers and cabanas
stretching out in front of La Maravilla, trying to place the voice.
Definitely not Mom or Addison, so that's good. Would Natalia
rat me out for being on the beach without a buddy?

"Over here!"

My head swivels toward the sound. Holly is stepping from
behind a cabana's semi-drawn curtains, smiling widely. She's
wearing an orange baseball cap and a gauzy orange-and-yellow

beach cover over the white bikini she had on at the pool the other day. Forcing my eyes to stay trained on her face, I return her smile with a small wave. She probably doesn't even know about the whole buddy system thing.

"Come join me for a bit?" She ties back the cabana curtains, exposing the cushioned lounger to the open air on all sides, clearly signaling, *There's nothing inappropriate about this invitation.* Not that I would have complained, but I get it. She's Uncle Corey's girlfriend, and she's twenty-four. Nothing's going to happen.

"Yeah, okay." I cross over and take a seat on the edge of the cabana bed. "Where's Uncle Corey?"

"Still sleeping." She laughs. "I'd chalk it up to vacation, but nothing gets that man out of bed before ten any day of the week. Unless he's on set, of course."

"Of course."

"So." Holly turns her baseball cap to the side, exposing her wide blue eyes, and takes a seat at the foot of the bed, keeping a respectable distance between us. She leans back against one of the canopy poles. "I'm glad I caught you this morning. After lunch yesterday, I'd been hoping we could talk."

"Oh. That." Is she going to scold me for accepting Uncle Corey's illicitly proffered beer?

"I overheard what Theo said to you at the buffet. About the fight, and getting kicked off your hockey team?"

Oh. My face goes white. Their table was nearby, but I didn't think they were in earshot.

"Don't worry, I would never say anything. To anyone."

"'Kay," I say warily, shifting uncomfortably on the mattress.

The waterproof cover squeaks beneath my butt. Maybe I should have pretended not to hear my name and made a beeline for the resort.

"The thing is," Holly continues, "I can relate."

I snort. I can't help it. "You beat some kid within an inch of his life too?"

She gives me a sympathetic smile. "Not exactly. But I'm an athlete. I *was* an athlete. Until I got kicked off my college swim team—and off campus."

My jaw unhinges. "What—what happened?"

"I was on an athletic scholarship. Top student, team captain, the whole thing. Then I blew it." She shrugs. "Pretty spectacularly. I showed up late and beyond wasted to swim finals and destroyed my team's chances of qualifying for state. And it was a dry campus, so I lost my housing, too."

"Oh damn."

She grimaces. "Not my finest hour. I could get into all the whys of what happened, but that's a story for another time. The point is, I screwed up for my team and for myself. And when I overheard you talking to Theo yesterday, it sounded like you might know something about that."

I shrug. "Yeah, kinda."

Opening up to Theo this fall was a mistake I never would have made had I realized who he was. Now he's the keeper of my biggest, worst secret, which he could deploy against me at any time. But Holly doesn't seem like the threat-wielding type. In fact, she seems like an entirely different kind of stereotype: pretty, young blond dating a rich older guy. I'm not sure Uncle Corey is old enough for Holly to qualify as a gold digger, but my family obviously assumes she's in it for the Mayweather money.

I'm not so sure, though.

As if reading my thoughts, Holly says, "I don't know if you've looked me up, and no shade if you have, but I've spent the past four years turning things around for myself."

I shake my head. At one point, I'd meant to google Holly Bird, but I never did.

"I lost my scholarship, but I got a job and a sublet off campus. Fortunately I only had one semester left. I finished out my senior year, graduated cum laude, and launched Pivot Point."

"What's Pivot Point?"

"It's a start-up," she says. "I like to describe what we do as 'second chance' life coaching for people at a critical juncture. At a pivot point. We're three years out the gate and going strong."

"Oh wow." *Now* I'm going to google Holly Bird. I feel guilty admitting it, even to myself, but I totally assumed she was a model or beautician or something. Not that there's anything wrong with modeling or painting nails or whatever. But I did not figure her for a self-made entrepreneur. "That's really cool."

"Thanks. But I'm not telling you this to brag. Or because I think you should hire me. Trust me, I wouldn't accept money from someone who's practically family! But I do think I might be able to help. If you wanted to talk. If you'd let me." She flashes me a warm smile.

"Oh." I scrub my hand across the back of my neck. I've never been big on talking it out or listening to advice or whatever. But Holly seems really genuine, and she's easy to talk to. And easy on the eyes, although I remind myself for the hundredth time—off-limits. "I'll think about that. Thanks."

Just then, my phone pings, and I dig it out of my pocket.

NATALIA

All the poolside cabanas are taken when I emerge from brunch, but I find an open lounger near the restaurant deck and post up. My parents are down at the beach, as they are every morning, but I don't feel like joining them. I don't want to talk to anyone. I just want to wallow.

Seth and I texted a bit last night, after I told Addison I was going to bed, and everything *seemed* normal, but it's not. Seth has been lying to me, I'm sure of it now. Still, I couldn't bring myself to raise Theo's suspicions about the location of his hike or to ask about the two photos of Seth posing with another girl that mysteriously appeared on my camera roll yesterday afternoon. Not over text.

How did those photos get on my phone? It's clear Theo doesn't trust Seth, but why be up-front with his suspicions in the morning and then mess with my phone a few hours later? It doesn't make sense.

Which means there's someone else here who wants me to doubt Seth is for real. And it's working.

At nine thirty, my phone vibrates with a FaceTime request from Seth. Last night, when we were messaging, I asked if we could talk sometime this morning. I need to see his face. I need to ask him in person—or as close to in person as we're going to get—what's going on.

I accept the call.

Seth's face appears on my screen. He looks the same as always—reddish-brown hair dusting his forehead, brown eyes flecked with green, cheeks melting into smile lines at the corners of his mouth.

"Hey, beautiful."

I blush, in spite of myself. *He's not who you think he is. He needs to start telling the truth.*

"Hey," I say back.

Seth's in his room, like he usually is when we talk. He straightens up against his headboard. In Spokane, it's only six thirty in the morning, but his face is free from pillow creases; his hair isn't wet from the shower or matted from sleep. And I can't tell for sure, because of the camera angle, but it looks like his bed is made up. Theo has me noticing these things now.

"What's wrong?" he asks. I've barely said anything, but whatever I'm feeling—a mix of hurt and nerves and disappointment and sheer curiosity—must be written all over my face.

I draw in a deep breath. "You're up early," I say. "Even for you."

"Oh." He frowns. "Right. My aunt and uncle are in town, and my parents are having them over for brunch. I promised I'd help straighten up downstairs and set up the dining room before they get here, so I figured if we were going to talk this morning, it had to be now."

"Okay," I say. "Makes sense." And it *does* make sense. That's the thing. Despite what Theo said yesterday, despite the mysterious photos, everything always makes sense with Seth. Sure, we met online, but there's a perfectly reasonable explanation for that. And yes, we haven't met in person yet, but again, we're two teenagers with no cars and a five-hour drive between us. It's really not that weird.

But I requested this call for a reason. I have to clear this up—right now—one way or another. Even if the truth is devastating.

"Here's the thing," I say. "Yesterday afternoon, these photos showed up on my phone." I press my lips between my teeth, again wondering who wanted me to see those pictures and how they got there. Then I shake my head. "They were of you and some girl I didn't recognize. White, long brown hair, wearing a pink-and-white-striped top?"

A shadow passes over Seth's face. "Samantha? That's my ex. We broke up a couple months ago."

"Okay," I say, a tendril of relief unfurling in my chest. Seth's not cheating. A couple of months ago, we hadn't even met.

"Can you send them to me?" he asks.

"Sure." I message them over, then return to our FaceTime.

"This is so weird," he says. "Those are her photos. I didn't even know she had them posted anywhere, but maybe they're still up on Facebook."

"Strange," I agree, even less sure what this all means than I was a few minutes ago.

"How did you find them again? Are you, like, cyberstalking me?" His tone is teasing, but there's a hint of concern on his face.

"What?" I sit up straight in the lounger. "*No.* They appeared out of nowhere on my camera roll. Someone in my family must have gotten into my phone, I'm not sure how."

"Okay," he says slowly.

"Seriously," I insist, suddenly on the defensive when Seth's the one who should be explaining himself. Right? "Someone found the photos, got access to my phone, and downloaded them for me to see. I'm not sure why—maybe they didn't know she was your ex."

"I don't get it," he says. "Did I do something? Why wouldn't they trust me?"

I sigh. Suddenly Theo's whole argument about the mountains in the background and the level of the light seems incredibly thin. Seth was up early yesterday because he's always up early. Mountains look like mountains. And so many things—the camera angle, a filter—could easily account for the light.

The whiplash is real. Once again, I'm sure I let Theo make me doubt Seth for no reason.

"I have no idea," I say. "I'm sorry. The photos freaked me out, but it's just someone in my family being overprotective. Let's forget it."

"What's up?"

My head snaps up from my screen. Mason is standing in front of me, phone clutched in one hand.

"I have to go," I tell Seth. "Chat later?"

He nods and gives me a small smile, then the call beeps to black.

"That your internet boyfriend?" Mason asks.

I roll my eyes. I am so not in the mood to dignify that comment with a response. The thought that Mason could be the one who downloaded those photos to my phone crosses my mind—he has been dismissive and frankly, a little rude about Seth—but whoever wanted me to see the pictures of Seth with another girl actually cares about my happiness and safety in some twisted way. And my cousin has barely been around this whole trip; it's hard to imagine him making the effort.

"You going to breakfast?" I ask, tilting my chin behind me, toward the restaurant.

"Yeah." But he doesn't make a move toward the deck. Instead, he clicks on his screen and frowns down at something on his phone.

"What's up?" I ask.

"Nothing," he says quickly, switching his screen off. He starts to leave, then turns back toward me and takes a seat at the foot of my lounger.

"Have you gotten any weird texts on this trip?" he asks.

I shake my head no.

"Huh," he says. "'Kay."

I frown. Mason can be so closed off. "But I'm assuming you have," I prompt after a beat, when he's offered up nothing else. "Can I see?"

He keeps his phone clutched tightly in his fist. "It's from some bogus-looking email address. I'm sure it's just spam."

I nod slowly. "Addison said she's been getting a lot of those too."

"Right." He jams his phone into his pocket and stands. "She mentioned that."

And then he's walking up the wooden steps to the restaurant deck without so much as a "see you later" or a wave goodbye.

21

With Mia at camp and Natalia down at the pool, I head up to our room after lunch to change into my suit and check on the box.

Because I'm obsessed.

Because last night, when I came back to the room after Mia and Natalia were both in bed, it looked like my laundry bag had been messed with. In the dark, the shape seemed wrong. Disturbed. My cousins were both breathing deeply, but I couldn't be absolutely sure they were asleep, so I resisted the urge to paw through it. Instead, I lay in bed for over an hour, stressing, before I finally drifted off to sleep. And this morning, Mia dawdled in the shower, then changed her outfit three times, so I didn't get a chance to check before I had to leave to meet Mom and Austin for breakfast.

Now I sling the dead bolt over the door and peer inside the closet. My laundry bag is slumped against the back wall, exactly where it was last night. Does it look different? Is it a little farther to the right than it was before?

I squat down and pull open the drawstring, then grope through the pile of dirty clothes until my fingers make contact with the wooden cigar box buried inside. My shoulders relax a bit. I pull it out, then slide open the latch and peer inside. Nothing is missing. Everything is fine.

I exhale.

But I need a new hiding spot. I eye the little pass-through compartment between our room and the hallway. It's the perfect size, but far too exposed. I try sliding it under my mattress, but any way I position it, the box leaves a conspicuous lump. In the bathroom, I slide my fingers beneath the sink one more time, but there's no hidden shelf, nowhere to tuck it.

Finally I settle for opening the doors to the top part of the dresser and sliding it behind the TV. It fits back there perfectly, nestled on top of the cables. I check from all angles, and when I'm satisfied you can't see even a glimpse of wood, I shut the dresser doors again and sit down on my bed.

Reluctantly, I pull out my phone. The messages have been piling up, yet again, and there's one more thing I need to do before changing into my suit and heading back into the sunshine.

I start to type.

> No one has breathed a single word
> about the Incident. It's like it never
> happened. You can chill.

"Please, please chill," I say out loud. "And *stop texting me*."

Not that I'm brave enough to say it over text.

Without waiting to see if a response comes in, I switch off my phone. We have a day and a half left in paradise, and I've been letting all these secrets ruin my vacation. The box, the Incident three summers ago, the texts. I need to relax. I reach for the little tablet on my cousins' nightstand and pull up the afternoon activity schedule. There's a yoga class on the beach starting in fifteen minutes. Perfect.

Quickly, I change into my comfiest two-piece, then add a pair of cropped leggings and my flip-flops. Armed with my beach bag and a bottle of water from the mini-fridge, I unlatch the dead bolt and step outside.

I freeze. A few doors down, toward the end of the hall, Mason and Holly are walking toward her room, their backs to me. Uncle Corey is nowhere in sight. Holly presses her key card to the sensor, then pushes the door open, and she and my brother disappear inside. Alone.

THEO

It's late afternoon, and the sun is beating down on the pool deck. Not that I'm down there. I'm stretched out in the hammock in the shade of our balcony, eyeing all the resort guests happily sweltering through the hottest part of the day. I pluck my water bottle from the wide balcony rail and take another gulp. After tonight, we've got one more full day in sunny Mexico, and then I can finally go back home to Jay and skiing and winter as it should be—nice and cold.

For the third time this afternoon, I reach into my pocket and retrieve the note I found sticking out from beneath my pillow after housekeeping had been through the room. It's printed on hotel stationery, presumably from the small business center on the second or third floor.

8:30 p.m., tonight, the fire pit. Let's talk.

No signature, no further indication of what this is about.

Just then the lock clicks, and the door swings open. I crane my neck around in the hammock to see Mason stepping into the room. The door bangs shut behind him, hard. With the balcony doors open, this place is a wind tunnel.

"Jesus," he says, starting at the sound, then kicks off his sandals and flops down on his bed.

I slide out of the hammock and step back into the room. "Hey."

He gives me a small chin tilt, but his eyes are fixed on the ceiling.

I sit on the edge of my bed, note pinched between my fingers. "You get one of these?" I ask.

Mason peels his eyes from the ceiling and turns his head slowly to face me. I hold the note open so he can read it.

"Nope." His eyes return to the ceiling. "Looks like you've got a secret admirer."

I snort. "Maybe. But seriously, you don't have any idea what this is?"

"None. And I definitely didn't write it."

"Yeah." I fold it up and stick it back in my pocket. "Didn't think you did."

If Mason wanted to talk, we could be doing that right now.

But I've been trying all week, and he'd rather let a stupid grudge fester between us.

"So," I say after a minute when Mason's still silent, still sprawled out on his back and staring at the ceiling, "you going to the Mexican Street Market tonight?"

If we can't have a real conversation, maybe we can at least graduate to the level of friendly small talk.

"Have to," he says. "It's an all-Mayweather activity."

"Right."

He doesn't say anything else, and god, this is so frustrating. We don't need to be best friends, but he could at least make the tiniest effort.

I try again. "Do anything fun today?" The question sounds childish, but whatever. I'm grasping at straws over here, and I'm done trying to be "cool" in front of Mason.

"Nah," he says. "Mainly just hung with Holly."

My eyebrows arch up, not that Mason is looking at me. "I didn't realize you and Holly had been hanging out."

I swear a small smile flickers across his lips.

"A little," he says. "Turns out we have a lot in common. And I think my uncle's been pretty wrapped up in family stuff on this trip. She needed someone she could be real with."

The irony.

Also, *has* Corey been "wrapped up in family stuff" this week? Every time I see him, he's partying by the pool with Holly, or they're eating at one of the hotel restaurants, usually just the two of them. I definitely hadn't gotten the impression that Holly was being neglected. But what do I know?

"There's a lot more to Holly than you might think, based

on her looks," Mason continues. "She's cool, when you get to know her. On a personal level."

I get the sudden sense that Mason is baiting me. He wants me to ask if there's something going on between him and his uncle's much younger girlfriend. But there can't be, right? Anyway, it's none of my business. And I'm not about to give Mason the satisfaction.

"That's great," I say noncommittally. "That you're bonding, or whatever."

Never mind that we're the ones supposed to be bonding on this trip. But at this point, I'd settle for cordial disinterest, which I guess is how you'd classify this conversation.

Hooray, progress.

But for whatever reason, I can't let things lie. "Just, careful around your uncle, you know?"

Mason snorts. "It's fine. I can handle Uncle Corey."

I'm not exactly sure what that means, but I press my lips together and remind myself I do *not* want to stir up more shit with Mason. He's a big boy.

"Right," I say, shoving up from the bed. I already put my foot in my mouth with Natalia yesterday, and in that case, I had every reason to believe my warning about Seth was legitimate. Whatever's going on between Mason and Holly, it's probably not romantic, even if Mason wishes it was. And if he gets on his uncle's bad side, that's a whole lot of his problem.

Witness: Natalia Mayweather (minor accompanied
by mother, Kiersten Mayweather)
Statement Taken by Oficial Juan Parra
Sunday, January 7, 4:48 p.m.

Natalia Mayweather: That news story was a kind of bogeyman
throughout the trip. Our parents were very worried. They put
a "buddy system" in place, which I'm not sure any of us really
followed. [Glances at Kiersten Mayweather.] Sorry, Mom.

Oficial Juan Parra: You did not feel in danger?

N. M.: I was worried at first, mostly for my little sister, Mia. She
was bored on the trip, and I didn't know what she might get up
to. But she's smarter than that, and it's a luxury resort. Whatever
happened to those two American girls seemed far removed from
our vacation. Until early Tuesday morning, when we learned
Mason was missing, La Maravilla seemed very secure.

Oficial J. Parra: But Mason Acker-Mayweather sought out the
surf school, Escuela de Swell?

N. M.: Apparently Mason had been going there most mornings.
We didn't know. But it's his signature on their rental logs, and
he's never been much of a rule-follower.

Oficial J. Parra: He didn't say anything about going surfing or
his interactions with the employees at Escuela de Swell to you or
anyone else in your family?

N. M.: Definitely not to me. He didn't tell anyone, as far as I know. Our parents would have shut that down if they'd found out.

Oficial J. Parra: I see.

N. M.: You really think the surf school had something to do with . . . whatever happened to Mason?

Oficial J. Parra: It's possible. But please, Ms. Mayweather, tell me what you remember about the night of Monday, January the first.

N. M.: Okay. [Clears throat.] When Mason went missing, we were all at the engagement party. It was ten thirty or eleven, something like that. We had a toast for Aunt Elizabeth and Austin, and someone noticed Mason wasn't there. Uncle Corey, or maybe it was Holly. It's a bit of a blur. Anyway, we all assumed he'd gone back to his room without telling anyone. He'd been late coming up to the party in the first place, and he was upset about his mom's engagement, so it didn't seem strange that he would have ducked out. Addison texted him, but he didn't respond. At that point, no one was very worried.

Oficial J. Parra: What happened next?

N. M.: The party went late. We all went back to our rooms around one in the morning. Theo was sharing a room with Mason, and when he realized Mason wasn't there, he texted his dad to let him know. But I guess Austin didn't check his phone until the morning.

Oficial J. Parra: What time was that?

N. M.: Eight a.m. That's when Austin woke up, saw Theo's message, and called Theo to ask if Mason had returned. Theo said he hadn't, and Aunt Elizabeth started panicking. She texted the whole family while Austin went down to Guest Services to alert the hotel staff.

I have no idea what happened. But I really don't think the surfers had anything to do with it.

Oficial J. Parra: And why not, Ms. Mayweather?

N. M.: I guess Mason could have gone to meet up with them, if they'd all gotten friendly during the week, but wouldn't they have been arrested by now if they did something to those two American girls?

Oficial J. Parra: I'm sorry, Ms. Mayweather, but I cannot share details of an ongoing investigation.

N. M.: Right. Of course not. It's just, Mason didn't run off and join a cult. He *died*. And from what you've told us, it wasn't an accident. I don't think a couple local surfers had anything to do with that.

22

One Day Until the Engagement Party

MASON

If we were spending New Year's Eve at a *real* Mexican street market, that might be kind of cool, but the "street" is the hotel lobby, and the various food and souvenir stalls are staffed by the resort restaurants and gift shops. It's the same food we've had all week, the same tchotchkes laid out on tables to look like "local crafts." I'm sure it's all authentic as hell.

But tonight's street market is a mandatory all-Mayweather event, and no one's going to venture away from the resort to party, not that I particularly want to party with my sister or cousins anyway.

A quick glance around the lobby, and everyone's here: Holly and Uncle Corey are examining maracas and clay marionettes with Aunt Kiersten and Aunt Paola at one of the souvenir tables; Mom, Austin, Mia, and Theo are eating tostadas and grilled corn on the cob over in the seating area; and Addison and Natalia are standing in separate lines at two food stalls. My eyes drift to my phone. It feels like forever, but it's only eight o'clock, which means we've somehow only been down here for half an hour. There's still so much night left.

I bet I could hook up with the guys from the surf school to find the real action, but I don't have their numbers, and Escuela de Swell must have closed hours ago. I grip my phone, hard, resigned to the most boring New Year's on record, but I make a mental note to grab their numbers in the morning—in case I need an escape from the engagement party from hell tomorrow night.

Mia bounces up to me then, all smiles. "Have you tried the churros? There's chocolate sauce, mango sauce, and dulce de leche."

I force my lips to part into a grin. I'm in a shitty mood, but I've barely spent five minutes with my little cousin all week, and she's a cute kid. I should put in some hang time.

"I have not. Lead the way?"

Mia takes my hand, and I let her bring me to a cart in the far corner of the lobby. There's a long line, and I can see why. The smells wafting from the cooking station—fried dough, cinnamon, and sugar—are undeniably delicious. Maybe I've been too hard on this fake market situation.

While we wait, Mia launches into some story about her friends from home involving a cute boy sighting, a trip to the trampoline park, and a Squishmallow. I try to follow along, I really do, but as we inch forward in the churro line, my mind trips back to the text I got this morning, right as I was leaving Holly's cabana on the beach.

The message was a link to a listicle of athletes, student to pro, who've been kicked off their teams for serious infractions ranging from sexual assault to drug use to fighting and other forms of violence. Someone is taunting me—anonymously. My first thought was obviously Theo, but why would he make up a bogus email address to harass me over text? If he wanted to hold my secret over me, he'd have a thousand other ways to do it. But someone else knows what I did, which means Theo has ratted me out, despite his promise.

My hands clench into fists at my sides. Over the past couple of months, I've painstakingly intercepted all communication home from Coach, then gritted my teeth and asked Dad to sign the required forms. It's the most interaction I've had with Dad since the supervised visits stopped, and while I hate owing him any favors, I knew he'd be so desperate for an excuse to be part of my life, he'd be willing to play along. So far, I've succeeded in keeping my epic fail from Mom.

But the fight is public knowledge at school; everyone in the league knows I beat that kid to a bloody pulp and got permanently banned from Division 1 athletics. And I've received plenty of hate for it—kids who think I disgraced the team, disgraced our school, gave credence to stereotypes about the sport—but no one's hiding behind anonymous messages. People openly gossip about me, and some outright say shit to my face.

This is different. This isn't one of my former teammates, or someone from school. I can't be one hundred percent sure, but my gut says Theo told someone in my family, someone who was never, ever supposed to know the truth.

My eyes rove around the lobby again. They land first on Aunt Paola; I've seen Theo spending time with her this week, but she's an adult. Would Aunt Paola really send me an anonymous text? Natalia or Addison are more likely candidates, or even Mia, although why Theo would go blabbing to my little cousin about me is hard to fathom.

My thoughts turn then to the Mayweathers absent from this vacation. Gigi Gloria and Pop-Pop barely know how to turn on a smart phone, but my cousin Beau is a possibility. My jaw begins to clench, until I remember Theo and Beau haven't even met.

"Hey."

As if I've conjured him, Theo appears beside us in the churro line. We're nearly at the front.

My hands clench and flex. "We need to talk."

He gives me a small shrug. "Okay."

"Sorry, Mia." I step out of line and nudge Theo toward the registration desks in a deserted part of the lobby.

"Where are you going?" Mia asks, voice pitching up. "Don't you want churros?"

"Maybe later." I march up the three stairs separating the lobby floor from the fleet of desks on the street side of the resort. Theo follows me.

"What's up?" he asks when I've posted up against a column and pulled out my phone.

"What's up?" I say back, sneering. "What's up is this."

I open the text and click the link, then hold my phone out and watch as he scrolls through the list.

"I don't get it," he says after a minute, holding my phone out toward me. "I don't know any of these people."

My jaw slowly unhinges. Sure, some of the student players are a little obscure, but how has Theo never heard of Josh Brown or Michael Vick?

"They're athletes, genius. Who got kicked off their teams."

He flinches, just slightly. "Okay. And this has what to do with me?"

Guess I'm going to have to spell it out. "Someone found this very relevant listicle online, then sent me the link. Someone who *knows*. Which means you couldn't keep your mouth shut after all."

"Whoa." Theo takes a step back, then another, until he smacks into one of the empty desks. "Not it." He leans down to rub at his leg. "I didn't tell anyone, and I definitely didn't send that text."

"Not buying it," I snarl. "Someone found out somehow."

"Sure," he says, straightening up. "But that . . . run-in . . . between you and the other player—that happened at a scrimmage? In front of your teams? No offense, but literally dozens of people saw it go down, and most of them are probably mad at you."

I open my mouth to explain why that's not what's going on here, how no one at Rhyne Ridge needs to taunt me anonymously when they could—and have—just told me how I'm a massive loser to my face, but Theo keeps going. This time, his voice has lost its waver, and there's a flinty gleam in his eye.

"I follow the stats. Without you playing center, Rhyne

Ridge has been having a terrible season. Most likely, some angry fan got your number."

He takes a step toward me, and this time, I'm the one flinching.

Theo exhales sharply. "When are you going to start seeing that I'm not the bad guy?"

NATALIA

Aunt Elizabeth's been raving about the elote, and I don't feel much like sitting with everyone else and keeping up with the conversation, so I join the line and watch the vendor douse a steaming ear of corn with lime juice and salt, then roll it in mayo, queso fresco, and a dusting of chili powder. My mouth waters.

I haven't been waiting long when I realize the twenty-something woman in line in front of me is Marisol, Mia's counselor at Kids Kamp. My sister hasn't said much about the tens-to-twelves group since Friday, the day she snuck away to the spa and wound up grounded for the night, and I figure I should check in.

"Hi." I step into Marisol's peripheral vision. "I'm Natalia, Mia Mayweather's sister?"

"Oh, hi." She gives me a small smile. "We miss Mia at camp."

My head tilts to the side. "Excuse me?"

"It's a shame she decided not to stick it out. We're taking a field trip down to La Piscina *Splash!* tomorrow. I think she'd really enjoy the water park."

"I'm sure she would," I say slowly, heart beginning to thud. "Remind me, what was the last day she came to camp?"

We step forward in line; the middle-aged couple in front of Marisol ask for two ears of corn without any of the traditional toppings. What a waste.

"Thursday," she says after a minute. "Mia started on Wednesday; that's the day we made pineapple candles and emoji rock paintings."

The crafts Mia had found so childish.

"Then she came for one more day before your parents pulled her out." She frowns. "You did know she'd dropped out?"

"Sure." I nod gamely, but my mind is racing with visions of Mia wandering the beach alone, chatting naively with ill-intentioned strangers. "I just forgot."

I suck in a deep breath and remind myself that Mia is fine. The instinct to cover for her is strong, but she has a lot of explaining to do. I know what she was up to on Friday; she spent the morning at the spa, then the afternoon with Holly. But if she hasn't been at camp, what the hell has she been doing for the last two days?

Marisol steps up to the vendor, clearly a friend, and they launch into a conversation in Spanish too rapid for me to follow. My eyes skate around the lobby until they land on Mia. She's standing with Mom and Mami at one of the dessert stations, filling a plate with Mexican sweets. She turns to look over her shoulder, straight at me, and our eyes lock. Then she whirls back around.

Marisol steps aside with her elote, and I turn to the vendor. "Uno con todo," I say.

Before she can walk away, I tap Marisol's shoulder, and she turns to face me.

"Sorry, one more thing. When Mia dropped out, did our moms sign off on something?"

Marisol nods. "Of course. When Mia told me she wouldn't be coming back, we left a voice mail on the room phone and delivered a letter to your parents. Mia brought it back signed the next day. We will also, of course, be issuing a refund to their account for the unused days."

I smile. "Thanks so much. But Mia will be coming back tomorrow, actually."

"Oh great." She beams. "Then we'll see you in the morning."

The vendor hands me a red-and-white cardboard tray with my elote. I accept it with a smile, but I've lost my appetite. There's no way Mom or Mami know about any of this.

My eyes return to the dessert stations. Mia is pulling our moms toward a table on the far side of the lobby. I weave my way quickly through the crowd, arriving just as they're pulling out chairs.

"Hi, baby," Mami says. She gives me a warm smile. "Come join us."

"I actually need to talk to Mia for a second." I place the elote down on the table. "But I brought you this."

With a wide grin, I place my palm firmly between my sister's shoulder blades. "We'll be right back."

Mia looks like she wants to protest, but seeing as the alternative is having this out in front of our parents, she allows herself to be steered away from the table. I guide her to the side of the lobby adjacent to the pool deck, and we settle onto an empty love seat just as Theo walks through the sliding glass doors, looking rattled. My eyes follow him for a moment as he crosses the pool deck and takes the short set of stairs down to the fire pit.

Then I turn back to Mia. "Explain," I say.

She gives me an exaggerated shrug. "I don't know—" she starts to say, but I cut her off.

"Enough with the BS. You haven't gone to camp *since Thursday*? This is so beyond ignoring Mom and Mami's buddy system."

She slumps back against the couch cushion and crosses her arms over her chest. She knows I'm right.

"Start talking."

"Camp was for babies," she mutters. "I told you. But Mom and Mami wouldn't listen, so I just . . . quit."

"Uh-huh. And what about the voice mail on the room phone? And the letter they supposedly signed for Marisol?"

She pulls her knees up to her chin. "I gave them our room number. It wasn't rocket science."

I scowl. La Maravilla is the type of place that can afford to have more security "theater"—rules that appear to keep guests safe and their belongings secure—than actual security. Until some twelve-year-old kid wanders off or drowns.

"And what exactly have you been doing for the past two days?" I picture Mia at Escuela de Swell, chatting with the guys who might be perfectly nice surf instructors or might be part of a cult.

She glares down at her feet. "None of your business."

"Oh, excuse me. Should I go tell Mom and Mami right

now, or wait for them to see the refund for your unused days of camp when they check out?"

My sister's head snaps up. Her eyes are huge. "What?"

Now I have her attention.

"I will help you get out of this mess on two conditions," I hiss. "First, you need to tell me *exactly* what you've been up to. And second, you go back to camp tomorrow, for the full day."

"Natalia." Her voice is pure whine.

I lean back into the cushion and wait. We check out early Tuesday morning. For one more day of "baby camp," Mia is going to accept my offer.

"Fine," she says after a minute. "I'll go back for the last day."

"Good. I will be walking you over and checking in with Marisol throughout the day. So don't get any ideas."

"Fine," she says again. "And I haven't been doing anything dangerous, so you can breathe. I've been walking to the hotel next door, chilling at their pool. I met these two girls from Florida; they're really nice. We hang out, that's it. Please don't tell Mom and Mami."

I sigh and shake my head, the muscles in my neck and shoulders slowly relaxing. I feel ancient and boring, but what the hell was Mia thinking?

"Mom and Mami would absolutely lose their minds if they found out what you've been up to," I say. "After those two girls went missing last month? They'd have matching heart attacks. We would *all* be grounded. So no, I'm not going to tell them."

"Thanks," Mia says, voice small. "But what about the refund?"

"Let me worry about that." Tomorrow morning, I'll go to

Guest Services and get them to convert it into resort points or switch it to a different credit card. I'll figure something out. "But if you ever pull something like this again, I am throwing you to the wolves. Got it?"

Mia nods. Her eyes stray to the wall of windows behind us, to the pool deck and beyond. I know what she's thinking—she won't even get to say goodbye to her friends from Florida.

Too bad.

"Come on." I stand and gesture for her to follow me. "I'm getting back in the elote line. Meet you over at Mom and Mami's table in a minute."

She tears her eyes away from the window and shoves herself to her feet.

"This trip sucks," she says.

"Being twelve sucks," I reply. "Thankfully, the condition's not permanent."

23

Ten Hours Until the Engagement Party

ADDISON

Usually I spend the last full day of a trip squirming out of Gigi Gloria's itinerary to make room for anything left undone on my own vacation checklist. But Gigi isn't here to meticulously schedule our time, and at this point I've abandoned my own agenda—one real conversation with Mason and Natalia. So on Monday morning, I find myself wandering through the brunch buffet, filling a to-go box to take out to the beach, resigning myself to the fact that tomorrow we're all going to fly home, and things will remain woefully unresolved.

I luck out when I get down to the sand. A young couple has just left their cabana to head back toward the pool, and I slip inside, drawing the side curtains closed for some privacy but keeping the front flap open to the gorgeous expanse of ocean before me. It truly is beautiful here. And a lot more peaceful down on the beach, removed from the clamor of the swim-up bar and nonstop beach volleyball game. The water isn't exactly calm; choppy waves disrupt the ribbons of blue, but I like it this way. Because it's not safe for swimming anywhere except in the roped-off area farther down the beach, with the side curtains drawn, I can almost imagine I'm out here alone with the gulls and my thoughts.

I spear a thin slice of papaya on my fork and watch the foamy waves churn and swirl. Above, the sky is a perfect, cloudless cerulean blue.

I've polished off the contents of my take-out box, and I'm contemplating which souvenir I should buy for Rebecca and Logan today—a marionette, maracas, a Day of the Dead mask, or maybe all three?—when a pair of familiar voices swell from down the beach. Uncle Corey and Holly. And they don't sound happy.

"I can see what's going on here, and it's not cool, Holls."

"He's sixteen. He's your nephew. I promise, it's not like that."

I part the side curtain just wide enough to peer out in the direction of their voices. My uncle and his girlfriend are standing by the water, a few yards farther down the beach, glaring at each other. Uncle Corey is in swim trunks, his bare chest gleaming golden in the sun. Holly's wearing a sheer, silvery beach cover over a plunging floral one-piece.

"I'm sure it's not like that for *you*. But Holls, come on. You know you're gorgeous. And he's a teenage boy with raging hormones. You can't be hanging out in our room with him, alone."

"Christ, Corey!" She's almost yelling now. "Did it ever occur to you that I might have more to offer than my looks? *These*"—she gestures pointedly at her breasts—"are *not* why Mason's been hanging out with me."

"Fuck, sorry, okay? I didn't mean to imply—"

"I'm sure. And I'm done with this conversation."

She turns away from the water, and I shrink back from my slit in the cabana curtain, knowing full well I shouldn't be eavesdropping on this lovers' spat. But it *is* about my brother. And they *are* shouting at each other on a public beach.

"Wait," Uncle Corey says. "I'm sorry for what I implied. But can you at least tell me what's going on with Mason? Maybe I can help."

"Huh-uh," she says. I'm not looking out anymore, but their voices are drawing closer. They're walking back toward me, toward the resort. "That's between me and Mason. You're just going to have to trust me, Corey."

"I *do* trust you."

They're standing right outside my cabana now. I hold my breath and fumble in my bag for my AirPods. It's not too late to claim plausible deniability if they look around the front and spot me.

"Great, fine," she says. "I'm going to take a walk."

"Want me to come with you?" he asks.

"No. I want to be alone."

A minute later, Holly passes in front of the cabana, and I shrink back into the pillows. For a tense moment, I think she might spin back around, but she keeps walking. She doesn't see me. Then I listen as Uncle Corey's feet slap the stairs up to the pool deck, and I watch Holly's back retreat, silvery beach cover fluttering gracefully behind her.

Once more, I'm alone with my thoughts.

I saw Mason going into their room yesterday with Holly, and I definitely had the same worries Uncle Corey just shared. Does that make me sexist?

I've made a few assumptions about Holly, and that's on me, but also, I know my brother. He wouldn't try anything, but *of course* he's into her. So it's not like Uncle Corey was way off base. My thoughts circle back to something Holly said to him just now: *Did it ever occur to you that I might have more to offer than my looks?*

Maybe she was talking about being a good listener, or generally being nice. But her tone implied something more than that, and curiosity piqued, I pull out my phone and google Holly Bird.

The first thing that pops up is a link to something called Pivot Point, a life-coaching business. I go to the site; looks like Holly is an entrepreneur. The site's content is a little woo-woo self-helpy for my taste, but it looks professional, and Holly has a staff of four coaches working under her and a whole slew of gushing testimonials from satisfied clients on display. Pretty impressive for someone no more than three years out of college.

I switch off my screen and try to relax against the pillows. Maybe Holly offered Mason an internship with Pivot Point, not that my brother has ever expressed interest in being anything other than a pro athlete. It's hard to imagine him using her coaching services, but then again, my brother never talks to me anymore. If he's looking for a "second chance" for some reason, it's not like he'd tell me about it.

I slip in my AirPods and stare hard out at the water. It's great that Mason's bonding with Holly; I hope she can help him with whatever it is. But there used to be a time he'd come to *me* if something was bothering him. And I have to admit, I'm more than a little jealous.

THEO

It's after eleven when I pry my eyes open. I expect to find the room empty, as it has been basically every morning when I wake up at a normal-for-vacation time and Mason's off doing whatever he does alone on the beach, but today I shove myself up in bed to the sounds of the shower running in our bathroom and the nearby thrum of music I can't quite make out.

My thoughts rove back to the "street market" in the resort lobby last night. At eight thirty exactly, after Mason pulled me aside to accuse me of sending that anonymous text, I went out to the fire pit as instructed, but no one was there to meet me. I still have no idea who sent that note. *8:30 p.m., tonight, the fire pit. Let's talk.* The thought that it could have been Mason after all crosses my mind. When I showed it to him yesterday afternoon, he brushed it off with some crack about a secret admirer, but who else would have sent it? Maybe he was planning to have a real conversation with me, finally, but after he got that text, he changed his mind?

I grit my teeth and pad over to the dresser. I've spent this whole trip trying to talk rationally with my future stepbrother, but after last night, I think I've had my fill of "bonding time" with Mason Acker-Mayweather.

I select the last semi-clean T-shirt from my drawer and pull it over my head. One more day of Mayweathers, culminating in Dad and Elizabeth's engagement party tonight. Then in the morning, we can finally check out and head to the airport. I tug on my jeans and walk over to the closet to grab my belt off the hook, nearly tripping over Mason's sandy swim trunks and crumpled shirt on the floor. His phone spills out of the laundry pile, and the music hitches up a notch. The screen displays an in-progress playlist.

I reach down to scoop it up, planning to toss it onto his bed, grab my belt and room key, and get out of here. But once Mason's unlocked phone is in my hand, it hits me that this is an unexpected gift I'm unlikely to get twice. I'm overcome by the urge to go into his texts, find the one with the link to the list of athletes. Try to figure out who sent it.

Because it *definitely* wasn't me, or anyone I told. No matter what Mason believes, I've shared his secret with exactly no one. He said the text came from some bogus-looking email account. It's probably untraceable, but even the tiny chance I might be able to figure it out is too tempting to resist. Proving who sent it means getting Mason off my back.

My eyes stray to the closed bathroom door. The shower is still running; I have a minute or two before I have to ditch his phone and get out of here. And I *need* to exonerate myself in Mason's eyes. Because our parents are getting married this summer, and whether he likes it or not, we're going to be stuck with each other for all eternity.

One eye still on the bathroom door, I navigate to Mason's texts and tap open the list of messages, scrolling down through his history. But before I find anything from a weird email address, I freeze. Because there's something else here, something that makes absolutely no sense at all.

Witness: Holly Laurel Bird
Statement Taken by Oficial Juan Parra
Monday, January 8, 11:33 a.m.

Holly Laurel Bird: I'm not a letch, if that's what you're implying.

Oficial Juan Parra: No one is implying anything, Ms. Bird.

H. L. B.: I'm sure.

Oficial J. Parra: We are simply asking you to tell us why the victim was seen entering your hotel room on the afternoon of Sunday, December thirty-first, the day before the engagement party.

H. L. B.: Fine. But this has *absolutely nothing* to do with what happened the next night. With his death.

Oficial J. Parra: Let us determine what is relevant, Ms. Bird.

H. L. B.: [Sighs.] Mason and I bonded over similar mess-ups from our past. I told him about a mistake I made a few years back, which resulted in my removal from my college swim team. The story's public knowledge; it's part of the pitch for my coaching business, Pivot Point. You can look it up.

Oficial J. Parra: Go on.

H. L. B.: Mason's more recent actions had gotten him banned from his school hockey league. Unlike me, he hadn't made his peace with what happened. He came to me to talk, that's all.

Oficial J. Parra: And what did you talk about, specifically?

H. L. B.: Me, mostly. If you want your clients to trust you, you have to be open with them. Honest. Not that Mason was a client; we were just talking, as friends. I thought I could help him. So I opened up to him about why I showed up intoxicated to swim finals that day. I'd been sexually assaulted the night before, by my boyfriend at the time. The next day, I was reeling. I drank to try to block out what had happened, instead of going to the police or my coach. [Pause.] Maybe it's different here, but in the United States, sexual assault survivors are rarely believed.

Oficial J. Parra: Mmm.

H. L. B.: It's taken time, but I've gotten to a place where I'm not hard on myself anymore about how I chose to cope. I do regret how my actions impacted my teammates, though. I derailed something important for a lot of people I cared about that day. It's a complicated set of emotional truths.

Oficial J. Parra: I see.

H. L. B.: The reason I shared this with Mason, the reason I share this story with a few select clients, is because I want the people I work with to be able to recognize that the actions we've come to regret, which have negatively impacted our lives in some way, can't simply be dismissed as "bad behavior" or uncharacteristic mistakes. There's almost always a reason behind our actions that needs to be confronted before we can move forward.

Oficial J. Parra: Ms. Bird, is it correct that the information you shared privately with Mason Acker-Mayweather about your assault is not part of the public story you share on your business website?

H. L. B.: That's right. I don't want people to perceive me as a victim without getting to know me. As I said, it's a personal story that I choose to share with select clients, depending on the circumstances. And I chose to share it with Mason that afternoon. That's why we were in my hotel room. Nothing more.

Oficial J. Parra: I see. And the conversation with the victim, it angered your current boyfriend, Corey Mayweather? You were seen arguing on the beach the following morning.

H. L. B.: Corey didn't know the nature of my conversation with Mason that afternoon. Frankly, it was none of his business. When you work as a life coach, you respect client confidentiality.

Oficial J. Parra: But as you've stated, Mason Acker-Mayweather was not a client.

H. L. B.: No, but—

Oficial J. Parra: Mason was known to have quite a temper. Did he threaten to share your secret with others? Did you regret sharing your private history with him, Ms. Bird?

H. L. B.: No, not at all.

Oficial J. Parra: Ms. Bird, this week was your first time meeting your boyfriend's family, was it not? You've stated that people's perceptions are important to you. After sharing sensitive information about your past with Mason Acker-Mayweather, did you ask your boyfriend, Corey Mayweather, to make sure his nephew would stay silent?

H. L. B.: What? No!

24

Nine Hours Until the Engagement Party

MASON

When I step out of the bathroom, towel wrapped around my waist, my clothes have been shoved into the closet with the rest of the laundry, and my phone rests on my bed, open to the playlist I had on earlier. What the hell? I glance around the room for Theo, but he's gone.

I switch the music off, then tap open my texts, then my email, then Instagram. Nothing looks like it's been messed with, but it's hard to tell. If I was in a generous mood, I'd say my phone fell out of my pocket when Theo was needlessly straightening the room, but by the final draining day of this vacation, I'm feeling anything but generous when it comes to the Hunts.

On the other hand, if Theo was deliberately snooping, why leave my phone on the bed instead of returning it to my pocket where he found it?

I get dressed quickly, wrestling with the thought that yesterday's anonymous text—all those athletes kicked off their teams—has made me a little paranoid. If Theo really didn't tell anyone what I did, then that means someone else has been digging up dirt. And it's not someone from school, no matter what Theo might believe. At school, my secret's not a secret. It's public knowledge. No one knows I've been concealing the truth from my family, my mom in particular. They might hate me for kicking that kid's ass and spoiling Rhyne Ridge's prospects for the season, but they don't have any reason to hide behind an anonymous text, to treat it like a big secret.

Which leaves my family—most likely the people right here at this resort. Addison? Mia? Natalia?

It's hard to believe it could be one of the adults, but Austin's face flashes across my mind. Even if Theo didn't rat me out to his dad, Austin could have easily overheard something Theo said. Or maybe after the tension at lunch the other day, Austin decided to do his own research. No doubt Mom has told her fiancé exactly how I feel about him. All the color leaches from my face. Was the text Austin's way of trying to keep me in check? Play nice, or I'll tell your mom what I know?

Well, fuck that. Whether or not he sent the text, Austin Hunt is bad news for our family. Bad news for Mom. My eyes drop back to my phone screen. It's getting close to noon; Mom and Austin will have finished breakfast long ago. He's probably back in their room, doing his all-important magazine work, which means Mom is either at the pool or the beach.

We need to talk before the engagement party tonight. I need to find her—now.

I check the pool first, then the beach, but Mom is nowhere. I shoot her a text, then head to the typically deserted indoor pool where I can swim some laps, burn off some of this nervous energy. Thankfully, I'm the only one there. I throw on my swim trunks in the locker room, then dive into the deep end.

It's almost one thirty by the time she texts me back.

> Sorry, hon! Addison and I were getting our hair done at the spa, but we're all finished now. Would you like to get lunch?

I frown down at the screen.

> Just you and me. Cantina Victoria. Meet you in 10.

Cantina Victoria is a sports bar and grill type place on the fourth floor. It's loud and the food's mediocre, which leaves very little chance any other Mayweathers will be dining there this afternoon. It's perfect.

Mom meets me at the entrance. Her hair looks the same, maybe shinier and half an inch shorter. I'm sure the cut cost a couple hundred bucks.

"You look great," I tell her, because I know it's what she'll want to hear.

"Thanks, hon." I tilt my head down so she can give me a peck on the cheek. Then she peers through the door at the large flat-screens and sticky-looking tables inside the cantina. "Are you sure this is where you want to eat?"

"Definitely," I say. "I'm in the mood for nachos."

Mom gives me a small smile, the kind that means, *I don't understand you, but I love you*, and I hold the door open for her. My heart is doing crossovers in my chest. I don't want to make her life harder—the exact opposite. She's not going to like what I have to say. But throughout the week, the feeling in my gut has gotten stronger and stronger: Marrying Austin would be a massive mistake.

When we've ordered and Mom is dipping a greasy tortilla chip into the mildest of the trio of salsas, I clear my throat.

"I'm worried about you," I say, and she lays the chip down on her plate.

Her eyes search mine. "What's wrong, hon?"

"At lunch the other day," I say after a moment, "I didn't like what I saw between Austin and Uncle Corey. If you hadn't been there to intervene, Austin would have hit him."

And I should know because I've been there.

Mom presses her lips between her teeth, and I want to say everything: That I've been that person, but I'm trying to be better. That if she marries Austin Hunt, he will *not* be good for us. Not for me, and not for her, either.

But I need to tread carefully. I take a big gulp of ice water.

"That's not your job," I say out loud. "With Dad, you were always on patrol. I saw what it did to you. You were miserable."

And in the end, Mom couldn't keep him from getting in the car drunk, endangering all four of us. But bringing that up now will only make her feel guilty, which is the exact opposite of what I'm trying to do. I'm sure parents never stop worrying about their kids, but protecting us from other supposedly responsible adults shouldn't be part of the deal.

She reaches across the table and places her hand on top of mine.

"You're right," she says after a minute. "I was miserable. And I'm so, so sorry your father and I put you and Addison thorough that."

"Then you get it," I say, riding this wave of mutual understanding. My heart is doing double time now, but I'm not going to get another chance. "You have to break things off with Austin. I know you're into him, Mom, but—"

"No, no." She withdraws her hand from mine, looking horrified. "That's not at all what I'm saying. Austin is *not* like your father. This trip has been stressful for him, more than I realized it would be, and what you saw at lunch the other day was that stress boiling over. But hon, *nothing happened.* It was a heated moment, but Austin would never have hit Corey. I promise you that."

I shake my head, hair whipping in my eyes. She's not listening to me, not at all. She is one hundred percent in denial.

And then the waiter is approaching our table with my nachos and Mom's taco salad, but I'm standing, chair scraping against the wooden floor.

The words are out of my mouth before I've thought them through, before I can swallow them back.

"It's him or me, Mom. You can't have it both ways. You have to choose."

NATALIA

After lunch, I clean up Mia's mess at Guest Services, ensuring the Kids Kamp refund will go to Gigi and Pop-Pop's bank of resort points instead of Mom's credit card, then I find an open cabana on the peaceful side of the pool. I spend the next couple of hours with all the curtains drawn, texting back and forth with Marisol. Fortunately, Mia is holding up her end of the bargain at camp. Marisol texts me a series of photos of my little sister, clearly enjoying herself on a waterslide, then releasing a little tree frog she found by the water back into "the wild"—a grassy area beyond the parking lot. Mia's been very into frogs lately; if Mami wasn't so squeamish around them, she'd probably already have a tank filled with the little hoppers at home.

It's midafternoon when Theo finds me down by the pool. He's been texting me for hours, and if I'd wanted to talk, I would have responded. But now he's impossible to ignore, standing outside the cabana, whispering my name and rapping lightly on the curtain as if it's a door. My beach bag, which has slumped from the mattress down onto the deck, must have given me away.

"Fine," I growl. "Come in."

Theo parts the curtain, a sheepish smile on his face.

"I know you're mad at me," he says. "But I think you'll want to see these."

He perches on the edge of the mattress and digs his phone out of his pocket.

"Hold up." I extend my hand toward him, blocking his

screen. "If this is about Seth, I truly don't want to hear it. Or see it."

Theo's face crumples. "It is, but—"

"Seriously," I cut him off. "I talked to Seth yesterday. You were way off base, okay? Mountains are mountains, and you cannot get an accurate read on the position of the sun from one iPhone photo. You made me doubt him over nothing!"

And ruined the second half of my vacation. I like Theo, I do, but I can't just forget what happened and move on.

He leans back against one of the cabana's four wooden posts, clutching his phone. His knuckles are white around the case, and his face is still twisted up. He looks like he's in pain.

I let out a deep sigh. "Fine. What is it?"

His face relaxes. "Please trust me. You need to see this."

He taps at his phone, and a series of new messages appear on my screen.

At first I'm not sure what I'm looking at. It's a series of screenshots, text messages between Mason and someone named Seth Bayer.

"Seth's last name is Bates," I say to Theo. "Not Bayer."

He nods. "Just read."

A prickly feeling creeps across the back of my neck. "Where did you get these?"

"Mason's phone. He left it unlocked when he was in the shower this morning. I was looking for something else, which I probably shouldn't have been doing, but I found these in his text history. And then Seth being on the East Coast, what I said on Saturday, it all clicked."

I draw in a deep breath and read. The first screenshot displays texts from early September. Mason initiated the exchange by telling this Seth—Seth Bayer—that it's time to pay his dues. Seth asks him what he wants, and Mason says he needs help playing a prank on his cousin.

The prickly feeling shoots all the way down my spine, and I scroll to the next image. In the messages that follow, Mason says he's going to put Seth in touch with Derrick Gaff, that Derrick can tell him what I'm into. My mouth goes dry. Derrick transferred to Hamilton last year, from upstate New York. I had no idea he knew Mason. Now we're in wind ensemble together; it was Derrick who introduced me to Branca's Symphony No. 13 (Hallucination City) for 100 Guitars just days before Seth responded to my playlist post on Twitter, suggesting Branca.

At the time, I'd thought it was such a weird coincidence. And then I'd stopped wondering about it at all.

My phone tumbles down to the mattress. I'm not sure I can keep reading.

"It's the same Seth," Theo says quietly. "Mason first texted him on September third. That's the same time @sethybgoode joined Twitter."

I nod. I don't need any more convincing.

"But why?" It comes out half whisper, half croak.

"I have no idea," Theo says. "But there's a sophomore on Rhyne Ridge's JV hockey team named Seth Bayer. I found photos online. I'm sorry, Natalia. It's him."

I swallow hard, and Theo reaches for his phone. I know he wants to pull up the photos, to prove once and for all that Seth is a fraud, but I don't need to look.

"I believe you," I say, and my heart shatters into a thousand splinters that can never, ever be repaired. Seth—my Seth—is from Rhyne Ridge. He knows Mason through hockey, and Mason used his seniority on varsity to get Seth to pretend to like me. To catfish me.

"I just don't get it," I say, tears collecting in my eyes. "Why would Mason do this to me?"

But in my heart, damaged as it is, I think I know the answer.

Witness: Mia Mayweather (minor accompanied
by mother, Paola Ortiz)
Statement Taken by Oficial Juan Parra
Monday, January 8, 4:26 p.m.

Mia Mayweather: They were pranks, that's all. Not *even* pranks.
Just . . . messages. It was stupid.

Oficial Juan Parra: And what was the exact nature of these
pranks slash messages, Ms. Mayweather?

M. M.: [Sighs.] I put a tree frog in Addison's bed. That was Friday
night, while she was down in the hot tub with everyone else, and
I was grounded. On Saturday, I went into my sister's phone and
downloaded a couple photos of her boyfriend with another girl. I
wasn't even being mean; if I was her, I'd've wanted to see that.
Then on Sunday, I sent an anonymous text to Mason, and I left a
note for Theo, asking him to meet me that night. But then Natalia
cornered me at the street market when I was supposed to be
talking to Theo, and the conversation never even happened.

Oficial J. Parra: And what was the purpose of these pranks slash
messages, Ms. Mayweather?

M. M.: I was bored, okay? They were all blowing me off or
straight-up ignoring me. They act like they're so much older than
me, so superior. I was trying to get their attention, I guess. Like I
said, it was stupid.

Oficial J. Parra: Tell me more about the text you sent Mason.

M. M.: Mason had been ignoring me all week. Barely said hi, never hung out. I was mad, okay? So I thought maybe I could get back at him somehow, and I started searching around, following the people he follows on social. That's how I found out about Mason getting kicked off ice hockey. I thought maybe if he knew that I knew his secret, he'd have to hang out with me.

Oficial J. Parra: So you blackmailed him?

M. M.: I guess? It didn't work, though. I set up a fake email account, and I sent him an anonymous text that I knew would make him sweat. I was going to tell him it was me, after he stressed about it for a few hours, but then he ditched me at the street market to hang out with Theo, and then I didn't see him all day Monday. Until the engagement party.

Oficial J. Parra: Would it be correct to say you were pretty angry with Mason Acker-Mayweather when you saw him at the party on Monday night?

Paola Ortiz: Don't answer that.

M. M.: It's fine, Mami.

P. O.: No, it isn't. This interview is over.

25

ONE WEEK AGO
MONDAY, JANUARY 1

Three Hours Until the Engagement Party

THEO

After I break the bad news about Seth and Mason to Natalia, she understandably wants to be alone, so I leave her to the shade of her cabana and head back inside the resort. I feel bad—really bad. But I keep telling myself it would have been worse not to share the texts with her. She deserves to know that Seth's been playing her, that for some cruel reason, Mason set her up.

I knew he could be violent, and he can definitely hold a grudge. And sure, cousins play pranks on each other some-times. When we were in grade school and my older cousins Nick and Danny came to visit, they were all about playing tricks. But it was silly stuff—a whoopee cushion on my seat at the dinner table, fake bugs in the bathroom. What Mason's been doing to Natalia feels less like a prank gone too far and more like a vendetta.

I spend the next half hour wandering aimlessly around the resort. I don't want to go back to the room and risk running into Mason, whose phone I left in the middle of his bed this morning. At the time, I was amped up on the adrenaline rush of my discovery. I actually *wanted* him to confront me about snooping so I could tell him what I'd found, defend Natalia. But now that seems like a mistake. I've already meddled a lot; I need to let Mason and Natalia work this out on their own.

I'm standing outside the gym with zero intention of going inside when my phone chimes. Dad.

> Can you meet me in the room,
> please?

I can't get a read on his tone; am I in trouble? It crosses my mind that he's somehow found out about the whole Natalia-Mason-Seth thing. If Mason suspected I was snooping around his phone, would he seriously tattle on me to my dad? Guess I'm about to find out.

> Five minutes.

When I arrive to Dad and Elizabeth's room, it's only Dad inside. He looks off somehow—red-faced and puffy. At first I think he's been in the sun too long, but then it hits. He's been crying.

"What's wrong?"

Dad is pretty emotionally available, but he's not a big crier. Could I have possibly made him that upset?

He sighs, his whole body swelling and deflating. Then he takes a seat on the edge of the bed and nods toward the wicker desk chair. I pull it out.

"It's Mason," he says after a moment, and my throat tightens. Sure, I violated Mason's privacy, and if Dad wants to ground me, I'd deserve that. But I'm positive I deleted those screenshots after forwarding them to Natalia, and I can't imagine she would have showed my dad. Besides, my small role in this isn't even close to the whole story.

I don't even understand the whole story. That's between Natalia, Seth, and Mason.

But when Dad continues, it's not about the screenshots.

"He laid down an ultimatum. To Elizabeth. About me."

"What?" I clench the side of the chair, mind spinning. "What kind of ultimatum?"

Dad sighs again, shoulders visibly heaving. "Mason has become convinced I'm a bad influence on his mom. Elizabeth's first husband had anger issues, which led to their divorce, and it's no secret that controlling my emotions is something I struggle with too. So I understand how Mason feels, I really do."

"I don't," I growl. Yes, Dad has lost his cool on occasion. But never *violently*.

Unlike Mason.

"Mason has asked Elizabeth to break off the engagement," Dad continues. "He wants her to choose her family over me."

"What the fuck?" I spit out.

"Teddy, language."

"Sorry. But seriously, where does he get off? He doesn't even know us!"

Dad's face crumples. "I'm afraid that's my fault. This was supposed to be a chance to bond, and I've spent most of the week in here." He gestures limply around the room. "I'm embarrassed admitting this to you, but the truth is, until we got to Cancún, I had no idea how intimidated I would feel by Elizabeth's family. Their wealth, their history. Burying myself in work was a kind of avoidance, not to mention the extra cash. But in the meantime, I've alienated Mason."

"And Elizabeth's taking Mason's side?" I ask.

"The engagement is still on," he says. "But it's a little more complicated than that. Mason's her son; it's not about taking sides. I have a lot of repair work ahead of me, and I'm not sure Mason is open to that. At least not right now."

My jaw clenches. I've put up with *a lot* this week when it comes to Mason Acker-Mayweather, but laying down an us-or-them ultimatum on the day of the engagement party crosses a line even I didn't see coming.

"I'll talk to him," I say, an angry tremor shooting up my cheek. "Let me handle this."

ADDISON

When I walk into our room on Monday evening, Natalia is sitting crisscross in the middle of the bed—my bed—waiting.

She pats the comforter and scoots up so her back is against the headboard, making room for me.

"Hi." My beach bag slumps to the floor. I've wanted to secure some alone time with my cousin this entire trip, but despite sharing a room with her, she's been impossibly elusive.

Now here she is on the very last evening, two hours before the engagement party is set to begin, ready to talk.

I'm still wearing my damp suit and a beach cover, but something tells me this is a limited-time offer, and if I insist on a quick shower first, it might expire. I take a seat.

"What's up?"

"Mia will be back from camp any minute now," she says. "So we need to make this quick."

"Okay," I agree, still not sure what "this" is.

She lets her head fall against the headboard and raises her eyes to the ceiling, looking pained. "We need to talk about the Incident. And Mason."

"Oh." My pulse instantly spikes. Ideally, Mason would be here for this conversation, because this involves all three of us. But I'll take what I can get. "I agree. We definitely should."

But what Natalia says next doesn't seem to connect to what happened three summers ago.

"It turns out, Seth isn't who he says he is. He's a friend of Mason's, from Rhyne Ridge. Mason's been using him to catfish me."

"What?"

"Here." She holds out her phone. On the screen is a text exchange between my brother and someone named Seth Bayer. Natalia motions for me to scroll through the screenshots, and I start to read.

"I don't know what to say," I say, unhelpfully, when I've finished. I place her phone delicately on the comforter between us. "This is beyond horrible."

Natalia presses her lips together, and her eyes lift toward

the ceiling again. It's then that I realize how red-rimmed they are, how much she's been crying.

"It's because of everything with Beau," she says after a moment, and *now* I see the connection to the Incident. "Why else would Mason be so mad at me?"

All at once, it's acutely clear that the conversation I'd so desperately wanted to have at the start of this Mayweather family reunion would have come far too late anyway. Mason's already been punishing Natalia for what her older brother Beau did three summers back—and how Natalia drew us into it.

It started that spring, when Beau got into NYU but didn't get anything in the way of financial aid. This was when Natalia and I were still inseparable, when Mason and I were still "Maddison," when Natalia's family still lived nearby, before Beau left for college and everyone else moved to Portland the following fall.

At thirteen, we were all a bit too young to understand how the whole FAFSA process worked, but Natalia whispered to Mason and me, hush-hush, that between Aunt Kiersten and Beau's dad, his parents made too much for the family to qualify for a grant, but not quite enough to comfortably bankroll four years at Beau's very expensive dream school in a very expensive city. If he wanted to go to NYU, he'd need to take out sizable student loans.

Beau lobbied for Aunt Kiersten to ask Gigi and Pop-Pop for more to support his college plans, but Aunt Kiersten has always been weird about asking her father for money, or maybe she did ask and he turned her down. For whatever reason, it's Mom and Corey who have always been the golden children in

Pop-Pop's eyes. I don't really know how it all played out, but by that summer, Beau had developed a deep resentment over the looming student loan debt—and a scheme for staging a home invasion at Gigi and Pop-Pop's gorgeous Naples ranch that would solve all his problems.

The Incident.

Under the auspices of attending an orientation session in New York, Beau flew to Florida while Gigi and Pop-Pop were summering in southern France, as they used to do when Pop-Pop could still easily travel, and lifted several valuable antiques from the vault in the back of their home. Most of the Mayweather family money is secured in investments and the bank, but apparently Gigi and Pop-Pop had been lax about renewing the insurance policies on their antiques, something Beau had overheard Aunt Kiersten griping about earlier that year. And so he took advantage.

Natalia took advantage too—of her big brother's absence. He'd been acting so secretive and weird in the weeks leading up to the NYU orientation, refusing to answer her curious questions about his trip to the city, hiding his phone screen when she came into the room, calling his student host Brad, then Chad, then Thad. It wasn't like Beau to lie to Natalia, or shut her out, and she complained to Mason and me about it for days.

After he left, Natalia was determined to find out what he'd been hiding from her. If she hadn't snooped around Beau's room while he was away, if she hadn't found his flight reservations or web searches for antiques dealers who wouldn't ask a lot of questions, if she hadn't come over to our house to breathlessly spill everything to Mason and me . . . I can still see it so vividly: Natalia rushing up to my bedroom the moment her moms dropped her off, Mason closing the door behind the three of us and Natalia divulging everything in hushed, reverent tones.

If none of that had happened, we wouldn't have spent the next three and a half years shouldering Beau's secret—and living under his thumb.

Of course Natalia couldn't keep a straight face around her big brother when he came back from Florida, and she immediately confessed both to snooping and to telling Mason and me what she'd found. Beau managed to convince Natalia that what he'd done wasn't really wrong, that the money was all going to go to their parents and then to them in the inheritance anyway; he was taking a portion of his share in advance, when he needed it. In Beau's eyes, our grandfather's refusal to establish trusts, his propensity toward playing favorites, and their mom's pride were not good enough reasons to saddle him with a lifetime of loans.

Beau wasn't entirely wrong. We all knew what he'd done was illegal, that it was a *crime*, but it was hard to argue with his logic. And besides, Gigi and Pop-Pop still had plenty of money. The invasion was jarring, the loss of the antiques a wake-up call about their home security, but financially it was hardly a setback. So we promised Natalia we'd never tell a soul.

Beau seemed satisfied his kid sister wouldn't rat him out, but when he found out Mason and I knew about the theft too, no amount of swearing we'd keep our mouths shut was enough to make him breathe easy. Throughout eighth and ninth grades, while Natalia settled in on the West Coast with Mia and their moms, far away from her brother and his guilty conscience, Beau bribed Mason and me with trips to visit him at NYU and fun outings in the city. He cemented our complicity in his crime, and for a time, we went along with it, no questions asked. Over and over, Mom praised him for being the *best big cousin*. But by our sophomore year, Beau's paranoia reached new heights. That's when the bribes turned to threats—what would happen to Mason and me if the family found out we'd known his secret all along. Pop-Pop would stop funding Mom's shop in Rhyne Ridge. She'd have to close the business. We'd go broke. We'd get cut out of the inheritance. The Mayweathers would be torn apart.

At some point this fall, Mason blocked Beau's number, and the frequency of Beau's paranoid texts to me doubled. I've been dealing with it, sparing Mason from the stress because I knew he wouldn't be able to cope, but it's reached a fever pitch this week—Beau harassing me nonstop, my phone constantly pinging with yet another reminder to keep my mouth shut during the reunion.

I suck in a deep breath and turn to Natalia on the bed across from me.

"Mason's angry. Really angry," I say. "But it's been a long time since he's opened up to me. I thought his resentment was focused on Beau, for obvious reasons. But clearly it doesn't stop there."

"Clearly not," Natalia says, eyes downcast.

"You did draw us into this," I say gently.

"I was thirteen!" she splutters. "If I could go back, I never would have burdened you and Mason with any of it. Do you understand how guilty I feel about that? Why do you think I've been avoiding this conversation all week? Why do you think I let your emails sit for weeks and weeks before writing back? Sometimes I feel so bad about how I messed things up for you, I can't bring myself to reply at all."

Oh. Natalia doesn't hate me. She feels *guilty.*

Because she made us complicit, then moved away, leaving us. It wasn't her fault, but that's how it happened. And to add insult to injury, Beau trusted his sister like he never trusted Mason and me, sparing her from the paranoia that followed. I never blamed Natalia for any of it; I just wanted my best friend back. But of course she feels guilty. And Mason is beyond bitter.

Shame floods my cheeks, hot and bright. I've been so focused on trying to press the reset button with my cousin and brother, I've been oblivious to their feelings.

I place my hand, gently, on Natalia's arm.

"We were all kids," I say. "I never blamed you. What happened was *not your fault.* But Mason . . ."

I let my voice trail off. It tracks that he's mad at Natalia for drawing us into this. But catfishing her? Deliberately setting her up to have her heart broken? It's *cruel.* For the first time, it hits me that Mason and I have become more than distant. I don't have any idea who my brother is anymore.

"But Mason," I repeat, "has never been great at managing his emotions. The way he sees it, I think, is that you got off the hook while we took all Beau's heat. And he's lashing out at you because Beau is a threat, but you're an easy target."

"I'm sorry," she sniffs, wiping wet streaks from her eyes. "I can't control my brother."

"I know all about that."

Control is exactly what I've been trying to exert over this situation all week, and I've failed epically. But this conversation has been eye-opening in multiple ways. Natalia doesn't hate me after all, and my brother has changed far more than I ever imagined.

"But why come after me now?" Natalia asks. "It's been more than three years."

I nod. "Things didn't get really bad with Beau until last year. And it seems like, from those screenshots, Mason jumped on an opportunity when that guy Derrick moved to your school."

"Looking back," she says, voice hardening, "I never should have supported Beau like I did. I was so unbelievably gullible. I let him convince me that what he'd done was okay, and because he was my big brother, I trusted him. We used to be so close, Beau and me. He ruined all that."

Her chin is quivering.

"I'm so sorry," I say.

I know all about losing the people you love. With Natalia, there's hope, but with Mason, I wonder if the rift is permanent. My stomach clenches.

"Now," Natalia continues, "it's hard for me to trust people. It took a long time for me to make friends in Portland. And I've never dated before. All of which Mason knew. So when I met Seth, it was a really big step for me to open up, let him in."

"I'm sorry," I say again. "On Mason's behalf. I honestly never would have guessed he could be so cruel."

Our heads turn in unison toward the door. Outside, there's the sound of voices—Mia and Aunt Paola—then the click of a key card against the scanner.

"Me either." Natalia squares her shoulders against the headboard. Her face is tear-free, the sadness around her eyes replaced by something colder, harder. Pure anger.

As the door swings open, Natalia leans toward me, voice dropping to a whisper. "Tonight, Mason and I are going to talk. Alone."

Witness: Theodore Hunt (minor accompanied
by father, Austin Hunt)
Statement Taken by Oficial Juan Parra
Monday, January 8, 6:17 p.m.

Oficial Juan Parra: Tell me about the ultimatum.

Theodore Hunt: Um, okay. Well, Mason had some pretty off-base
ideas about my dad and me. He wanted his mom to break off
the engagement. Earlier that day—the day of the party—Mason
told her she had to make a choice: him or my dad. [Glances at
Austin Hunt.] So Dad was understandably upset that night. And
I was too—about the ultimatum, and the trip in general. I'd been
trying really hard to get on Mason's good side all week, and it just
wasn't happening. But I didn't hurt him! And neither did Dad.

Oficial J. Parra: Mmm.

T. H.: I'm serious. By the night of the engagement party, pretty
much everyone on the reunion trip had a reason to be angry with
Mason.

Oficial J. Parra: Mind breaking that down?

T. H.: Oh—I'm not here to point fingers. It's just, Mason had a
way of getting under everyone's skin.

Oficial J. Parra: Please, go on.

T. H.: [Sighs.] Fine. All week, there was tension between Addison, Mason, and Natalia. I don't know exactly what was going on, but it seems like Mason had been carrying a grudge. That morning, I discovered he'd been using a friend of his to catfish Natalia. She was devastated. But again—I'm not saying she did anything to him. Just that he'd made a lot of enemies on the trip.

Oficial J. Parra: Mm-hmm. And the others? There were eleven of you at the party that night.

T. H.: Elizabeth was upset about the ultimatum, of course—but she never would have hurt her own son. And Mia was mad at everyone. We'd all been ignoring her a little. But she's only twelve!

Oficial J. Parra: And Corey Mayweather and Holly Bird?

T. H.: There was some drama there. I don't know all the details, but Mason and Holly became close toward the end of the trip. He was into her. And she might have overshared some stuff with him, I don't know. Maybe she regretted it? Anyway, Corey got upset. Jealous. You'll have to talk to them about it.

Oficial J. Parra: Which leaves Kiersten Mayweather and Paola Ortiz.

T. H.: I don't think Paola spent much time with Mason on the trip, but she did tell me this story about getting back at some parents in her community who had let their kid bully her younger daughter, Mia. When I found out that Mason had been playing this cruel prank on Natalia, I wondered if she'd told her mom about it. . . . But Paola's so nice. I really don't think she would have lashed out at Mason.

Oficial J. Parra: And Kiersten Mayweather.

T. H.: Something happened right before the party. I don't know what, but when I got to the Vista Hermosa deck that night, Kiersten was on the phone with Beau, her oldest son, in New York. She sounded upset, and I heard Mason's name come up. But I don't have any idea what it was about.

Oficial J. Parra: Thank you, Theo. That'll be all for now.

26

One Hour Until the Engagement Party

MASON

I'm sitting alone by the cold fire pit, going back and forth between seething anger and tears I won't let spill. Not because boys don't cry or whatever bullshit, just because what's the point of melting into a snotty puddle right now? Mom's made her priorities clear. There's no sign of the party being canceled. She's made her choice—and it's not me.

Despite her repeated texts assuring me we'll talk more after this trip, and everything's going to be fine, then imploring me to please give Austin and Theo a chance, I don't feel better. At all. Life with Mom and Austin is going to be just like life with Mom and Dad. A complete regression.

I feel ill.

In an hour, everyone's going to congratulate Mom and Austin and act all happy about our families merging because they're too blissed out on vacation vibes or too happy about watching Mom find love again to see Austin Hunt for who he is. And there is absolutely nothing I can do about it.

My phone chimes, and I dig it out of my pocket. Addison.

> Where are you? Everyone's in
> the rooms getting ready.

My fingers hover over the screen. What if I just didn't go tonight? Would anyone aside from my mom and sister even notice? But before I can decide or think up what to say, a second text comes in.

> And Natalia's beyond pissed,
> btw. You've been catfishing
> her?!?!? What the hell, Mase?

Oh. Shit. I click off my screen without responding and slide my phone back into my pocket. Wonder how she figured it out. My mind flashes to my phone sitting out in the middle of my bed this morning.

Theo.

My fingers grip the cold concrete bench. Only staff have the keys to open the grate, but if I could, I'd light up the pit, then set this whole place on fire. I don't even know where to direct my rage right now: Theo or Natalia. Beau or Pop-Pop.

They're all to blame.

Over the past year, everything has gotten worse and worse. Constant check-in texts from Beau. Monthly trips into the city to "hang out"—i.e. sit there while he threatens me with every bad thing that would happen to Mom, Addison, and me if I ever let it slip that the Naples home invader was none other than Pop-Pop's oldest grandson.

And then I lost it.

I'd just been down at NYU over Labor Day weekend, suffering through three days of Beau's paranoia and threats. Assuring him, yet again, that my lips were forever sealed, no matter how bad I wanted to expose him out of sheer spite. Then, not more than a week later, junior year was kicking into gear in Rhyne Ridge and preseason was just getting started when Beau texted me during a scrimmage demanding I come down to NYU again that night. He'd just found out about the planned Mayweather reunion in Cancún, and because of some internship orientation over his winter break, he couldn't go. Which would mean Addison, Natalia, and me all in one place for a whole week, free from Beau's watchful eye, free to discuss the Incident as much as we pleased. Free to, he was sure, tell on him like the babies we were.

I was fucking pissed. I'd just paid my dues down in the city, and there was no way I was going again that night. I texted Beau back, telling him to get lost. Then he started calling. I switched off my phone, but I could see the calls piling up, and my temperature started to rise. Coach called me onto the ice, and fifteen seconds into play, Landon Murphy, this kid on the opposing team who'd been on my ass since the first period, cross-checked me.

I snapped.

For a moment, Landon and Beau blended into one, and I started whaling on him. If Coach and three of my teammates hadn't pulled me off, I think I would have kept going until Landon stopped moving.

When they dragged me away, there was blood all over my hands, my uniform, the ice. I scared the shit out of myself.

After my brief school suspension and permanent removal from the league, I blocked Beau's number and got a new phone. Beau was at least temporarily off my back, but I was still furious at Natalia for putting me in this position in the first place, for getting off with zero consequences out in Portland. So when I learned Derrick Gaff had transferred to my cousin's same high school, I got an idea for shaking up her life, for serving up a tiny taste of the harassment her brother had rained down on me since the Incident. Recruiting Seth Bayer from JV to fake interest in Natalia wasn't my most mature moment, but when he reported back that they'd hit it off, that she was totally smitten, I can't lie.

It felt amazing.

Now, though, the whole Seth and Natalia thing has taken on a life of its own. Our deal was simple: he would send my cousin a minimum of three texts a day and video-chat with her once a week. In return, I'd use my muscle to make sure Seth got a spot on varsity next year, something I might have been able to pull off in my former life as team captain, but can't possibly hope to make good on now. I kind of led Seth to believe I still had some leverage at first, but now he knows the truth. He must actually like Natalia a lot, because even though the deal is off, he's still talking to my cousin.

Which means ironically, I did her a solid. Guess that serves me right.

I shove up from the concrete pit and head up the stairs, back onto the pool deck and toward the hotel lobby. Time to change. Going to this engagement party is still the last thing I want to do, but I should probably suck it up and talk to Natalia before reunion week is over and we don't see each other in person again until the wedding. If the cursed event happens. I owe her an explanation—she was an easy target when I was at my lowest, but really, this isn't her fault.

I'm stepping out of the elevator when Aunt Kiersten's room door swings shut behind her, and the two of us are alone on the fifth-floor hall. She gives me a wide smile.

"Mason." She's wearing a formfitting black dress cut above the knee and a brightly colored shawl. She takes in my sandy shorts and T-shirt. "Headed in to change?"

"Yeah." I'm about to continue on past her, go to my own room, but something stops me. Aunt Kiersten is at least as much to blame as Natalia. If it wasn't for her strained dynamic with Pop-Pop, her constant competition with Mom and Uncle Corey, maybe Beau wouldn't have felt like stealing from the family was his only option.

I've been carrying around his secret for three and a half years. Am I going to do this forever? If I tell, if everyone finds out that I let Beau buy my continued silence with Rangers games and concert tickets and other bribes acquired with Pop-Pop's money, the consequences are huge: Pop-Pop will pull his support from Mom's shop. It will go belly-up, and we'll go broke. Addison and I will get disinherited, Beau and Natalia too, and soon the whole family will be shattered. It won't matter that I only accepted Beau's gifts to keep his paranoia in check. Gigi and Pop-Pop won't see it that way. They'll just see how we all betrayed them—Beau, Natalia, Addison, and me.

Then my thoughts skip back to my conversation with Mom at lunch. How it took no time at all for her to choose Austin over me. That *hurts*. The second after I opened my mouth, I regretted laying down the ultimatum, but it's a good thing I did, because the result has been eye-opening.

For three years, I've been suffering under Beau's thumb for the sake of our family, to make sure Mom keeps her shop. What was it all for if Mom isn't willing to put Addison and me first anymore, to keep our family together? I feel like a fool for trying so hard.

Maybe I've spent too much time hung up on the consequences when I should have been peeling back the curtain. The Mayweathers are damaged goods either way. Maybe what we all need is to have our eyes pried open.

The urge to burn it all down sears through me, stronger this time.

Aunt Kiersten is headed for the elevators. As she brushes past, I reach out and grab her wrist. "Wait."

She spins, surprised.

"What is it, Mason?"

The hallway is empty aside from the two of us, but I drop my voice to a whisper and lean in close. "There's something you need to know about the robbery at Gigi and Pop-Pop's house. There was no home invader. *Your son* stole those antiques."

For a moment, a flash of surprise lights up Aunt Kiersten's eyes. Then her face softens into something that looks like resignation.

She already knew.

"Come here," she says, beckoning me away from the row of doors, behind which the rest of our family is changing into their party clothes, and into the elevator lobby.

"I should have realized Natalia wouldn't be able to keep Beau's secret," she says when we're seated on the little bench opposite the elevators. "You all were only thirteen."

"How long have you known?" I ask, head spinning.

"Almost since it happened. But by the time I found out, Beau had already sold the items. It was too late to go back."

I shake my head slowly back and forth. All this time, Aunt Kiersten has known the truth. Which explains why Beau has gone so easy on Natalia; their mother chose to be complicit in her son's crime, and she's not going to let Natalia spill to Gigi and Pop-Pop, risk getting cut out of the will. Addison and I were the only liabilities.

"I could tell Pop-Pop the truth," I say to her. Suddenly the weight of keeping this secret seems far worse than what we'd lose when it comes out.

She nods. "You could. And maybe Dad *should* see exactly how badly his favoritism has driven his family to behave. But if you tell him, Mason, who wins? If Dad and Gloria learn the truth about what Beau did, we all suffer."

"I've been suffering for over three years," I hiss. "Keeping your son's secret. Enduring his endless stream of threats."

Aunt Kiersten's eyes narrow. "I didn't realize he'd been

threatening you. I'll talk to Beau, but please, Mason, think about this. Don't do anything rash."

Her voice is calm, but there's a flash of something wild in her eyes.

Panic.

Just then the hard slam of a room door reverberates down the hall, and both our heads turn toward the sound.

"Christ. I will never get used to this wind tunnel." It's Addison's voice.

Aunt Kiersten stands, and I follow suit. In a moment, Addison and Natalia emerge into the elevator lobby with Aunt Paola. Natalia is wearing a dressy pair of shorts and a cherry-red top with the kind of strappy sandals I don't know how girls walk in; the others have on flowy party dresses. A minute later, Mia scurries down the hall after them.

Natalia's gait halts a minute when she sees me, then she stiffens and keeps walking.

"Headed over?" Aunt Paola asks, and Aunt Kiersten nods.

"I just need to change," I mumble, shouldering past them and starting down the hall toward the rooms. "Be there soon."

"You want me to wait?" Addison asks.

Without turning around, I give her a head shake and a wave. The elevator dings.

When the doors have closed behind them, everything is silent again. For a moment, I stand frozen in the hallway, fingers wrapped around the key card in my pocket. But my eyes are fixed on the door to a different room. A kid's sandal—presumably Mia's—is wedged between the base of the door and the frame, propping the door to Addison, Natalia, and Mia's room slightly ajar.

Addison's voice from a moment ago travels back to me. *Christ. I will never get used to this wind tunnel.*

I take a step toward the door, planning to kick Mia's sandal back inside and let the door latch. I'm sure Mia thinks she's helping, but keeping their door unlocked for hours while everyone's at the party is a dumb move.

But then I hesitate.

My sister has been acting weird all week—first refusing to let the hotel porters handle her luggage, then trying to rent a locker at Guest Services, then lying about the constant stream of texts blowing up her phone, which are so obviously from Beau. Ever since I blocked his number, I bet he's been using her to keep tabs on me. The back of my neck grows hot.

All week, I've had a vague hunch that Addison has been hiding something, but until now, I haven't really cared.

Now I care. Because given her relentless campaign to get Natalia and me to talk about the Incident, my gut says whatever she's hiding is connected to the secret I'm sick of keeping. And the luggage thing, the locker . . . I'm nearly positive it's something she stashed in her suitcase, something she doesn't want the rest of us to see.

Mind made up, I grab the door handle and shove it open. Somewhere in this room, Addison is keeping a secret. And I'm going to find it.

4

THE ENGAGEMENT
PARTY

27

THEO

The sky is a deep, inky black spattered with heavy gray clouds, but the Vista Hermosa terrace glitters beneath hundreds of string lights. Two black-clad servers circulate with canapés, and a third pours drinks at the bar. It's almost too much wait-staff for our party of eleven guests, but their presence is comforting. With the staff here, I feel like a bit less of an outsider at this Mayweather gathering, even if they are just working the party.

Nonetheless, fifteen minutes into the evening, I'm sitting alone on one of the deck chairs, swallowed in the shadow of a large shade umbrella no one bothered to take down after sunset. "Signed, Sealed, Delivered" trumpets through a set of speakers up by the bar. I sip my Coke and watch Dad and Elizabeth chat with Paola. Big smiles light up all three of their faces. Corey and Holly are at the bar getting a fresh round of drinks, and Addison, Natalia, and Mia are absorbed in conversation by the stone fountain in the center of the terrace. I could go join any of them, but I'm not in the mood. The only Mayweather I want to talk to right now is Mason, and either he's running late, or he's decided to skip the party altogether.

I check my phone for the third time in as many minutes. 8:16. If he's not here by eight thirty, I'm going back to our room to root him out. He does not get to drop an ultimatum bomb and then simply not show up tonight like messing with Dad and Elizabeth's happiness comes with zero consequences.

At the beginning of the week, I wanted nothing more than to clear the air, to forget our false start this fall and make this trip a redo. But I have given Mason so many chances to do that, and he's obviously uninterested in a chill relationship. Far from ideal, but that's fine. We don't need to be friends. But despite his best efforts, we *are* going to be family. And he needs to stop treating Dad and me like the enemy and start accepting reality.

My eyes travel back to Dad and Elizabeth. His arm is cinched around her waist, and she's beaming while Paola selects a tiny ceviche cup from a silver platter and says something complimentary to the server. Dad is happier than I've seen him since Mom died, and it's pretty obvious to everyone but Mason that Elizabeth is happy too. My fingers curl around the arms of the deck chair until the wood digs into my flesh. I will not sit back and watch Mason destroy that.

"Finally. Are you ignoring my calls?"

The voice behind me is hushed, but I can just hear the

speaker above the party playlist, and she sounds pissed. I straighten up in my seat.

"This isn't a game. You need to stop treating Mason like a pawn. It's only going to backfire."

My head swivels slowly around. At first I can't find the source of the voice, but then my eyes land on Kiersten. She's on the phone, back pressed against the wall behind me. Her pale hand rests on the small white ladder leading up to the roof, and her black dress and dark brown hair blend in with the vine-draped wall at her back. I'm similarly camouflaged under this umbrella; I should clear my throat or something to let her know she's not having this conversation in private, but rabid curiosity stops me.

"Beau Edward McCardle." Her voice is a low hiss. "I should not have to tell you, of all people, how much is at stake."

My eyes close, mind searching for the name, until it clicks. Kiersten's oldest son, with her ex-husband. That must be him on the phone.

"Teddy." Dad's hand lands heavily on my shoulder, and I start. My eyes fly open, and I almost drop my Coke.

"Sorry." He laughs, then beckons for me to get up. "What are you doing hiding out over here? Come on." His chin dips toward Elizabeth and Paola, who have now been joined by Corey and Holly on the opposite side of the terrace.

I strain to listen behind me, but either Kiersten has ended the call, or she's gone somewhere quieter to continue her conversation with her son. Her conversation about Mason.

Either way, my cover is blown. I knock back the rest of my Coke and shove up from the deck chair. Mason's still not here, but I'll have to put in some face time with the grown-ups before going to find him. I give Dad a smile and follow him across the terrace.

NATALIA

Nearly an hour into the party I am trying to have fun, really I am, but my eyes keep returning to the hotel doors. Every time they glide open, I look up from my seltzer, look away from Addison and Mia, but it's always just one of the waitstaff coming or going with an hors d'oeuvres tray. Above the blare of "Crazy Little Thing Called Love" piping through the speakers, Mia is chattering on about the water park—*of course* she actually loved camp today once I forced her to go back—and Addison is dutifully listening and laughing in all the right places, but the clock has run out on my ability to engage in casual chitchat.

I have a singular focus right now: Mason.

My fist clenches around the napkin I've been holding until I realize I'm dribbling tortilla crumbs onto the terrace floor.

"Be right back." I flash them a big grin, then hurry across the terrace, through the doors, and into the resort. Suddenly it's silent, and I draw in a deep breath. There's a ladies' room to the right, and I step inside, stick my hands under the faucet. On TV, the main character is always escaping to the bathroom and splashing water on her face to calm down, but how does that even work with eyeliner and mascara? I let the cool stream run over my wrists, will the tick of my pulse to slow.

I don't think it's helping, because my thoughts stay locked on Mason. Leave it to my cousin to roll up over an hour late to his mom's engagement party. If he doesn't turn up soon, I'm going to his room to hunt him down.

And say what? *I know you've been using Seth to catfish me? You're a bully? You're mean?*

Each possibility is more childish than the next.

If we're really going to have it out, we'll have to talk about the Incident. What does he want me to say? I'm sorry I told you a big secret when we were thirteen?

Because I *am* sorry. If I could go back, I wouldn't tell Mom, wouldn't tell Addison or Mason. I'd keep what Beau did locked away tight, or better yet, I'd never go into his room to poke around at all. But I can't go back, and I can't control what my brother does—then or now. I've spent the past three and a half years racked with guilt, but what I did was a childish mistake with unintended consequences. What Mason's been doing to me is intentional, and that's so much worse.

The anger shoots through me again, hot and sharp, and I yank my hands away from the tap. The water shuts off. Its cooling properties aren't working. I don't know what I'm going to say to Mason when he finally gets his ass up to the terrace, but it's not going to be pretty or nice or forgiving. He doesn't deserve any of that.

I liked Seth—a lot. In a way I've never liked anyone before. And it was all fake, all a trap to hurt me, so they could laugh at me. My mind flashes to Mason on the night of the bonfire, right at the start of the trip. His eyes flicking across the four of us by the fire. *Who's dating an internet rando?* He'd played it off so well, I never would have believed he set the whole thing up.

I snatch a paper towel from the dispenser, scrub it across

my hands, and hurl it into the trash. It lands in the can with an infuriatingly gentle *pff*. Then I storm out of the bathroom and back onto the terrace, feeling more heated than when I came in for a break.

Outside, I halt. Mason is here, finally, standing by the bar with Uncle Corey and Holly, who have broken away from the other grown-ups, presumably to get yet another drink. Not that it's any of my business, but this must be their third trip to the bar in the hour or so we've been up here, and I don't think my uncle and his girlfriend are drinking soda.

But I don't really care what they do. My eyes are locked on Mason. He's changed into respectable party clothes—jeans and a button-down—and looks freshly showered. For some reason, a bulky gray messenger bag is slung across his chest. Maybe he's planning to ditch this party and head somewhere else for the night. He's leaning back against the bar, elbows propped on the counter, and laughing at whatever Holly's saying. Like he hasn't spent the past three months plotting my heartbreak and humiliation. Like he doesn't have a care in the world.

"Natalia."

My head jerks to the right. Mami is standing with Addison and Mia by the fountain now, and my little sister is waving for me to come back over. I cast one more glance toward Mason, but he's flanked by Uncle Corey on the left and Holly on the right, and pulling him aside right now would be very conspicuous.

I'll wait. I've got all night.

28

MASON

I get to the party a lot later than I'd planned, but once I'm here, all I want to do is turn around and leave. "Walking on Sunshine" pumps at max volume through the speakers hooked to the bar, and the sappy, bright lyrics are the exact opposite of my mood. The chorus starts again, and my jaw ticks.

Hanging with Holly and Uncle Corey feels like the path of least resistance through this all-Mayweather event, but we haven't been talking long before it's obvious Uncle Corey is kind of tense and a little too drunk. It's something I wouldn't have even clocked a couple of days ago, but my uncle's level of intoxication lands a little differently tonight. Apparently a too-deep love of booze is in the Mayweather blood, only one of many secrets I found hidden in Addison and Natalia's room an hour ago. My fingers clench around the strap of my messenger bag, and I adjust its weight against my hip.

When Holly gets a call and signals that she needs to step away for a minute, I leave Uncle Corey with the bartender and head for the doors leading back inside the resort. I know I've barely talked to anyone tonight, but I just want to be alone to think about everything I've found. To plan my next move.

Mom, apparently, has other ideas.

"Mason." Her hand lands lightly on my shoulder. "Come sit with us."

Her voice is gentle, but it's not a suggestion. Reluctantly, I drag my feet over to the floral-print deck set where Austin and Aunt Kiersten are sitting, three glasses of wine and a picked-over plate of cheese on the table in front of them. Mom settles back into her seat beside Austin on the couch, and I take the open chair beside Aunt Kiersten. I slide my bag off my shoulder, but keep it tucked tight to my side.

At first I think someone's going to bring up the ultimatum I laid down at lunch, and my shoulders tense, ready to defend myself. But Austin says something about the snow we're apparently getting back in New York and Mom says she hopes it won't affect our flights tomorrow, and it's clear that no one's going to talk about anything real. I don't know if I'm disappointed or relieved.

I contribute a few "yeahs" and "uh-huhs" to the conversation, but soon my eyes start to wander back to the bar, where Holly has rejoined my uncle. Addison is with them now too, seltzer in hand, and they're all looking at something on Holly's phone, presumably photos from the way Holly keeps swiping right and pausing to zoom in. She hands it over to Addison, and my sister's head tilts back in open-mouthed laughter at something on the screen.

A part of me wonders if it's too soon to break away from Mom, Austin, and Aunt Kiersten. Addison's pissed at me over the Natalia and Seth thing, but after what I found in her room tonight, I need to put in some quality time with my sister.

Tucked behind the flat-screen, a wooden cigar box. And inside, a chilling collection of Mayweather family history she was presumably planning to keep hidden.

My phone buzzes in my pocket, and I push my bag aside to dig it out. Holly.

> Meet me on the roof in 5? Something to
> tell you.

My chin jerks up. After a minute, Holly looks up and smiles, then her eyes drop back to her phone. She points at something on the screen, and Uncle Corey shakes his head and plucks it from her hand to scroll furiously back through her camera roll while Holly and Addison both laugh.

"Tacos al pastor?"

A waiter with a silver platter of tiny pork tacos resting on equally tiny silver stands leans down between Aunt Kiersten and me, and everyone takes one with a thank you and a smile.

"Mason?" Mom asks when I still haven't moved.

"Oh right." I'm not really hungry, but I lift one from the platter to be polite.

The waiter heads toward Aunt Paola and my cousins, and I pop the taco into my mouth.

"What makes these sweet?" Austin asks, and Aunt Kiersten says something about diced pineapple and a spit grill.

I tune them out and turn slowly in my seat to look around for the stairs up to the roof. My eyes land on a small white ladder on the vine-draped wall at the back of the terrace. It's washed in darkness and half-concealed behind a large sun umbrella that's been left open, but that must be the way up.

"Excuse me," I mumble, standing and slinging my bag back over my shoulder. "Gotta hit the restroom."

Mom nods, then turns back to Austin and Aunt Kiersten. They're debating the merits of corn versus flour tortillas.

I slip across the terrace to the back wall. No one is watching me. No one is paying any attention. When I'm swallowed in shadow, my fingers close around a thin white rung, and I begin to climb.

ADDISON

I've been at the bar for a while, wedged between my uncle and Holly, the feel-good oldies playlist I made for Mom and Austin—"You're the One That I Want," "Happy Together," "Daydream Believer"—piping from the speakers overhead, but now Holly's week-in-review photo show seems to be coming to an end. Holly glides past three artfully snapped shots of today's lunch from the hibachi place and a dozen more beach selfies, then switches off her screen.

"That's it," she says above the music. "We've been thinking about hiring a professional photographer for the reboot of

Pivot Point's website, but I wonder if I could do the photography myself?"

"You definitely could," Uncle Corey says. His words are a bit thick around the edges, and not for the first time since we've been standing here talking, I wonder how much he's been drinking. "But shouldn't most of the photos be of you?"

"Hmm, true."

My eyes trail around the terrace, and with a start, I realize Mason's seat beside Aunt Kiersten is empty. I glance over to the wall just in time to see my brother's back disappearing up the ladder and onto the roof.

"That was amazing," I say to Holly, angling my shoulders so I can slip out between the two of them. "But if you'll excuse me for a sec?"

They both nod, barely paying me any notice. The animosity I observed between them down on the beach this morning seems to be gone, or at least they're putting on a good show in front of the family. Uncle Corey wraps his arm around Holly's waist and pulls her in close.

"It would save us a lot of cash," she's saying, "but I want the new site to look professional."

I don't stick around to hear his reply. I slip toward the back of the terrace, behind the large sun umbrella. Then, when I'm sure no one's watching, I follow Mason up onto the roof.

The sky is clear, the roof washed in moonlight. My brother is sitting on the low wall overlooking the beach, a bulky messenger bag resting beside him.

"Adds?" He looks confused. "Where's Holly?"

I walk over and brush aside a few vines from the cold stone.

The music travels up from the terrace below, swallowing our conversation in Van Morrison's "Brown Eyed Girl."

"Not coming," I say when I've adjusted my dress to swing one leg over the lip, straddling the wall so I can face him. "That was me, texting from her phone. I've been trying to talk all week, and you keep brushing me off. Seemed like the only way to get your attention."

He frowns. "Okay, secret agent Acker-Mayweather. I kind of want to talk to you, too."

My brows arch. All week, my brother has been flatly uninterested in a conversation. Why now?

"Fine," I say. "But I'm going first. What the hell were you thinking, messing with Natalia like that? You crossed a line."

He rolls his eyes—*literally rolls his eyes*—at me. "Not my finest moment, okay? But we have a lot more important things to talk about."

"More important than the Incident?"

He grabs the messenger bag and pulls it up onto his lap. The moonlight catches the outline of something rectangular and boxy through the gray fabric—and my heart goes still in my chest.

No.

My brother's eyes are locked on me. "You're so goddamned determined not to ruffle any feathers, you don't ever take a stand. Can't you see that 'being Switzerland' is its own kind of choice?"

I can barely breathe. "What's in the bag, Mase?"

His fingers tighten around the strap. "I learned a few things tonight. Like that Grandma Serena is alive—and you *knew*. All our lives, we've been told she died on that camping trip with Pop-Pop and their friends, when Mom and Aunt Kiersten were babies. Except she didn't, and you've been keeping her secret. What the hell, Adds?"

All the blood rushes to my head, and I feel suddenly dizzy. "You stole my cigar box."

Mason grins, cold and joyless. His white teeth flash in the moonlight. "And this party is the perfect occasion to share what's inside." He juts his chin toward the ladder leading down to the terrace. "I thought Beau and Natalia were the worst of it—the mess they got us into. But the Mayweathers are made of secrets and lies." His face twists into an ugly scowl. "Can't you see it's killing us?"

I clench the wall with both hands to keep myself steady. The beach rises and buckles below. "Mason, you *can't.*"

Because inside the box is everything I've uncovered about the Mayweathers over the past three years. Photos, letters, news clippings, genetic genealogy results. It would kill Mom and Aunt Kiersten to learn the truth. It would tear our family to shreds.

Mason starts to stand. "Try me."

29

ADDISON

"Wait." My hand shoots out, snatches for his wrist. "Let me explain."

My brother hovers for a moment, then sits back on the wall. When he speaks, his voice is flat. "Start talking."

I draw in a deep breath. "Fine. I found out about Grandma Serena—and the rest of it—in eighth grade. I was getting really into genetics, as you know, and I did one of those online test kits. That's how I found Rebecca Joy, Serena's third child. She's in her late thirties now, and she teaches at Tipton Academy. She's the main reason I applied."

And now I can't imagine my life without her, without Tipton.

"We have another aunt?"

I nod, and the night breeze whips my hair into my eyes. I

brush it away. "Grandma Serena had Rebecca after she and Pop-Pop split. She remarried a few years later, just like he did."

Mason scrubs his hand across his face. "But how is Serena *alive*, Addison? And why don't Mom and Aunt Kiersten know? She's their *mother*. She's our grandmother, and she what, just never wanted to know us?"

He shoves up from the wall, and I swing my leg over the lip, back to the roof. The ground is still unsteady beneath me, and I stumble a little getting to my feet.

"It's not that simple." I snatch again for his wrist, partly to keep him here, keep him talking, partly to steady myself.

After I discovered the box inside my suitcase, I should have found a better hiding spot. Maybe I should have pitched it into the ocean. But it's too late for that now.

"After Mom was born," I continue, "Grandma Serena suffered from severe postpartum depression. It's still not well understood, even now, and back in 1977, it was stigmatized and misdiagnosed by a lot of doctors."

"Fine," Mason says. "So she was in a bad way, and the patriarchy sucked even harder back then. That gives her license to walk out on her family?"

My hands turn to fists at my sides. This is precisely why I've kept Grandma Serena's secret, why I knew I could never tell Mason or anyone else. But now that he knows, he needs to see the larger picture, how all the pieces fit.

"You read the clippings?" I ask. "About the boat crash?"

Mason nods. "Pop-Pop's obsession with swimming. That's where it comes from."

"Assume so."

"He *killed* a woman."

I nod. According to local news articles from the year Mom was born, Pop-Pop was driving a small boat that crashed during a flash storm near his vacation home on Lake George. But Mom and Grandma Serena weren't with him; his boating companion was a young woman named Carol B. Jones, who fell overboard and drowned. It was deemed a tragic accident, and that was the end of it.

But a bundle of letters that Grandma Serena saved, which Rebecca passed on to me, tell a different story. Pop-Pop was having an affair with Carol, and they were both drinking on the boat. The sudden storm that cropped up on the water probably contributed to what happened, and Carol couldn't swim. But the crash was Pop-Pop's fault—he was drunk, and he lost control. He should have been prosecuted, probably thrown in jail for manslaughter. But he was white and wealthy and a man, and from what I can tell, the local police didn't want a criminal case, and the Jones family didn't want their daughter's death tainted by rumors of an affair. Calling it an accident and chalking it up to the storm was by far the easier path for all involved. And Grandma Serena agreed to keep Pop-Pop's secret—in exchange for her exit from their marriage.

For a Catholic woman, leaving your husband was very much frowned upon in 1977, no matter what the circumstances may have been. And leaving two babies? Unheard of. So Grandma Serena and Pop-Pop struck a deal: They would go camping with another couple, and Serena would leave the group in search of more kindling, then vanish—leaving only her backpack and a bundle of sticks at the top of a steep cliff. The other couple would be able to testify that Pop-Pop never left the campsite, that he had nothing to do with his wife's supposed death. And Serena would get her clean break.

Faking your death must have been a lot easier in 1977—no internet, no cell phones. They pulled it off.

And then Pop-Pop made up that whole story about how the smell of hot dogs cooking triggers his grief, which makes my blood boil. I understand why Serena did what she did, but I have a lot less sympathy for my grandfather.

Still, keeping the secret about what really happened to Grandma Serena is the only way to keep Mom and Aunt Kiersten from getting hurt. Mom especially—when I've probed, since discovering the truth, what she's said has always supported my conviction that I'm making the right choice. Sometimes I still have doubts about not telling her that Grandma Serena is alive, but I always return to Mom's own words, most recently from the spa this week: *I will always miss the idea of my mother, but I've been at peace with her death for a long time now. It was a tragedy, plain and simple.*

Who am I to shatter the peace Mom has found, to expose the thorny truth that there was no terrible tragedy in the woods that claimed her mother's life? That Serena *chose* to leave her all those years ago? My grandmother had good reasons for escaping her marriage, but the truth would still hurt Mom deeply. And protecting Mom, and Serena, feels a lot more important than exposing the dark secrets an eighty-year-old man has been keeping.

"Grandma Serena was dealing with some serious mental health stuff," I say to Mason, struggling to keep my voice steady, "untreated and unsupported by her doctors or her husband. And then Pop-Pop cheats on her and asks her to keep his secret after he accidentally—but irresponsibly and without suffering any consequences—kills the woman he was having an affair with. He put her in an awful position. Of course she wanted out."

"Fine, I get it," Mason says. "Grandma Serena had her reasons, and Pop-Pop's the bigger monster. But don't you think Mom and Aunt Kiersten deserve to know their mother is alive? And that they have a half sister and a nephew? Didn't you think *I* deserved to know? Or are you the only one who gets to have a relationship with Rebecca and her son?"

A hiss of air escapes through my teeth. Of course Mason feels slighted, left out. But I know what I'm doing—*knew* what I was doing. Now my brother holds the power; it's all in his hands.

My eyes travel again to the messenger bag at his hip, the outline of the box inside.

People love to glorify the truth above all else, as if its very existence blots out every other factor, but sometimes the truth only causes pain. Sometimes, secrets are meant to stay buried. And the cold, hard truth is this: whatever her reasons, Grandma Serena doesn't want a relationship with any of us.

So I ask Mason the same question I've been asking myself for nearly three years. "How would learning their mother didn't actually die back then help Mom and Aunt Kiersten now? Grandma Serena could have chosen to come clean to her daughters years ago, when she was safely out of her marriage and had started her new life. But she didn't. So it's not about who deserves to know what, it's about keeping Mom and Aunt Kiersten from getting hurt. Can you see that?"

"Sure," he says, and for a moment I think he really does understand, and we can both take the ladder down to the terrace and go back to the party. "She Loves You" comes to an end, and "Oh, What a Night" starts up on the speakers below. The knots in my shoulders begin to unfurl.

But then he says, "But in your bleeding-heart determination to keep Grandma Serena's secret, you've let Pop-Pop keep his, too. He got away with murder, Adds. And she let him walk free. Just like we let Beau walk free. Can't you see this is about all of us, how messed up we are? I am so done protecting people's *feelings*, as if that's the only important thing!"

"Mase—" I start to say, but he cuts me off.

"You want to talk about the Incident so badly? Let's go. Beau robbed Gigi and Pop-Pop, and he's scared us into keeping his secret ever since. We've been at his beck and call *for three years*. Want to hear a secret? He had me so fucking shaken up, I beat a kid bloody and got kicked off ice hockey. And I know Beau's been blowing up your phone this whole trip. Don't tell me you aren't messed up!"

My jaw hinges open, but no words come out. *Of course* I'm messed up. And Mason got kicked off hockey? But tattling on Beau and Grandma Serena and Pop-Pop won't change any of that.

Before I can respond, Mason takes a step toward me. Then another.

"No more Perfect Little Diplomat, Adds. Don't you know your Shakespeare? Truth will out."

The blood rushes to my head again, and I take a step back. "No. No, no, no." My leg hits the wall, and I sit down, hard.

"You need to give the box back. No one wins if you tell."

No one—including me. Protecting Mom and Aunt Kiersten may be selfless, but the stickier truth is, by keeping these secrets hidden, I'm also protecting myself. Because knowing that I've gotten close with Rebecca and Logan while keeping them from Mom would hurt her just as bad. Bad enough to pull me out of boarding school—if Pop-Pop didn't cut off my tuition money himself. Probably bad enough to ground me until college. My relationship with Dad is already broken. I can't let the truth destroy my relationship with Mom, too.

I have everything to lose here. Every choice I've made is for a very good reason.

Mason takes another step forward. He's gripping the strap of his messenger bag with both hands, knuckles white against the fabric. "No more secrets. I am done being this messed up. This ends now."

My eyes lock on the bag, the sharp rectangular outline beneath the gray fabric. Before I can think too deeply about what I'm doing, I lunge toward my brother, grab it with both hands.

Startled, Mason wrenches away from me, but I keep my grip on the bag. My brother may have seventy pounds and an entire foot on me, but I am strong. He twists again, to the side, and then we're both slamming against the cold stone wall, messenger bag between us.

"Let it go," he snarls.

"You let it go."

The dizziness has passed, and I scramble up onto the wall, still clutching the bag.

"What the hell are you doing?" Mason asks.

Hedging my bets. I don't say it out loud. The beach is eight stories below us, and Mason won't let me fall. He'll shrug the strap off his shoulders, let me win.

Instead, eyes flashing, he joins me up on the wall in one easy hop.

"Don't be stupid, Adds." He takes a big step back, pulling me toward him. "Let. It. Go."

That's not an option. I can't let go, and I can't let Mason get his way, do something he thinks would be noble but would only cause a world of pain.

But my traitorous fingers are cramping, and for a second, I relax my grip. Mason must think he's won, because he drops one hand, uses the other to shift the strap against his shoulder where it's been digging in.

I don't hesitate. I grab onto the strap with both hands and start to hoist it over my brother's head, except my arms are too short, or he's too tall, and it snags on the back of his neck.

"Fuck, Adds." He stumbles forward, and one of his sneakers catches in the vines. In the next instant, I'm staggering backward, off the wall, back onto the roof, while Mason careens the other way, over the edge, the bag still snared between us.

His weight yanks me forward, down to my knees, and I'm white-knuckling the strap, using the wall between us to keep me from going over too.

Oh my god.

"You need to pull me up," he grunts.

Tears spring to my eyes. There's no way I can pull my brother up; I can't even stand without tumbling over the side. He's too big, too heavy, and I am losing my grip.

"I can't," I gasp. "Can you grab onto the wall?"

"Addison, please." There's panic in his voice now. "I'm going to fall."

I can't let that happen. I squeeze my eyes shut, block everything out until a plan forms: I'll call for help, loud enough to cut above the peal of "Sweet Caroline" from the speakers below. Then I just need to hang on for a few more moments while the others figure out we're up here, climb onto the roof. Help me hoist Mason back up.

But when my eyes fly back open, my brother's words from earlier boomerang back to me: *Can't you see that "being Switzerland" is its own kind of choice?* I hesitate.

My mouth opens, but no sound comes out. The realization that I hold the power now crackles through my veins like electricity, and my grip on the fabric loosens. I press my eyes shut again, and across the backs of my lids, I see the Mayweather family secrets laid bare, my life at Tipton yanked away from me, our family's world blown apart. But I could make sure that doesn't happen.

I could let go.

And then there is a ripping sound, and suddenly all the weight is gone. The bag snaps against my chest with a thwack, and I tumble backward, the torn strap smacking me in the face.

"Mason," I gasp. I heave myself up, and then I'm peering over the side of the wall to the beach below.

I didn't let go. But I didn't call for help, either. And in doing nothing, I made my choice.

I could have saved Mason, and I let him fall.

My eyes strain to pierce eight stories of darkness. For a

moment, I don't see anything on the beach, and I let myself believe that maybe, possibly, he's okay.

Then, on the sand, the shape of a boy, twisted unnaturally. Unmoving.

My fault.

My stomach heaves, and bile fills my throat. Did I wish this into being? I wanted our fight to end, the problem to go away, but not this—the indelible, horrible fact of my brother on the sand below, dead. *I didn't get help. I killed him.*

The shock hits me everywhere. Beneath my skin, blood and muscle and bone are twisting, changing. Becoming something new. I shudder, fight the urge to claw through my dress, get inside, make it stop.

Then there's a break in the music, and voices trickle up from the terrace, snapping me back to the world outside myself. Mia is laughing. Aunt Kiersten says something about champagne flutes. I breathe in, then out, clutching my arms to my stomach until I know what I need to do. *Be normal.* Slip like a shadow back to the party. Act like nothing has changed and hope against hope no one's noticed me missing. My hands rise to my mouth to hold in a sob. The task feels impossible, but I'll do it because I have to. Because I can't tell the truth, can't reveal the killer I've become tonight, up on this roof. Not to my family. Not ever.

The tide is coming in. I need to go, but for two minutes that feel like an eternity, I linger at the wall, hands clamped to my mouth, watching the dark water creep up from the ocean to tug my brother's body slowly, slowly out to sea.

30

One Hour Until the Wedding

NATALIA

The low hum of the ceiling fan is the only noise on the top floor of the Oak Lodge at Rhyne Ridge. From my vantage point in front of the wall of windows, the wedding guests are a silent film playing on the lawn below, chatting and sipping champagne before the ceremony begins.

I hang back, alone here in the reception hall where later we'll all gather for dinner and dancing, the inn's dark eaves stretching above me. Down below, I watch Mami weaving little white flowers into Mia's hair, Theo introducing his boyfriend to Aunt Elizabeth's friends, and Uncle Corey, single once more, flirting with a young, auburn-haired woman by the champagne table.

Gigi and Pop-Pop have already taken their seats in the front row of white wooden chairs set up before a matching white trellis, and while Gigi fiddles with a clunky pink digital camera, I follow Pop-Pop's gaze across the lawn, across the sea of faces, Mayweathers and Hunts comingling, until his eyes land on Beau.

Maybe it's my imagination. Pop-Pop could be looking at someone standing near my brother. But the prickling feeling that took residence at the base of my spine four summers ago and never left tells me otherwise. Pop-Pop is watching Beau with heavy eyes, and I wonder, not for the first time, if he has known the truth all along. If Pop-Pop has chosen to keep my brother's secret, to keep this family from blowing to pieces.

The truth is, we're already shattered.

I step back from the windows, smooth my hands down the front of my peach bridesmaid's dress, thoughts traveling from the people on the lawn to the people who aren't here today. First Mason, who over the past five months I've seen in glimpses again and again, broad shoulders and dusty blond hair rounding a corner or disappearing behind a tall, leafy tree. Who died before I could stop being furious with him, who I never got to scream at or freeze out, or, eventually, forgive.

Then Seth. Who swore that what started as a prank turned into something real, who promised he wanted to meet me in real life, who cried when I told him it was over, that I could never, ever trust him.

After Beau, after Mason, after Seth—after someone at that engagement party *killed Mason* and lied to the police—how can I trust anyone ever again?

I pull out a chair from one of the round reception tables and take a seat. I'll go down when I need to, put on a happy face, but until then, I'd rather be up here, alone with the one person I can count on, always.

THEO

It's him or me. You can't have it both ways. You have to choose.

That's what Mason told Elizabeth on the afternoon of the engagement party, five months ago. Now Mason is dead and the rest of us are gathered at a rustic-chic lodge in Rhyne Ridge for Dad and Elizabeth's wedding. Jay and I stand at one of the little round cocktail tables on the lawn. I give his hand a squeeze, an uneasy feeling gathering in the pit of my stomach like it does every time I think about Mason, how I wanted to kill him—*metaphorically*—that day, how he died before I got the chance to accuse him of being a selfish, hotheaded prick.

Bile rises in my throat, and I choke it down. I know better than to speak ill of the dead, especially at a wedding. But I can't control how I feel.

"You okay?" Jay asks.

I clear my throat, stifling a cough. "Just a little thirsty. Could you grab me a sparkling cider?"

Jayden takes off across the lawn, and I draw in a deep breath. It means a lot that he's here today, as my date. As my boyfriend. When the hockey season ended in February, Jay decided he was done keeping his sexuality a tightly guarded secret. Little by little, he's been coming out to a few more friends. Last week, he came with me to queer youth alliance. When I invited him to Dad's wedding, I fully expected him to say no—too much, too soon—but here he is, charming Elizabeth's friends and picking flowers for Mia's hair and heading back across the lawn, now, with two glasses of sparkling cider and a huge grin on his face.

I match it, trying to push my thoughts of Mason firmly aside, but it's impossible. I didn't kill him. Dad didn't kill him. So who did?

For a while after he died, after we all returned home and tried to move on with our lives, I was sure he'd ditched the engagement party to meet up with the guys from the surf school. But this spring, Sophie Fletcher—one of the sisters who disappeared off the beach last November—released a statement about her experience with the eco cult, in which she cleared Escuela de Swell and everyone who works there from all responsibility. Sophie revealed that she and her sister Julie had been groomed by a woman from the commune for months before the Fletcher family traveled to Cancún, that the group had arranged for the sisters to "disappear" while on vacation to throw their family off track. The fact that they'd last been seen taking a surf lesson that morning was an unlucky coincidence for the school, whose reputation is probably tainted forever despite Sophie's statement.

Which leaves the Mayweathers. Everyone who was on the terrace that night is here today. I sip my cider, mind cycling once again through the possibilities. I don't want to think of my stepfamily as *suspects*—and there has never been enough evidence to charge anyone—but the truth no one is willing to say out loud is this: someone right here at this wedding killed Mason.

A shudder wrenches through me, and I hope Jay doesn't notice. Quickly, I knock back the rest of my cider.

After Mason died, I thought Dad might change his mind,

but he and Elizabeth insisted that calling the wedding off would be letting tragedy win. So here we are, fifteen minutes until the ceremony is set to begin, on a bright green lawn under a deep blue sky, surrounded by the beautiful, wealthy, smiling members of my new family.

And one of them is a killer.

MIA

Natalia, Addison, and I stand under the trellis in matching peach dresses, our nails glossed in matching peach polish, our fingers wrapped around matching peach-and-yellow bouquets. It's a perfect June afternoon, the perfect day for a wedding. Everything is sunny, warm, bright. On the other side of Aunt Elizabeth and Austin stands Theo, a peach pocket square poking out of his jacket.

For the first time since Mason died, since his case went cold and the Mexican cops released us all to go home, everyone is together again. Everyone is smiling. If you can forget that my cousin is buried in a cemetery not far from here, it's the perfect Mayweather family reunion.

Despite the warm sun on my shoulders, I shiver.

My eyes trail to Addison, her dusty blond hair swept into an elegant knot at the base of her neck, her blue eyes shining.

The police only wanted to talk about the pranks. The frog in Addison's bed, the photos on Natalia's phone, the messages I sent Mason and Theo. They didn't ask about what I saw that night. Mason climbing the ladder to the roof, then Addison going after him a few minutes later. Only Addison climbing back down to the terrace, joining the rest of us for a toast.

If they had asked, would I have told?

The question buzzes around my brain like it has every single day for the past five months. I didn't tell the police, or Mami, or Mom. At first I thought there must be some good explanation. And I didn't want to get Addison in trouble. But now, I've had loads of time to think. Something happened on the roof between my cousins. Something bad. My fingers cramp around my bridesmaid's bouquet, and I remind myself to relax. Smile big.

It's a wedding, after all.

For the first time in months, everyone is happy. *Be happy, Mia.*

The officiant, a friend of Aunt Elizabeth's, turns to Addison and asks her to share her reading. My cousin slips a piece of paper from beneath the ribbon of her bouquet, then passes the flowers to me with a smile.

I take them. While she reads one of Shakespeare's sonnets, voice cool and clear, I study her face. What am I searching for? Some sign my cousin is a killer. Or that she watched her brother jump, then kept her lips sealed.

Who are you, Addison Acker-Mayweather?

I hold our bouquets together tight.

Addison is keeping a secret. Dark as night and bloodred as the sun rising from the ocean outside La Maravilla.

She looks up from her paper and smiles, eyes traveling between her mom and her mom's new husband. Then she keeps reading: "'But thy eternal summer shall not fade, / Nor lose possession of that fair thou ow'st; / Nor shall death brag thou wander'st in his shade, / When in eternal lines to time thou grow'st: / So long as men can breathe, or eyes can see, / So long lives this, and this gives life to thee.'"

She turns to me, and I hand her flowers back.

For now, I want to say, *I am keeping your secret.*

But I'm not sure I can keep it forever.

ACKNOWLEDGMENTS

The Reunion was as fun to research as it was to write. Passionate, heartfelt thanks must first go out to my dear friends and longtime travel companions, who will surely notice many similarities between La Maravilla Cancún and our 2022 vacation destination. (Murder aside, of course.) Special shout out to Dora for your fiscal savvy and resort points. Long live Ladycation!

Thank you, just as heartily, to the team at Margaret K. McElderry Books for giving me license to dream up another thrilling murder mystery and for throwing your support behind this story. Nicole Fiorica remains a keen editor and fantastic champion; I am so lucky to have had you in my corner across multiple books now! My gratitude to everyone else at MKM and S&S who has had a part in the making of *The Reunion*, especially Elizabeth Blake-Linn, Justin Chanda, Lindsey Ferris, Bridget Madsen, Alissa Nigro, Kate Prosswimmer, Emily Ritter, Nicole Russo, Valerie Shea, Caitlin Sweeny, Nicole Valdez, Karen Wojtyla, Jasmine Ye, Anne Zafian, and the tremendous sales force.

Big thanks to Levente Szabó for your genius rendering of Mason, Addison, Natalia, and Theo on the cover and to Debra Sfetsios-Conover for the brilliant design.

As ever, an abundance of thanks to my agent, Erin Harris, for your sharp editorial eye and fierce support. My gratitude also goes to Folio team members Mike Harriott, Kat Odom-Tomchin, and Chiara Panzeri.

Thank you a million times over to my husband, Osvaldo Oyola, for everything you do. And especially for your eye on the Spanish and Spanglish in this novel! Ramona, thank you for napping, sometimes for longer than thirty minutes at a stretch, so I could revise.

Special thanks to Felix F-R for lending your expertise to a tricky sentence!

To Jessica Goodman, Kate Alice Marshall, Kathleen Glasgow, Rebecca Barrow, Wendy Heard, and Liz Lawson: thank you for taking the time to read *The Reunion* early and lend your support!

To my writer friends, who make this career so much less solitary, especially: Rachel Lynn Solomon, Anica Mrose Rissi, Maxine Kaplan, Kara Thomas, Sara Shepard, Carlyn Greenwald, Derek Milman, Karen M. McManus, Sarah Nicole Smetana, Katie Henry, Amelia Brunksill, and all the Electrics. And to my family—Mom, Dad, Aunt Sally, Sonia, and Lissette—for all your support and enthusiasm for my books. In loving memory of Angel Garcia.

Last but definitely not least: to the booksellers, educators, librarians, and bloggers across platforms who have supported and promoted my books—you are so appreciated. And to you, reading this book—whether this is the first or fifth book of mine you've picked up, thank you for spending your time in the twisty world of the Mayweathers.